# *Troubles*

★

The sheriff sighed, pulled the chair beside me out a ways, sat down, tilted back and parked his hat on his lap.

"Okay, Wilcox. Stop and think. All your life women been trouble for you. Both times you went to prison it was because you were trying to get money for women who needed money—or thought they did—and you were drunk. Half a jug and you're Robin Hood. The point is, you got to remember that young girls' pas have got rabbit ears so you'd better try to see things from their view if you're gonna stay out of trouble. Now take Fin. Sure he's got more money than most around here, but he's got worries you and me never dreamed of—"

"Uh-huh. Like a wife that won't die."

# MURDER

## THE CARL WILCOX SERIES

Paint the Town Red
The Missing Moon
The Naked Liar
The Fourth Widow
The Barbed Wire Noose
The Man Who Met the Train

Published by
THE MYSTERIOUS PRESS

# MURDER

## a novel by
## HAROLD ADAMS

**THE MYSTERIOUS PRESS**

New York • London • Tokyo

MYSTERIOUS PRESS EDITION

Copyright © 1981 by Harold Adams

This Mysterious Press Edition is published by arrangement with the author.

Cover illustration by John Jinks

Mysterious Press books are published in association with Warner Books, Inc.
666 Fifth Avenue
New York, N.Y. 10103

A Warner Communications Company

Printed in the United States of America

First Mysterious Press Printing: March, 1988

10  9  8  7  6  5  4  3  2  1

# * Chapter *

# I

It was one of those summer nights in Corden when the sidewalk glowed after dark from all the heat soaked up through the long day. I was at slow bake in a straight-backed chair, tilted against the white hotel front under the balcony, hoping for a breeze while I watched moths, June bugs and God knows what, wildly circling the corner streetlight. It made me dizzy enough to feel near sozzled and I was half enjoying it until Wilt Bowman slithered along and plunked his skinny butt in the chair on my right.

"Hi, Carl, long time no see."

I grunted and asked if he had a smoke. He wasn't happy about it but dug a pack from his shirt pocket and passed it my way. I took two, stuck one behind my ear and lit the other.

He wriggled around, got his own smoke started and asked had I heard about Fin Larson?

"No—is he pregnant?"

"Fin? How could he be—?"

"I don't know, but that's about all he could do that'd interest me."

He gave me a gummy grin. "They didn't change you none in jail, did they. Still always kidding."

"It was prison, not jail. I been in jail a dozen times—prison only twice. You better note it down—there's a lot of difference."

"Sure," he said but he wasn't really interested in learning

1

from me, he was in the news delivery business. "How about his wife, Iris. You interested in her?"

"I hope *she's* not pregnant."

"No sir, what she is, she's dying." ·

He watched close as I let out smoke slow and easy and kept my eyes on the bug halo around the streetlight.

"And you know what Fin's done? He's brought in this cousin from the cities—Cora—no more'n twenty or so—real dark—a looker! Fin claims she's there to take care of Iris and the house, but why couldn't Angie do that?"

Angie was Fin's sixteen year old daughter. The last time I'd seen her she was spending all her energy on growing tits. She was having great success but for some reason it only made her sullen as a one-balled bull.

"There's some," said Wilt, "that figures Iris ain't normal sick. She didn't have no problem till Fin started sashaying to the cities every week. That's where Cora come from, you know."

"Yeah," I nodded, "you already told me. I know something else, too."

"What?" he asked, leaning closer.

"If Fin gets wind of your talk, Iris won't be the only one not normal sick in town."

Wilt tried to scowl but only managed to look worried.

"I ain't afraid of Fin Larson," he said, looking around.

"Then you're one of a kind," I said, trying not to sound too grateful.

"Come on. You ain't afraid of him, are you?"

"I'm only afraid of my enemies, Wilt, and all I got is friends."

He waggled his head and grinned. "No, sir, they didn't change Carl Wilcox one bit. You ain't scared of nothing."

He stood up, shook his balls loose and started drifting off. He could see I was about through with my smoke and was afraid I'd bum another.

No sooner had I got adjusted to the loss than Hank, my sixteen year old nephew came out of the hotel. His hair's black and wavy and he's got eyebrows you could trim with a scythe if he'd hold still long enough.

"How'd you like to go swimming about now?" he asked.

"About now, that'd beat getting laid."

"Granpa says we can take the Dodge if you drive. You mind if Clayt Doppler and a couple girls come along?"

"Wouldn't have it any other way. Unless you can come up with an extra girl or two—"

"Well—" he said, looking embarrassed.

"I'm kidding. Let's go."

"Okay. I'll call before we go pick them up."

He wanted to warn them that I'd be along so there'd be no awkwardness. Hank wasn't too worried about my readjustment to society, what concerned him was society's readjustment to me.

While Hank was telephoning I lit Wilt's second cigaret and thought about my nephew's powers of persuasion. He never begs or coaxes, he just starts little talks with people and before long, what he wants is what they want. I think he could talk a sultan out of his wives. If I were to ask Elihu, my old man, for an axe to cut his own wood, he'd turn me down flat, but ten minutes of Hank's oil and suddenly I was welcome to his precious Dodge. Given another ten minutes, Hank could've talked him into giving me the hotel and maybe even Bertha, the cook.

A part of Hank's technique is, he almost never seems to want anything for himself. In this case he was worried about my rehabilitation—and at the same time he was picking up a chaperone who wouldn't cramp anybody's style at the swimming hole.

When everybody'd been called and warned we drove to Clayt's house. Clayt was about six four with meat platter hands and feet big as snowshoes. He always looked worried —probably because he couldn't always tell where the feet were going.

Next we picked up Ellie, Hank's girl, a brown-haired, slim kid with wide blue eyes and filly legs. She casually called me Uncle Carl as though she went riding with ex-cons every day.

Fin's daughter, Angie, met us on the street corner a block east of her home. Under the white summer dress her hips and tits looked round as melons and her waist didn't seem stout enough to hold the top steady. Her worried look matched Clayt's when we drove up and then they were both smiling as she scrambled into the car. Hank said she probably remembered me, his cowboy-carpenter uncle and she said yes without glancing my way because she was too busy looking out the rear window as we took off. It didn't take any Sherlock Holmes to guess she'd left home without permission. At the moment I foolishly figured it was probably just as well.

Our route to the swimming hole took us back past the Wilcox Hotel and as I turned south on First, Wilt Bowman, who was standing under the hotel sign, bugged his eyes as he spotted me and my gang. Again I didn't worry. I was sure Wilt was too scared of Fin to go blabbing.

The gravelled road to the swimming hole runs through rolling hills—hell, it's more like lumpy prairie—and after three straight miles makes a west jog around the end of what used to be a lake but now's mostly slough. Late in the twenties, villagers built an earth dike enclosing the main springs and formed a swimming pool about a hundred by two hundred feet. The dike walls are steep except on the west side where there's a shallow beach under a row of old cottonwoods.

As I turned into the parking area our lights flashed across the dark water and caught the diving tower I'd built two summers before. It looked old and tired.

All four kids popped out of the Dodge before I set the brake and began stripping to swim suits. They raced up and down the beach a couple times, yelling and laughing, before Hank and Ellie charged into the water which exploded before them and sparkled in the starlight. Angie said she wanted to get wet slowly so of course Clayt had to pick her up and charge in while she screamed bloody murder. The way he carried her you'd have thought she weighed no more than a balloon although I'd guess she went at least one hundred and fifteen pounds.

All four kids were heading for the north end by the time I got down to my trunks, made a running dive into the cool water and rolled over on my back to kick along, looking at the stars.

In South Dakota, on clear nights, stars hang lower than

any place else in the world but that night, seen from the black pool, they just looked clear and forever away, leaving the earth lonely and me empty. I rolled to my belly, swam to the diving tower and climbed up. The platform trembled like a nervous bride but the board, which had lost its burlap pad, still had all its bounce and threw me over when I tried my first jacknife in two years.

Back on the beach I toweled off, rolled a smoke, lit up and sat down. The kids had quieted down by then and mostly I could hear bullfrogs hooting all over the slough. It was lovely peaceful.

At first I didn't pay much attention when I saw the lights coming from Corden. Then I realized they were moving damned fast and wondered why anybody'd be in that big a hurry on a nothing road to nowhere. The answer was a maniac parent rushing to the rescue of his innocent daughter. I stood up as the headlights swept down the easy slope toward the jog. The driver hit his brakes a little late and the car slewed wildly, held, then came skidding around the incline above the beach. When it halted the headlights pinned me alone on the sand.

As both doors flew open, I decided to go swimming. Two long steps and a fast jump put me in the water. I dug for the bottom, cut sharp left and plowed strong until I had to come up. Light was all around me when I surfaced so I took a deep breath and went down again, angling toward the opposite bank while keeping a northerly direction. By the time I came up I'd cleared the lights and was able to make out shadows along the beach I'd left.

It was some relief to see the rescuers weren't carrying shotguns, but not much . . . because they had baseball bats.

"Wilcox!" yelled Fin. "Where's Angie?"

I looked north and for a second thought I'd lost directions since there was no one in sight. Then I realized the kids must have hidden in the cattails beyond the dike.

"Circle the south end," hollered Fin in his drill sergeant's voice. He wasn't as big as Goliath or quick as David and he had a gut made for body punches, but being armed with righteousness and a baseball bat made him a damned dangerous playmate. The only comfort I could find was that he only had one stooge along. If he'd taken the time he could've rounded up the entire mob of Veterans of Foreign Wars and maybe the Legion too.

I dove, headed for the north bank and when I could touch the rocky bottom, worked up a step, got decent footing and stared around. Fin was out of sight. His partner was barging through thickets along the marshy south end which made him harmless for a while. I picked up a rock the size of a baseball and hunkered down with only my head above water. In a few seconds Fin crashed into the open and charged along the west bank, peering at the water and bobbing his head for a better view.

"Wilcox," he hollered, "you son-of-a-bitch, I know you're there—what've you done with Angie?"

He looked bigger than Paul Bunyan in high-heeled boots as he staggered along the high bank waving his baseball bat. I crouched lower and hung on to my rock.

By then Hank had had all the hiding he could tolerate so he stepped up on top of the bank.

"Angie's here," he yelled, "what's the matter?"

Fin wheeled, stumbled and glared.

"Angie?"

"I'm right here, Daddy."

"Well, Goddamnit—come up where I can see you!"

The three other kids stood up and joined Hank.

"When'd you put that suit on?" demanded Fin.

"At home—"

"Where's that Wilcox son-of-a-bitch?"

"I don't know."

"My name's Wilcox," said Hank. He was too mad to be scared.

"Is Angie with you?"

"I came with Clayt Doppler," yelled Angie whose anger was beginning to wipe out fear.

"You trying to tell me Carl Wilcox ain't here?"

"Sure he's here," said Hank, "he gave us a ride out. What's all the excitement? Why've you got a baseball bat?"

"I got this bat to use on that ex-con for bringing my daughter out for a naked swim! Now where is he?"

"Who's naked?" demanded Hank. He was getting madder

by the second and considering what he faced he wasn't showing a lot of smart but I couldn't fault his guts.

Just then I heard a crashing in the willows behind me and Buck Dover, Fin's butcher cousin, came charging out of the brush hollering, "He's right down there, Fin! I can see the bastard!"

I straightened up and seeing me, Fin roared, waved his bat and started scrambling down the bank. Buck crouched to grab a rock. At the same time I heard another car approaching. It didn't look like it was going to be my night. Figuring there was no percentage in trying to pitch to two sluggers, I dropped my rock and hit the water like a kingfisher diving for a deep one.

They started pegging steady when I came up for air but were too excited or drunk for accuracy and the one hit caught me in the ribs and was some cushioned by the water. The second time I came up I saw Fin running along the west bank and Buck on the east, both grabbing rocks and throwing like kids in a snowball fight. As I took a deep breath for another dive, a woman's voice, sharp and clear as a whistle, called "Fin! Fin Larson!"

Fin stopped in his tracks and dropped the bat. Buck fired another rock and Fin turned, said "Stop that!" as if he were speaking to a child. A moment later a slender woman was above Fin on the bank, talking down too low for me to hear. The next thing I knew, the strange woman and the two wild men walked back to the cars and left me with the kids, including Angie.

"My gosh," said Clayt as I joined them on the bank, "old Fin really does go crazy, doesn't he? Angie'd warned me, but I didn't think he'd be that bad. What'd you think, Carl, when they were throwing rocks at you?"

"I thought the pool was too blamed small."

"Come on," said Clayt impatiently, "you know what I mean—you aren't going to let them get away with that, are you?"

"Don't worry," Hank assured him, "Carl will fix them— nobody messes with him and gets away with it."

It seemed to me that I could remember at least a platoon

or two who had but I didn't raise the point because it's no fun trying to spike myths about yourself.

We climbed back into the Dodge wearing damp swimming suits and sat on towels with our dry clothing in our laps. All, that is, but Clayt who had Angie on his lap. She sat stiff as a rheumatic goat and I could see in the rear view mirror that Clayt was hugging her close all the way.

It was interesting to me that no one said a word about the woman who'd shown up like the Seventh Cavalry and tamed wild man Fin. I guessed they were trying to avoid further embarrassment for Angie.

As we neared Main, Angie leaned toward me.

"Don't take me home—I'll stay with Ellie."

"I don't think that'd be very smart," I said.

"I will *not* go home." Her voice was tight. She was having a hell of a fight to keep from bawling.

"I understand—but you'll just make things worse—besides—your Dad's all calmed down—he won't whale you now—"

"You bet he won't!"

"So okay, think about your Ma some."

She sat back, took a deep breath and through the mirror I saw her staring out the car window. She ignored Clayt's squeeze.

"All right, I'll go home," she said.

"I don't know—" said Clayt, "what if he does beat you?"

"I'll kill him!"

She said it with enough heat to shock the whole gang. I think it even shocked her when she realized how strong it came out. Then Clayt said no—*he'd* kill him.

"We could draw straws," I said, but nobody laughed.

The minute I stopped in front of the Larson house, Angie jumped out and sailed up the walk with her head high. Clayt trotted along, trying to match her style but he was too awkward to make it. Lights were on in the house, upstairs and downstairs. It took a long time for the couple to say goodnight. I could barely see them but it looked like they were talking, not mushing. Finally she went in and he came back to the car. He didn't say a word.

As we drove off I remembered his egging me on to getting even with Fin and Buck for pegging rocks at me. Was it something he really expected, or was he trying to arrange it?

I decided to keep an eye on him, there might be more to Clayt Doppler than the reach of a giraffe.

# * Chapter *

# II

Hank sacked out the moment we got back to the hotel but I wasn't sleepy so I rolled a smoke, sat down in one of the chairs out front and surveyed Main Street. The first movement, aside from the bugs around the streetlight, was old Joey Paxton, lumbering toward me. Joey was the only guy in town bigger than Fin Larson so naturally he'd been made the town cop. He had a permanent slouch, a bloodhound face and arms so long his knuckles would drag if he didn't always keep his hands in his pockets. Some folks claim his slow movements can fool you—they say he can really go if he has to—but I don't know where that notion comes from because the only time I've seen his hands was when he took off his hat to wipe sweat from his forehead and that never called for a lightning move.

He leaned against one of the pillars supporting the balcony that runs along the hotel front and gave me a mournful, accusing stare.

"You're just the man I want to see," I told him. "I want to swear out a warrant against Fin Larson for attempted assault, abusive language and general disturbance of the peace."

He shook his head sadly. "You got Fin all tore up, Carl."

"I got *him* all tore up? *He* was the Goddamned assaulter —with deadly weapons—and besides that, he sicced his ape on me."

"What the hell'd you expect a man like Fin to do when he

10

found out you took his kid swimming at night—where folks claim kids been swimming nekkid?''

"Joey, the first thing that moron saw when he got out there was me alone and wearing trunks.''

"May be. But just the sight of you is enough to rile any Corden pa with a kid built like Angie.''

"Damn it, she wasn't with me!''

He sighed, pulled the chair beside me out a ways, sat down, tilted back and parked his hat on his lap.

"Okay. Stop and think. All your life women been trouble for you. Both times you went to prison it was because you were trying to get money for women that needed money—or thought they did—and you were drunk. Half a jug and you're Robin Hood. Now lately it looks like maybe you got the booze licked, but you got to remember that a man with your reputation had better watch his step with the ladies—''

"You make me sound like a Goddamned gigolo. For Christ's sake, look at me—do I look like a lady's man?''

"You look like a fighter who's led with his nose too many times—but from what I hear that never cramped your style in the hay. The point is, you got to remember is that young girls' pas have got rabbit ears so you'd better try and see things from their view if you're gonna stay out of trouble. Now take Fin. Sure he's got more money than most around here, but he's got worries you and me never dreamed of—''

"Uh-huh. Like a wife that won't die.''

He gave me a long, disapproving stare. "Now what's that supposed to mean?''

"It means I'm trying to look at things from Fin's view.''

He shook his head again. "You always got to be a smart-ass, don't you? Okay, let me put this real simple. Keep away from Fin. Keep away from Angie. Keep your nose clean—''

"How about my ass. Can I leave that normal?''

"If you don't do like I tell you, you may lose it.''

"Is that right? Lemme tell you something. If he so much as farts in my direction again, I'm gonna kick Fin's ass up so high his ears'll be brown—and after that I might get rough. And today—as a matter of fact right Goddamn now, I'm going up and visit his sick wife. If you got a law says I can't visit the sick, trot it out and show me, but you'd best find it in a hurry because I'm on my way."

He put his hand on my arm as I started up. He didn't take hold, just put it there, heavy and awkward, like a grizzly's paw, and his sorrowful face turned tragic.

"Now Carl, don't go flying off the handle. I ain't trying 'o boss you and I sure as hell don't figure to make you into anybody's floor mat. But Goddamnit, I got two madmen I'm trying to keep from killing each other and you got the most common sense when you're sober so I'm asking you, man to man—"

"It's got nothing to do with who's got sense, it's who's got the dollars. He has—I ain't. Now take your Goddamned paw off my arm."

"Not till we talk a minute."

I glared at him but knew if he really meant to throw his weight around he'd have drawn his gun or at least grabbed on with both hands. Besides, he was big enough and strong enough to make breaking loose a blood proposition so I hesitated.

"You don't have to prove nothing to me," he said, "and nobody's watching so there's no show. Now listen, eh?"

"You calling me a grandstander?"

"Well, let's say you're prouder than most."

That seemed like a reasonable compromise so I settled back. I knew it was too late to go visiting Fin's wife anyway.

"Okay," he said. "I'm asking you, man to man, be reasonable and hear me out and I won't try leaning on you again. Just as a favor to me, stay out of Fin's way. You're a big enough man to forget about getting even. If you don't, and you two tangle, somebody's gonna get hurt and you're bound to be the loser. I know you can whip him—he's fat and slow and you're all muscle and speed—but you're not a kid any more and you got to think about what happens *after* a fight."

He was too right to stay mad at—and the asking was an apology so I said okay and he took his hand off my arm.

"I'm not saying I won't go visit his wife, Iris, one day."

"Fair enough, but give him time to simmer down."

"He may be simmered down right now. That cousin—she

cooled him off faster than a fall through the ice. You never saw a dog called off quicker than she stopped Fin."

He looked thoughtful. "Tell me about it."

I did.

For several seconds he sat there, studying the empty street and blinking like a frog in the sun. Finally he sighed and asked, "You get a good look at her?"

"No. Light was in my eyes. She looked skinny—"

"She's slim—not much like our girls—kind of foreign looking. Real proud."

"She's not a blood cousin, is she?"

He shook his head.

"What I figured."

Joey put his hat on, tipped the chair forward and stood up slowly.

"Do me a favor," he said. "Keep your figuring off Fin for a while, okay?"

"I'll give it a try."

# * Chapter *

# III

The next day, Friday, right after 8:00 a.m., Judge Crawford called and invited me to his office in the court house. The last time we'd met he handed me a year in the pen, but I'm not a grudge-bearing man so I went around to visit.

He sat behind a desk about the size of a billiard table all surrounded by shelves of books you wouldn't want to read and squinted at me under beetled brows with his hard blue eyes.

"It's my belief," he told me when I was seated, "that when a man has paid his debt he ought to be given every decent opportunity to make good when he returns to society. I called early to see if you'd be up and was glad to find you were but it didn't surprise me much, considering you come from a fine family. Now, I know you're dexterous—when sober—so I'm going to offer you a job."

He paused, to allow me time for grateful comment, but I hadn't heard anything I was ready to make a speech about so I just nodded.

"We're going to have a county fair this fall. First in five years. Now, the problem is, the grounds are in very poor shape, need sprucing up. You'll go out there and handle that job. Repair the vandalism, maybe patch a roof or two, clean out the show barns, fix up the grandstand. You look it over, estimate what you need, make out a list and I'll take care of supplies and tools. Hire some help—two, even three high school boys should do if you handle them right. Take your

14

nephew and a couple of his friends, but keep in mind you have just two months. The pay is thirty cents an hour for you, the boys get twenty-five."

I wasn't all that impressed by the pay, but it beat nothing which was what I'd been drawing since I left stir. I said okay and the judge beamed at me and we went out, got into his black Packard and drove to the grounds for a look.

"I'd imagine the barns will take the most attention," he said. "They're full of straw, manure and trash. You won't have to do much with the grandstand. It needs paint but some bunting and banners will spruce it up. Maybe you could whitewash the back and sides."

I could see he had grand plans.

"It's gonna be a hot job," I said, looking across at heat waves squiggling over the dusty race track and the weedy center field.

He scowled at me. "If it's too hot for you, there are others who will be only too happy to take the job."

"Oh, I'll take it."

"Don't let me put you out any."

"I'll handle it."

"Without boozing," he said.

I came close to choking on that, but he was watching sharp and I managed to say I could handle that, too.

He grinned, gave me his hand and said, "Good. Now I'm going back to the courthouse. You look around, figure out what you need and bring me a list."

"How about I use my truck and haul the stuff?"

"No. Anything you need, I'll have delivered. You can pile trash by the barn doors and I'll see that it's picked up."

So he had his own connections and didn't plan to save money on anything but labor.

"You gonna have the weeds mowed?" I asked.

"Pop Tucker'll take care of that. All you have to do is clean and repair. I'll see you on Friday. That's payday."

I watched him drive off in his shining Packard and then walked past the stock barns. There were five of them, side by side, just north of the grandstand. They had clapboard walls, sliding doors at each end and steep saddle roofs. I noticed the first one, closest to the grandstand, was closed up while doors were open on the east side of the next two. They'd been nailed shut after the last fair and couples had broken into them. Probably lovers who figured they could get down to business better on the hay than in the back seat of cars. I stuck my head inside the first open doorway and looked around. It smelled of hot straw and musty manure. Sunlight leaked through vents near the roof peak and made dust motes sparkle like tiny stars. I looked into the stalls where cattle had stood and guessed that all the prize-winners, runners-up and losers had been butchered long ago. And then I thought of the lovers who'd coupled in the cleaner hay and probably got married and were busy with noisy kids and money problems—or had broken up and gone dividing ways. It made me think of when I was a snot-nosed kid, watching couples and thinking, Jesus, when they get married they can do it every night and mornings too if they want and he can see her naked and it's okay. I figured seeing a girl naked any time you wanted would be the great-est thing in the world. I started looking forward to that when I was six.

Back in town I stopped by the hotel and Elihu told me Hank was out so I had to wait till noon to talk with him. When he did show up and heard the offer he was all hot for the job; it took him about five minutes to convince his grandfather that he could still earn his board and room by cleaning out the lobby before going to the fairgrounds and washing the windows on the weekend. He'd also do the bell-hopping after dinner.

I suggested he could shove a broom up his ass and sweep the street to and from the fairgrounds, but he didn't think that was funny. At sixteen the world is a serious place, at least where work's concerned.

After lunch we drifted over to Drake's Soda Fountain. It was dark and cool inside under the big overhead fans and we sat in wire-backed chairs at a table near the front windows and drank root beer from heavy, frosted mugs while watch-ing heat waves shimmy over the gravel on Main Street. Pretty soon Clayt showed up with Angie. I expected her to apologize about her old man's attack on me the night before but she hardly looked at me. Hank right away told Clayt about our job and instead of picking up on it, he hemmed and hawed and looked at Angie who stared back at him with a steady, dark expression.

"You might as well do it," she said finally.

"Well, okay."

Hank said the third guy on our crew should be Chip Hanson, a half-pint friend who worked nights for Fin, running the popcorn machine at the theater. I said he wasn't big enough to help, but Hank said he was ready and quick as a squirrel and funny to boot so I agreed since having Clayt was like getting a man and a half.

I was about through with my root beer when Clayt glanced outside and said to Angie, "Hey, there's your cousin."

Angie looked with a "so what?" expression as the slim girl on the sidewalk peered through the window and saw us. The next moment she was inside.

I'd never seen anyone like her in Corden before and don't expect I ever will again. She looked about half Chink and half Spik—with black slanting eyes, high cheekbones, a long straight nose and black hair that swung just short of her square shoulders. She wore a plain white dress and looked sleek as a show cat.

"Do you know where your father is?" she asked Angie. The voice was low, almost husky.

"You'd more likely know than me," said Angie.

"He talked with you last night. Did he say anything about going somewhere today?"

"All he tells me is 'don't' and 'you can't.'"

"He didn't sleep at home—"

"You'd know, wouldn't you?"

"—and he's not at the theater. His car is still in front of the house."

Angie shrugged.

"Your mother keeps asking about him," said Cora, keeping her voice calm with obvious effort. "She's worried sick. She didn't believe me when I said he was at the theater. Where else could he be?"

Angie's eyes turned toward me. Hank and Clayt looked, too.

"Don't look at me," I said. "I haven't got him."

The cousin's eyes, dark and suspicious, took me in.

"You must be Carl Wilcox." Her tone was formal enough to starch me.

"Every inch," I admitted and stood up to face her. "You must be Cousin Cora."

She examined me without any noticeable signs of admiration.

"You're the one that Uncle Fin attacked last night."

"I'm the man you rescued, yes, ma'am, and believe me, I appreciated it."

"Have you seen him since then?"

She was taller than I'd expected. Her body was so slim and neatly done up I'd figured she was short but our eyes were only an inch shy of level with each other. Of course that didn't exactly make her a tower.

"No," I said, "I haven't seen him. I saw all I wanted to last night and didn't figure we had anything to jaw about."

The dark eyes narrowed. "I've heard about you. You're a practical joker and you believe in getting even. What've you done?"

"Nothing to Fin. Not that I wouldn't have if I'd found him handy and batless."

She studied me a little more, got no pleasure from it, glanced at the kids and said, "I think this is a matter for the police."

Nobody said anything as she turned and walked out. After a second I followed her and caught up as she approached the street corner.

"Look," I said, "maybe we'd ought to check a few places before we call in the law."

She gave me a flat stare and said, "Why?"

"Well, now, it could be embarrassing if there was a big fuss and Fin was only messing around or sleeping one off."

She looked across the street, apparently giving the notion some serious thought and finally, with a little effort, turned back to face me. "Do you have any idea where to look?"

"Well, nothing special, but I could check around—"

"I suspect you would very much enjoy finding him in

some embarrassing situation. Isn't that really why you're so helpful?"

"Well, now, that would be fun, but the fact is, I'd get more pleasure out of putting your mind at ease."

I smiled as innocently as I could and after a couple of seconds she shook her head.

"I'm afraid I don't trust you, Mr. Wilcox. I don't want your help and I'm certain Uncle Fin wouldn't either. Good day."

I watched her float away and decided a girl that looked so fine either coming or going deserved all the help she could get, whether she appreciated it or not.

I decided to start with a visit to Lil's.

# * Chapter *
# IV

Lil's place was well up on the west hill with a fine view of a graveyard on the north, a sandpit to the west and the whole town in the valley east. She was sitting on the front porch in a rocker, sipping what looked like pink lemonade when I strolled up her front walk.

"Well," she said, giving me a sleepy grin, "the prodigal son. You want a drink?"

"Why not?"

"Sit," she told me, stood up and swayed inside. Her round buttocks jiggled under the silver rayon housecoat and I could tell she was warm and bare under it. I could see the dirty soles of her feet as she walked away.

A few moments later she jiggled back, leaned down and handed me a cool glass filled with liquid and a good chunk of clear ice in it. I took a sip. It was about equal parts of sloe gin and lemonade.

"Too sweet?"

"Perfect," I lied. "Just like the mixer. Why don't we go upstairs?"

"Too hot. How you been, Carl?"

"What I've been is without."

"My, that must've been hard on you."

"It's been hard on me most of my life. Let's go up and work on it."

"You really that bad off? Haven't had any since you left?"

"I'm what you could call a reborn virgin."

She shook her head. "And at your age!"

"I'll tell you, it's a Goddamned crime. Come on, Lil, let's go see if it still works."

"It's awful hot," she said doubtfully but duty called and she answered.

It *was* hot inside, and taking off our clothes didn't cool me a bit.

After a while I remembered what I'd thought I'd come up the hill for and I had to wake Lil to ask if she'd ever serviced Fin Larson.

She shook her head without opening her eyes.

"Never?"

"That's right."

"The poor son-of-a-bitch."

She giggled and opened one eye. "Old blarney Carl."

Pretty soon she decided we were hungry, went down to the kitchen and cooked hamburgers even though it was early afternoon. When she built another drink I settled for beer. It was a brew she made herself and it wasn't bad.

"You ever hear any talk about where Fin went when he was looking for something special?" I asked.

"He goes to the cities for it—or did. Now I suppose he gets all he needs from that cousin he brought back from there."

She said "cousin" with sarcasm.

"I kind of doubt it. I think he wants to, but she's too cagey to make it easy. She's got a hold on him I don't think she'd have if she'd already put out."

"How do you figure that?"

I told her what'd happened at the swimming hole.

She turned over the hamburgers with a spatula and squinted as they sizzled. "You get into the damnedest scrapes, Carl."

"Yeah, but do you think I might be right?"

"Uh-huh. Fin's always been a fella reaching. You know, he married above himself and he's always after women he's had to chase. I'd guess he likes running the show house because he gets to fight with those movie people that think they're big shots—"

"Where'd you pick up that stuff?"

"Lotsa people. They like to talk about Fin Larson."

"How about Buck?"

"Yeah, mostly Buck. Fin treats 'im like dirt, you know."

"Nobody treats anybody like dirt. What does he do?"

"Well, you've lived in this town for God's sake—you know. He bosses him around and yells. I could really tell you a thing or two about that man—"

"Shoot."

She slipped the cooked hamburgers on buns and put them on plates before us.

"Eat," she said.

"I can eat and listen."

"I can't talk and eat."

"Does Buck come around regular?"

"Used to."

"No more?"

She took a bite of hamburger and shook her head.

"How was he?"

She shook her head again, swallowed and said, "Like a bear with a wooden dick."

"Sounds awkward."

"The best part was he didn't take any time to mention."

"Heavy, huh?"

"Like a hippo."

"You take on lots of them?"

"More'n I like to remember. Who the hell you trying to find out about?"

"Everybody. Now I know why you like me—I'm a light-weight."

"Not where it counts. You want another beer?"

I said no. If I had a couple more I wouldn't stop. I kidded around about another trip upstairs but she knew I couldn't afford it and said no. I patted her bottom and went back downtown.

Joey's Model T was parked in front of City Hall and I stopped in to see him.

"I figured you'd be out scouring the county with a posse," I said.

"So you rushed in to volunteer?"

"Right. Where do we start?"

"I don't start 'til he's been missing two days."

"Where you figure you'll look in two days?"

"I probably won't have to look because he'll be home, minding his own business like everybody else should."

"You figure Cora's a busybody?"

Joey shook his head and looked sorrowful. He was very good at that.

"She's got this notion somebody's done Fin in. Hell, he's only been gone a little over half a day. If I started a murder investigation every time some husband disappeared that long I'd be spending all my life at it."

"That's right—you got more important things to do."

That didn't score anything so I asked who he thought Fin might be messing with besides his cousin.

"Now don't go asking questions like that—Fin's been behaving himself quite a while now."

"Uh-huh. But before he got religion, who'd he mess with last?"

"That ain't in my line of investigation."

He liked that word. It was long and professional.

"Yeah, I know. Your specialty is checking parked cars for spooners. You talked with Buck yet?"

"About what?"

"Fin."

"I ain't talked to anybody but that Gypsy-looking cousin."

"Buck'd know if anybody—it wouldn't cost you to ask."

Joey shoved his chair away from the desk, got up and glared out the window at the baking street. That didn't soothe him any and after a moment he grunted and started off. I trailed along.

Buck ran a butcher shop two doors north of Second Street just off Main. His pa had been the town blacksmith and Buck learned the trade but later turned to butchering because it was lighter work, he got to meet the ladies and none of the animals kicked.

The shop was empty when we went in but the jangling bell on the door brought Buck out from the room like a shark to bait. His apron was bloodstained and his blacksmith arms were bare and sweaty. For just a second his face was a great study—something between fear, anger and just plain confusion. There was no way to tell whether he figured we were there because I'd made a complaint about the rock throwing or if he was worried about something else. He was still trying to decide between bluster and charm when Joey said hi and asked how business was.

"Can't complain," he said. "How's yours?"

"About the same. You know where Fin's at?"

His eyebrows went up. "Fin? He ain't here. Why?"

"Cora says he's missing. Didn't sleep home last night, car's out in front of his house. Seems funny."

Buck folded his massive arms across his barrel chest and scowled at me. It was enough to spook a marine sergeant.

"Why's this peckerhead with you?" he asked, tilting his head at me.

"I came in to apologize for getting in the way of your rock last night. I think I chipped it."

His blue eyes took me in for a second, then shifted back to Joey.

"I ain't seen Fin since last night. He mebbe decided to go to the cities."

"Without his car?"

"The Goddamn trains still run, don't they?"

"Not from Corden after midnight. Leastways not passenger trains. You trying to tell me Fin travels like a hobo?"

"How the hell do I know? I ain't his nurse."

"Seems to me you've put him to bed more'n once."

"I didn't last night. Ask his hot-ass kid, or Eddie Langer. Eddie'd probably know."

"Why'd you bring up Angie?" demanded Joey. His face getting red. "Why'd you call her hot-assed?"

"Hell, she's running around with that big stud alla time —why else'd she go with him—"

"You got a mind like an open sewer," said Joey. "Think what you like but don't let it spill out and stink up my town."

We went back out on the hot sidewalk and stomped around the corner—or Joey stomped. He was steaming. He never could stand bad talk about women, let alone a high school girl, and he was mad and depressed at the same time. His face was enough to choke up a wolf.

"I should've asked him more questions. I bet he knows more'n he's admitting," he said.

"Yeah. Why didn't you?"

"I'd had all I could take. Imagine a man saying stuff like that about his own cousin—"

We walked on to the theater and Chip Hanson, the kid Hank wanted to join us on the fairgrounds job, was sweeping out the lobby when we opened the front door. At first glance he looked about twelve, being so small, but his eyes had a wise glint and he moved quick and sure, as Hank said, like a squirrel.

Joey greeted him with a voice that held only a little of his anger at Buck. Chip nodded at him and grinned at me. For some reason feisty kids always grin at me.

"How long you been working for Fin?" asked Joey.

Chip squinted in mock concentration and said eight months.

Joey shook his head. "Beats all—I'd have swore you started last week. Is Eddie up in the booth?"

"Nope. Doesn't show until afternoon. Why?"

Joey ignored the question. "Seen Fin lately?"

"Not even early. You gonna pinch him for throwing rocks at Carl?"

"Hadn't planned on it. You know your boss pretty good?"

"Better than some."

"Any notion where he might be?"

The wise eyes became a little hooded. "Right now?"

Joey's face began to droop with annoyance. He nodded.

Chip grinned. "Lots of places. Why?"

"He didn't sleep home last night, his car's out front of his house and his family's worried."

"So what else is new? I bet he doesn't sleep home half the time."

"Even since Cora's been staying there?" I asked. Joey scowled at me and Chip's grin faded.

"I don't know that much about it."

"When'd you see him last?" asked Joey.

"Wednesday night. He came in about starting time and went up to give Eddie hell. It was about three minutes after show time. That always makes Fin mad. Then he came down, went out for a while and came back feeling pretty good. He stood out in front and talked with me by the corn popper, bummed a couple handfulls and talked."

"What about?"

"Mostly kidding stuff. Like was I getting any and how much. And then he asked would I like to learn about running the projector and I said not much more than being able to fly and he explained he needed somebody to fill in now and then for Eddie, like if he got sick or went somewhere, and if I was interested he'd teach me and I could take over whenever needed. He said he couldn't pay much, but the training would be worth a lot and I said that'd be great and we shook on it."

"Back up a little," said Joey. "He wanted you to fill in for Eddie if he got sick or went somewhere. What'd he mean, if he went somewhere?"

"What he said, I suppose." Chip was impatient with slow people.

"He didn't say any more than that about Eddie?"

"No."

"Did you get any notion maybe he was gonna can Eddie?"

"He didn't say anything like that, no."

"You said he gets mad when Eddie starts late."

"Well, sure, Fin likes to yell. He gives Eddie fits and in a minute it's all forgot. It's a game Fin plays."

"How drunk was he when he came back?" I asked.

"Pretty drunk. To tell the truth, I didn't set much store in his offer. I figured it was drunk talk he'd forget by Thursday—or he'd pretend to."

"Did he do that regular? Make drunk promises and forget?"

"Yeah. I got two raises like that. Never came through."

"That make you mad?" I asked.

"Naw. I kinda like him. He's awful screwed up, you know?"

"What's that mean?" demanded Joey.

"Well, he's just screwed up. Doesn't know what he really wants, but he wants it all, if you know what I mean."

Joey didn't get that at all but I thought I did.

We walked back across Main and on past the railway tracks about three blocks to Eddie Langer's place. The front screen didn't fit and rattled like a damned skeleton on resurrection day when Joey knocked. Doris, Eddie's blond wife, slopped up to the door in a tired pink kimono and green scuffs.

"Eddie here?" asked Joey.

"Out back," she said and slopped back to whatever she'd been doing in the kitchen. It didn't smell like much of a success.

We walked around the north side past untrimmed hedges flanking a dandelion lawn and found Eddie in a hammock strung between an elm and a box elder. He was reading a movie magazine with Jean Harlow on the cover. As we approached his head lifted and he peered over the tops of his glasses. He looked more curious than surprised or worried as his blue eyes shifted between us. He didn't speak.

"Workin' hard?" asked Joey.

Eddie turned the magazine upsidedown on his flat belly and didn't bother to answer. We stopped a couple feet away from the hammock.

"Was Fin around the show house last night?" asked Joey.

"No." His voice was soft and flat.

"You didn't see him at all last night?"

"That's right."

"When'd you see him last?"

"Wednesday night."

"Is that usual—him not showing two nights running?"

"Sometimes he doesn't show for a week."

Joey looked skeptical. "Even when he's not out of town?"

"Not usually, no."

Joey glanced around the yard, taking in the crab grass, dandelions and bare dirt. He looked at Eddie again.

"How do you and Fin get along?"

"Good enough so I been with him seven years."

"Would you say he was an easy man to work for?"

"Easier than Simon Legree."

Joey gave him a schoolmaster look. "I get the feelin'
you're bein' cagey. How come I feel that?"

"I imagine because you're a cop asking cagey questions. I
don't know where Fin is, yeah he yells at me, no we don't
get drunk together and yes I'd rather work for Santa Claus.
Okay?"

"Why'd Fin yell at you Wednesday?"

"Because I started his movie two and a half minutes late."

"How come you did that?"

"I made a mistake putting the reel on and had to change
it. They'd been packed out of sequence."

"Does it make you mad when Fin yells?"

"It bores my ass off."

"You ever yell back?"

Eddie swung his legs over the hammock edge and sat up,
carefully holding the magazine against his belly. His hair
was thick and curly and a blue shadow covered his lean jaw.

"A man doesn't yell back at his boss, not if he wants to
keep his job. Why're you asking me all these questions?"

Joey smiled at him for the first time.

"You know, Eddie, I was beginning to wonder if you'd
ever ask. What do you figure's the reason?"

"I'd guess he's missing."

"You knew when we came around, didn't you? How'd
you happen to know?"

"Because his cousin Cora called and asked about him."

"Why the hell didn't you say so?"

Eddie smiled. "You never asked."

Joey gave me an exasperated look and turned back to
Eddie. "I'm gonna tell you something. People that want to
help a lawman tell him things without him having to drag
them out. Now do you think maybe you can tell me where
I'll find Fin without a lot more gab?"

"No. I mean I haven't got the foggiest where he might
be. I never been involved in his personal life—not when I
could help it."

"What's that mean?"

"It doesn't mean anything." Eddie hadn't smiled again

and he looked uncomfortable. When Joey just stared at him, he took the magazine from his lap and rolled it in his bony hands.

Without taking his eyes from Eddie, Joey asked me, "Why do I get this notion he's lying to me?"

I didn't answer.

"Sometimes," said Eddie, "when he's been on a real binge, he goes to Aquatown to dry out. There's a place for that . . ."

"You figure he was in the middle of a binge when he hollered at you Wednesday night?"

"Coulda been. He was generally drunk by night, though."

"He holler at anybody besides you?"

"Sure. Everybody—except that cousin from the cities— and the movie people from Chicago."

"Movie people?"

"The ones he dickers with for shows we run."

"He holler at Buck a lot?"

"Hell, yes." The recollection seemed to relax him a little, he quit trying to roll the movie magazine into a dowel.

"I guess maybe you don't like Buck much," said Joey.

Eddie looked him straight in the eye. "I got nothing against Buck."

Joey stared back and pretty soon Eddie's eyes slipped away toward the house. There was a change in him I couldn't put a handle on.

"Eddie," I said, "is it true Fin only wants hard-to-get women?"

He snorted. "Drunk, he'd mount a sow."

"Who's he been after lately?"

"Anybody—everybody."

"How about your Mrs.?"

"Hah!" He tried to make it sound ridiculous, but Joey's eyes narrowed and it made Eddie squirm and start twisting the magazine again. "Look, fellas, I gotta eat so I can get to work—okay?"

Joey, still scowling, said okay and we went our way.

"If we ever find the body," I told Joey, "there'll be another problem besides finding the killer."

"Yeah, what's that?"

"Finding six guys willing to carry the coffin."

"You can rent pallbearers."

"Who'll pay for 'em?"

"Well, let's not bury him til we know he's dead."

# ＊ Chapter ＊

# V

After dinner at the hotel I hunted for Joey and found him at the café counter polishing off a slab of apple pie.

"You checked out that doctor in Aquatown yet?"

He gave me a glum stare. "How'm I supposed to do that?"

"Ask a cop, for God's sake. They'll know where you send drunks with too much money to throw in the tank."

He finished his coffee, paid the bill and started back to the office with me tagging along.

Nobody on duty at the city police station knew anything, but they suggested he call a lieutenant at home. I had to rag Joey to make him follow that up. He kept saying, "It's Friday night, for God's sake."

"So it's too early for him to be drunk yet. Call now."

The lieutenant turned out to be friendly and fonder of talk than food or drink. He went on till Joey was squirming like a kid at half past pee-time, worrying about the bill and trying to cut the man off. Eventually he butted in, got across a description of Fin and told the lieutenant to call back if he got something positive. Then he hung up.

"So he knew the place," I said.

Joey took off his hat, swabbed his brow and said if that guy'd known any more, the call would've lasted a week.

"Well, it's not costing anything now. What'd he say?"

"There's this Doc Manley, an honest to God medical

man, who's got like a clinic in a big brick house with Finnish baths—"

"You mean Turkish?"

"If I'd meant Turkish, I'd've said Turkish—this here's Finnish. That's what Lt. Richter said, and fellas go there and sweat it out and drink fruit juice and stuff and wind up with a cold shower."

"That'd ought to cure a man of drinking."

"Well, you want I should get you an appointment?"

"You're funnier than bleeding piles—and no thanks. I can't picture paying money to stay sober."

Pretty soon he got restless and said he'd ought to go make his rounds. I told him it was too early for neckers and he got indignant, claiming his duties went a hell of a way beyond snooping on young couples and I allowed as how he did have a lot of watermelon patches and crabapple trees to protect but the fact was he wanted to get out of the office to avoid a collect call from the gabby lieutenant. He denied that too so I asked was it okay if I stuck around and answered the telephone.

"If you stay sober."

That was supposed to squelch my offer but I gave him scout's honor and he snorted and left. For a while I stood at the front door of city hall, gawking down the street. Everything was peaceful as a graveyard.

When the telephone rang I went in and agreed to accept charges. Lt. Richter didn't bother asking who I was or where Joey'd gone, he had a live audience and he wasn't going to waste it. What he said in a few million wandering words was that Fin Larson had made an appointment at the Doc's place Thursday night but never showed or canceled. The Doc was mad. That seemed to impress the Lieutenant a lot more than seemed natural to me and he went on till I about dozed off. Finally I just said thanks and hung up with him still in full sail. That's the greatest thing about a telephone—you don't have to knock the talker down to shut him up.

Joey came back after dark and I told him about the call. He didn't like it—even though I didn't mention how long it'd gone on. He stood by the desk staring out across the street and scowled.

"That gypsy was right, Goddamnit," he said. "Something *has* happened to Fin."

I told him his detecting talents would shame Sherlock Holmes but he paid no attention so I left him to sweat.

It seemed like time to get acquainted with the gypsy so I meandered up to Fin Larson's. The house stood on a sloping corner lot with a lawn smooth as a golf green which ran down to the edge of a three foot stone wall along the sidewalk. Steps cut through its center led up to a long straight walk flanked by dark blue spruce. Beyond the trees was the white porch doorway.

I found Cora sitting behind the screen on the porch. She was in a white dress.

"Heard anything from Fin?" I asked.

"No. I hoped you had news."

"Maybe I have. Did you know he went to a place in the city to dry out now and then?"

After a second, she nodded.

"He made an appointment for last night, but didn't show."

"Yes," she said. "I know."

"Huh?"

"I made the appointment for him. After he attacked you. He promised he'd go. Dr. Manley told me, when I called him the next morning, that Uncle Fin hadn't come. That's why I was so sure something was wrong."

"Well, damnation, lady, you'd have saved some people a lot of time and a little money if you'd told us that before."

"Us?"

"Joey and me. Joey called the city long distance, checking on the Doc."

"Are you telling me that you're working with the police?"

"No, but Joey and I've been known to speak now and again—and in this case it's been quite a bit. Why didn't you tell the whole thing before?"

"I hoped it wouldn't have to come out that he had to go to a detoxification center."

"My God, is that what they call a boarding house for drunks?"

She didn't like that and kept silent.

"Why don't you either come out or invite me in? I don't like talking to spirits and that screen makes you look like a ghost."

She apologized and got up to open the door. When I was inside we stood awkwardly for a moment before she offered me coffee or iced tea. It had cooled down to about eighty-five by then so I said coffee'd be fine if I could smoke. She left me sitting on the porch swing and went inside.

A moment later she was back. She was so light on her feet she seemed to float.

"I've put the water on—it'll be a moment. If you don't mind we'll stay out here—inside Aunt Iris might hear us talking and I don't want to upset her."

"She know Fin's missing yet?"

"I told her he went to the city on business."

"She believe it?"

"Of course. Why not?"

"Well, there're quite a few reasons she might be suspicious. You're young, a lot too good-looking and Fin seems to know your whip."

Her head jerked up. "What's that mean—knows my whip?"

"You snapped it at him last night and he heeled like a trained hound. You told him to see the Doc and he agreed . . ."

"He didn't go."

"Uh-huh. But you were so sure he would if he could that when he didn't you right away called for the cops."

"Well, I only brought him to his senses. He was drunk."

"I know. And the only way I've ever brought a drunk to his senses was knocking him stiff first. What you did—now that was impressive. Come to think of it, you're an impressive woman from every angle. Damned impressive."

"Generally you're a profane man."

"So maybe you can bring me to my senses."

"You're not drunk."

"I could fix that fairly quick."

"Not for my benefit, please."

"Okay. Where's Angie?"

"Up in her room."

"How's Iris?"

"Very restless—excuse me—I'd better check the coffee water—"

While she was inside I heard a call from upstairs and it was several minutes before Cora returned carrying a small tray with cups, sugar and cream. She apologized for taking so long—she'd had to go up to Iris' room.

"What'd she want?"

"She thought she heard voices. I said it was a friend of mine."

I grinned. "You keep telling whoppers like that and she's not gonna believe a thing you say."

The screens had been fitted on the outer edge of the porch railing which was wide enough to hold the little tray and she set it down and told me to help myself. I did, then rolled a smoke and lit up.

"I'd like to talk with her," I said.

"Aunt Iris? Why?"

"I used to know her pretty well."

"I thought she was much older than you."

"Seven years. That's not much. You figure she's dying?"

"What a thing to say!"

"Why? That's the word all over town."

"And everybody in town thinks that I—"

"Oh, that's not unanimous."

"What do you think?"

"I think you're a lady."

That kept her quiet only a few seconds. She sipped her coffee and kept her head down. When she spoke, it was very low, just over a whisper.

"I don't know what to think about her. The doctor seems uncertain—even a little suspicious. Of course he's careful not to commit himself, but I don't think he takes her problem seriously. There've been nights when I was convinced she wouldn't live till morning. Then suddenly there's a miraculous recovery, for no reason I can see."

"You like her?"

"Yes." She said it hesitantly, as if her own answer were a surprise, then said "Yes," again, with conviction. "She's a good person. There've been times when we talked and laughed like schoolgirls. It made Uncle Fin irritated. He said we sounded like a couple of giggling kids, and of course that made everything funnier to us."

I grinned in the dark, thinking of the town's version of life in the Larson house; the tyrant Fin bullying his dying wife, the beautiful mistress, waiting to take over, and all the time these females are giggling at this poor dumb man.

"What were you doing before Fin brought you to Corden?" I asked.

"I took classes at the University and worked part time."

"What kind of work?"

"Why do you ask what kind of work—why not what I was studying?"

"I know about work. Studying doesn't mean anything to me."

She laughed. "I suppose that makes sense. Well, I was doing clerical and research work for an English professor. He was the department head."

"You liked working for him?"

"Oh, yes. He was an old man—very witty—and a terrible flirt. We had good times."

"Why'd you quit and come with Fin?"

"Well, it was one of those things. I knew the professor was going to retire and I probably wouldn't be hired by his successor who was a fussy man with an older secretary who'd been doing his work for years. So when Uncle Fin convinced me I was needed here, I came."

"You think you made a mistake?"

"Sometimes, yes. Even hired nurses get little respect. Care-taking relatives are nobodies."

"I don't think you'll ever manage to be a nobody."

She was silent for several moments. I wished I could see her eyes. I couldn't tell whether she was looking at me or not. When she finally spoke her voice had lost some of its defensive hostility.

"Are you Irish?"

"Some. And English and Scotch and Welsh."

"Oh my. Well, if you like, I'll go see if Aunt Iris is willing to accept a visitor."

A few minutes later I climbed the stairs and entered the

bedroom. Electricity had been installed about five years before but there were still gas jets all over the house and from the softness of the light I'd guessed Iris still used them. Instead there was a candle burning steadily on a small stand beside the bed, casting a gentle glow over the near side of the spread but not quite reaching the head half-buried in a pile of pillows.

"Well, Carl," she said huskily, "don't I look a fright?"

I crossed the woven rag rug to a chair at the bedside and sat down. Iris's face, once round and pink, was thin and gray against the white pillowcase. Her eyes, which had so often taken me in with sharp disapproval, now stared with a bright curiosity—even amusement. They didn't look related to the woman in the bed.

"You look a little lean," I said.

"I'm a little more than a skeleton."

"What's wrong?"

"Atrophy of the spirit."

She said it again and I told her that was a new one on me. She smiled, showing long teeth and I thought of Little Red Riding Hood's grandmother as played by the wolf.

"Is Fin the real trouble?"

"What else?"

"You want me to get you out of here?"

The bright eyes considered me, then she laughed once and slowly rolled her head on the pillow.

"You'd do that? Get me out?"

"Why not?"

She laughed again. "You always were a madman, Carl. And what do you think Fin would do if you tried that?"

"Sue for divorce?"

"He'd have you back in prison, that's what he'd do."

"Not if you backed me up."

"My backing lacks weight—or substance."

"There're still plenty people in town think you married beneath you. There'd be help."

"I doubt it. And anyway, I'm too little to fight."

"Nuts."

"Of course—you'd think that was ridiculous . . . but

what's all your fighting ever got you but broken noses and jail?"

It seemed to me there'd been more than that but at the moment it was a little vague. Her eyes closed as if she found my face more than she could bear, then, after a few seconds, she rolled her head half an inch and stared at me solemnly.

"You can't answer?"

I shrugged. "I guess I just never believed in making it easy for the other guy. I got my satisfaction from that."

"I suppose that *is* something," she admitted. She stared up at the dark ceiling for several seconds and slowly licked her lips with the tip of her tongue. "I remember," she said softly, "coming to your house when I was very young—you were just a little boy with a straight nose and an impudent face and you opened the door when I knocked and just stared at me. And I became impatient and said, very smartly, 'I didn't come here to see you,' and you said, 'I don't remember sending for you—' and you closed the door in my face. I was so furious I cried."

"Yeah, I remember that. I got whaled for it."

"Poor Carl. At the time I wasn't a bit sorry—I guess I'm still not. It's very difficult to feel sorry for someone who never knows he's beaten. Somehow that makes him undefeated."

She rolled her head toward the wall. A moment later, as if she had suddenly remembered she was the hostess and shouldn't allow silence, she began talking in a distant, rustling voice, about times with my sister, places they'd gone, fellows they'd known, presents received. Gradually her voice moved off while I wondered if she believed a return to the past would wipe out the now.

Then she was asleep.

I got up, pussy-footed out and went downstairs. Cora, who'd been reading in the living room, got up and met me by the front door. She carried her book which looked big enough to give a weight-lifter cramps and I asked what it was.

"*Look Homeward Angel,*" she said.

"It looks like a library dictionary."

She glanced down and smiled. "It almost is. The author calls it the story of a buried life."

"There can't be much buried now."

"No. Did Aunt Iris fall asleep?"

"Uh-huh. Let's walk."

"I don't think I'd better. Would you like more coffee?"

Her turn-down on the walk made me ornery and I said no, I'd had enough. She didn't press me and it took some effort to keep from stomping out in a sulk but I managed to make the exit casual. If that broke her up she hid it well.

# \* Chapter \*

# VI

Louie, the judge's hired hand, was unloading our equipment when we arrived at the fairgrounds; four shovels, two hammers, a crow bar, a keg of nails, two saws, rip and crosscut, and some scrubby lumber. The one fine touch was a gallon of iced water in a stubby thermos jug.

"Heard anything about Fin Larson?" I asked Louie. He shook his head, got in his truck and pulled out quick, as if he'd been warned by the judge about the dangers of talking to ex-cons.

"Where we gonna start?" asked Clayt.

"The stock barns," I answered. "It's gonna be hot enough to blister lizards by noon so let's keep in the shade for a few days and maybe it'll cool off later."

My consideration didn't seem to cheer him any.

To my surprise we found the east door of the first barn wouldn't slide open even though the boards that had once been nailed across it were gone. I walked around the south side to the west end and damned if that door wasn't still boarded shut.

"Somebody must be in there," said Chip.

"Sure," I said, "it's probably Fin Larson with a girl friend."

"If it is," said Hank, "they're both baked by now."

I sent Chip after the crowbar and in a few minutes I'd ripped off the boards and we shoved the doors open. For a moment we stood in the entrance, breathing the hot air that stank of old manure and baked straw, while our eyes adjusted to the dim light. I walked down the center aisle between stalls heaped with straw which had sifted across the dusty floor and crackled softly underfoot. The east end doors had been propped shut with two-by-fours braced against the walls. We lifted the two-by-fours out and slid the doors open to let in a cross breeze and more light.

"We need a big fan," said Chip.

"No worry," said Hank. "With you around there'll always be a breeze."

"Nothing that'll cool us," I said. "Okay, we'll start with the loft. Shove everything down in the center, and remember—it's gonna get hotter every hour so the quicker we clear out up there the sooner we'll be down where it's cool."

"What I don't get," said Hank, "is how the guy that propped the doors shut got out. The boarded-up end hasn't been open in five years—I'd bet on it."

"I'll show you," said Chip, and he scrambled up the loft ladder, which was nailed to the east wall, moved south on the upper door frame, reached the loft door, pulled it open and pushed the hook through an overhead eye.

"How about that," said Hank. "He climbed out, hung over the end and dropped to the ground. How'd he unhook the door up there afterwards?"

"He probably didn't bother to hook it up," I said, "now, while you're up, Chip, go to the other end and open that vent."

The smell and heat eased off with the ventilation but the breeze raised dust that made our eyes water, our noses dry and our throats dusty. By noon the temperature was over one-hundred and we'd polished off the thermos of ice water and had dropped about five pounds apiece in sweat which we made up for with layers of dust. There was damned little talk as we trooped back to town for lunch.

When Hank and I appeared in the hotel kitchen, Ma gave us a look she usually reserved for tramps and drunken salesmen.

"Feed them out here," she told Bertha.

That tickled Bertha about as much as it galled Hank. It only annoyed me because the kitchen was ten degrees hotter than the dining room but I kept my mouth shut. Ma just couldn't tolerate blue-collar men, even when they were kin. She was white collar to the soul and a little beyond. Her biggest ambition (she never had dreams) was to see Hank graduate from college—with honors. She made a point of letting him see he'd better not get any notions that laboring, especially for me, would allow him to mingle with his betters.

"Heard anything about Fin Larson?" I asked Bertha.

"Sure, I heard he's missing."

"I might've known you'd be right up to the minute," I said, as she put plates before us loaded with potato salad and thick-sliced pork sandwiches. "Did he ever make a pass at you?"

"If he'd ever tried, he'd've been missing before now."

After polishing off lunch with about a quart of milk I ambled over to city hall. Joey was sitting in a captain's chair, propped against the wall looking energetic as a sunning snake. He was staring at his big feet in their dusty, high-laced shoes.

"Well," I said, "hot on the scent of our missing citizen, I see."

He gave me his old dog look.

"It's got me beat, Carl. Where the hell can you look for a fella like Fin?"

"The last fella I heard of who got a tour of hell had a Wop guide. Trouble is, we got no Wops in Corden—"

He didn't know what I was talking about and knew I knew he wouldn't and refused to ask for education. I sat down, rolled a smoke, lit up and closed my eyes.

"Pretty hot at the fairgrounds?" he asked.

"That's a shrewd deduction—how in the world did you figure it out?"

He scowled. "Work sure don't agree with you. You're ornery as a knocked-up witch."

I decided he was too right to argue with and went to work.

We'd finished nearly three-quarters of the loft before knocking off at noon and since it was getting hotter by the minute I said we'd work on the ground the rest of the day

and complete the top next morning. That suited the crew
fine.

The mixture of manure and straw on the ground level
wasn't quite as dry as in the haymow, but it was riper; Chip
and Hank started clowning around, talking in phony English
accents which Chip claimed eased the stink.

"How?" I asked.

"Well, you tilt your head back, narrow down the nose,
push words up in the top of your mouth and sort of let 'em
come out that way and it blocks the smeller. Cawn't chew
feel it, old boy?"

"I smell something besides manure," complained Hank.

"Like what?" I asked.

"I don't know. It comes along when we get wind from the
east."

"It's London, old boy," said Chip.

"Probably a dead rat," said Clayt. It was the first time
he'd spoken for a while and I gave him a close look. He
seemed a little peaked.

"You okay?" I asked.

"Sure," he said but he didn't meant it.

We went back to work and by a little after four we had
almost reached the end on the north side. By then Chip had
run out of chatter and we worked in silence except for the
whistling prairie wind and the barn's creaking. A sudden
gust came in the west door, raising a dust storm that caught
Chip full in the face.

"Oh shit, oh dear," he yelled, dancing around. "I cawn't
see!"

I looked around, not really worried because he was still
using his English accent, and watched as he dug a dirty
handkerchief from his pocket and swabbed at his eyes. Then
I noticed Clayt standing still, not watching Chip, but staring
at Hank who was backing away from a pile of hay in the last
stall.

"Now what?" I asked.

Hank turned his head a little, without taking his eyes
from the straw pile.

"There's something under there."

I walked over beside him. "Like what?"

He handed me his pitchfork.

"You check."

That's when I noticed the flies. They were all over the straw. I pushed lightly with the fork tines, spreading the straw, and the flies rose and buzzed and came back as if magnetized and I got a good whiff of the smell Hank had said wasn't manure. Two more passes with the fork uncovered cloth.

"Hank," I said. "Go get Joey—I think we've found Fin Larson."

# * Chapter *
# VII

"I don't get it," said Joey. "I just don't get one damned bit of it. Why in hell would Fin Larson be in a fairgrounds barn, and why in the hell would somebody barricade the doors and climb out a window after killing him there?"

"The barricading makes sense," I said. "Whoever did it figured it'd take years to find the body. He didn't know there was gonna be a fair after five years without one."

Fin had been hauled away by the county coroner and Joey and I were still in the barn, staring at sunbeams shafting through wall cracks. Hank and Chip stood by the door, solemn as crows. Clayt, who'd lost his lunch when we found Fin, had gone home.

The coroner told Joey that Fin was stabbed through the neck with a pitchfork from the front. He wasn't sure of the angle—said he hoped that would come out in the autopsy.

Joey was awful disappointed when we poked all through the straw where Fin had been and didn't find a clue. He figured you always found a matchbook or a cigaret case with the murderer's initials if you searched the scene of a murder.

We walked slowly back to town and the thirst I'd forgotten in all the excitement came back so we stopped in Bach's Creamery and had milk shakes at the fountain. The place smelled of sour cream but the concrete floor and the shading elms outside made it cool and restful.

Old man Bach's daughter-in-law waited on us. She'd worked at the Wilcox Hotel before she married young Bach

45

and I'd known her in the non-Biblical sense. It wasn't for lack of trying, but she'd been in love and there's no reaching a girl when she's in that state.

"Is it true you found Fin Larson murdered?" she asked with a whisper.

"Unless he committed suicide by stabbing himself with a pitchfork," I said.

She was properly shocked and begged for details. Joey tried to wave her off but she ignored him.

"It's must've been a tramp," she said. "Nobody in Corden would do a thing like that."

"She's right," I told Joey. "This bum tried to panhandle Fin in the barn and when he said no, the bum stabbed him with this pitchfork he was carrying and hopped a freight."

Joey scowled, bottomed out the milk shake and made with a Scotch burp. Wearily he pushed the glass away and stood up.

"I got to go tell the family," he said. "I just hope no big mouth's already up there making a report."

"I'll go along," I said, sliding off my stool.

"No. I'll handle it."

I wanted to argue but he was so sorrowful I didn't and settled for waiting in his office.

"So—what'd they say?" I demanded when he got back.

He sat down, put his hat on the desk and mopped his forehead with a blue bandanna.

"The cousin—Cora—she came to the door and I told her. Took it like a wooden Indian. I thought for a second she hadn't heard me right. When I started over she raised her hand and turned her head and said she understood what I'd said and she'd tell the others. That suited me fine."

"So you don't know how they took it?"

He shook his head without looking at me.

I shook my head too and went back to the hotel for dinner.

After dusk I went up to see Cora. It was a clear night and the Milky Way looked thick enough to walk on if there was a ladder to reach.

Cora was standing on the walk, star gazing when I came up the steps. Her dress was dark and simple.

"From the top of the west hill," I said, "it'll look even clearer."

"All right," she said, "let's go up there."

She kept her eyes on the sidewalk as we walked along and for nearly a block said nothing. Finally she spoke without looking up.

"When you were little, did you think you'd live forever?"

"Sure."

"When did you get over it?"

"I'm not sure I have."

"I got over it when mother died—as if my immortality were tied with hers. When people told me she was happy in heaven and waiting for me, at first I thought that was selfish of her, and later I just didn't believe any of it. I don't have the imagination to believe in fleshless existence—spiritual permanence—all that floating stuff seems such nonsense I can't accept it even if it's true."

"You don't figure Fin's gone to a better place?"

"No, nor a worse one either. He's gone to a crematorium, that's where he's gone. And he'll come back in a jar."

"Whose idea was that?"

"His. He told Aunt Iris he didn't want embalming or a casket or burial—I think he was afraid of dark places—"

"I can't picture Fin thinking about death. Not his."

"He didn't ordinarily. But when Iris became sick he got it on his mind and talked about it to me one night and then he told Iris."

"What else did he talk to you about?"

She glanced up at me. "Lots of things—like my future."

"Yeah? What'd he have in mind?"

The nearby streetlight showed me her face, very young and earnest.

"You'd be surprised, really. He said he'd teach me to run the theater. Everything about it—the projectors, bookings, promotion—I think he was bored with the show house and he said Eddie wasn't reliable and might run off any time and I could handle his job and then, after a while, just take over running everything. I said I never heard of a woman running a movie theater and he said there wasn't anything a smart girl couldn't do if she'd just go at it."

"That figures. I guess you liked Fin a lot, huh?"

"Of course . . . he was good-hearted at bottom—"

"I always figured that's where he had it."

Her expression darkened and she lowered her head. I felt like a damned fool for kidding at the wrong time. I was still trying to dream up a line for recovery when she said, "I'll tell you what. Just for tonight, why don't you try not being clever? Just allow him one night of no criticism or sarcasm. That's not too much to ask for a dead man, is it?"

"No, not at all. Tell me about him. I don't suppose we ever saw the same fella."

She looked into my face for a couple steps but we were away from the streetlight by then so neither of us could see what we wanted to.

"I don't think my talking about Uncle Fin would entertain you much."

"I didn't figure we took this walk to entertain me, so why not unload a little? It can't pain me and it might do you some good."

She smiled a little grimly. "Somehow you don't seem like a fellow a girl can use as a father confessor."

"So who's asking for confessions? Just talk. That's what you want, isn't it? People feel that way when somebody dies."

She examined me again with the wide and probing eyes that looked black in the dim light. We were still going uphill and she walked with an easy stride that kept her in step with me as we passed in front of darkened houses.

When we came to Trotter's place, an abandoned, half-ass mansion on the corner of the last complete block west of town, Cora walked up to the front porch steps, turned and sat down, tucking her skirt in between her thighs and calves.

"What did you think he was like?" she asked.

"I never thought much about him at all until the night he tried to crown me in the pond. He just didn't interest me much. So I'm asking you, what was he like close up?"

She crossed her arms over her knees and stared down toward the streetlight.

"It's very hard to be . . . honest . . . with him dead such a short time. . . . I know perfectly well he could be horrid—he said awful things to Iris when he lost his temper—and he lost it all the time. He acted as though she got ill to spite him. Actually he despised sick people. I think they frightened him, like the dark. He wanted everyone to think he was strong and undefeatable—he wanted to run everything—he'd loved to have had the power of a politician but he had no patience and couldn't put himself out to please people who couldn't help him in very direct ways. He desperately wanted to be loved just for himself but he was always offering things, like teaching me to run the theater, to gain advantage. To make me feel obliged. And the funny thing is, I think he'd have gone as far as he had to in keeping that promise if he really thought it'd work. I don't think he was really dishonest. He'd make an offer, see how you reacted, and then go ahead and follow through if he had to."

"Uh-huh. Did you know he offered to teach Chip, the popcorn boy, how to run the projector?"

She looked at me, at first in disbelief. Then she said "Really?" and laughed. "I guess I shouldn't be surprised—but it's hard to understand what he expected to get from him."

"Loyalty, admiration—maybe even a friend." I didn't mention it was probably just to put a squeeze on poor Eddie.

She smiled at me. "Maybe you're right."

"Did Fin ever make a pass at you?"

The smile became a frown. "Don't be naive."

"What's that mean? That of course, every man does—or don't be silly, you wouldn't tell me if he did?"

"I never encouraged him."

"I didn't say you did. From what I hear, nobody had to."

"Most men don't have the nerve unless you lead them on—or they're drunk."

"Well, Fin got drunk enough."

She turned to face me. "Did you hate him even before that night at the swimming hole?"

"Hating's not my strong suit."

"But you hated him that night, didn't you?"

For the first time it dawned on me that she might think I'd

killed Fin. That really threw me. I couldn't figure anybody, not even a stranger, could think I'd do a thing like that. I knew that was stupid—to think she would understand me so soon. And then I thought of the nerve of this girl, taking a walk with me, with such a notion in her mind.

"Look," I said, "I'm a get-even guy. I mean, if a man knocks me down, all I want to do is put him down harder. If he makes a fool of me, I want the whole country laughing when I get through with him. But I never in my life wanted to wipe anybody out. I wouldn't have stuck a fork in Fin unless he was coming at me with an axe. And he didn't and I didn't. Okay?"

She watched as I talked, nodded when I stopped and looked out toward the street.

"You believe me?" I asked.

"Uh-huh." It wasn't strong but it wasn't too doubtful.

I leaned a little closer to her. "I've got a notion. I've got this idea that somebody had to decoy Fin into that barn. Somebody made him think he'd find what he wanted there —and from everything I hear, that'd have to be a woman. And from what I see and hear—he'd have been most drawn by you. Now, on Thursday night, after the swimming hole business, did he drive you back to town?"

"I wouldn't let him drive. He rode with me and Buck drove the car they'd come in—Buck's."

"What'd you talk about on the way in?"

"I wasn't talking to him. I was too angry."

"About what?"

"Him making a fool of himself—what else? Well, and what he was doing to Angie—"

"You like Angie too?"

She sighed and shook her head. "She's impossible—but she *is* human and awfully young so you can't help feeling sorry for her when her father makes an idiot of himself in front of her friends."

"Is Angie real stuck on Clayt?"

"I'm not sure. He's her fella . . . a girl that age . . . it's hard to tell how deep the feelings go with a boy."

Or how deep the boy goes in the girl, I thought, but I kept that still.

"Did Fin talk to you during the drive?"

"Not after a while. He started off giving me all this big story he got from the village idiot and how a father had to protect his daughter's honor. I told him he was drunk and dishonorable and that shut him up."

"What happened back in town?"

"We went home, I went to my room and he stayed downstairs."

"Did you ever hear him come upstairs to bed?"

"He sleeps downstairs—in the den off the dining room. He started that when Iris got sick."

"How'd Angie and Fin get on, generally?"

"At the top of their lungs."

"What'd they scrap about?"

"Everything. He was insanely jealous—asked nasty questions, set rigid schedules for hours, criticized what she ate, wore, didn't do, did do. But I'm not really telling it the way it was—they did care about each other—it was always all-out love or all-out hate between them, but the hate was so loud it's the most I remember. The thing is, Angie wanted his approval so badly and then when he became critical she reacted against him."

It wasn't exactly an original story and I cut it off.

"So when Angie got home Thursday night what happened?"

"Well, I heard the front door open and then she came up a little later and went to her room."

"No yelling session with Pappa?"

"I didn't want to listen."

"If the telephone rang, would you have heard it?"

"Oh yes, it's very loud."

"And you didn't hear it?"

"No."

"Then what happened?"

"I went to sleep."

I stood up, stretched and stared west where the land leveled for half a mile before there was another little rise hiding a valley beyond.

"I can't believe Fin didn't have a woman regular. He was

that kind, he had to. So who was she during the last days—
you got any idea?"

"No."

"You think I'm right about him?"

"Probably."

"So somebody who knew that got word to him that this
woman he wanted was waiting for him at the fairgrounds—
and he went there and died."

Cora put her chin in her hands and stared up at me.

"I'd guess," I said, "it'd have to be somebody he knew
well, like Buck."

"No," she said. "He was completely dependent on Fin;
he'd never have done anything to him."

"So who else knew him that well?"

She shook her head.

"There's Angie, Iris, Eddie . . . and you. Right?"

Her eyes opened wider. "Me?"

"You're one of the people who knew him well, yeah."

"We were all dependent on him."

"Okay, so what if one of those people found out he was
cutting them off?"

She shook her head. "That's ridiculous. Are you suggest-
ing that Angie, Iris or I could stab a man as big as Uncle Fin
with a pitchfork?"

"No . . . but a very small lady could set him up for a man
to do it. The man could be anybody at all—but who got him
there? Huh?"

"If any one of us had told him there was a woman waiting
for him somewhere, he wouldn't have believed us."

"Yeah," I agreed. "It's a generally dumb theory."

She stood up and said she should get back, Iris might
need her. The return hike was slow and silent until we were
in the last block.

"Look," I said, "I don't think you set him up, I never had
any real idea like that. I just wanted to talk the whole thing
through, okay?"

"I understand." She smiled. "Besides, you had a turn
coming."

She gasped as we approached the stone steps and a man
who'd been sitting on them stood up before us.

"Buck," said Cora, "what in the world?"

"I came around to see if you needed anything. Iris said you'd gone for a walk with somebody—I wanted to see who."

"I don't think," she said icily, "that it's any of your concern who I walk with."

"I was only worried about you," he said.

He sounded so woeful she was right away sorry and apologized and it was all touching as Tiny Tim. She even took his big paw and patted it. There was some more gab before she finally wished us both a good night, letting me know that she didn't need an escort to the door. We stood and watched until she went inside.

Buck gave a big sigh and scowled at me.

"Why," he asked, "would a girl like that go for a walk with a guy like you?"

"That's funny," I said, "I was just wondering why she'd want to pat your paw. If you get it all figured out, let me know."

"A con, a boozer, and a half-pint at that."

"Boozer—when the hell did you take the pledge?"

"I'll tell you what, Wilcox. If I ever see you so much as talking to that girl again, I'm gonna bust your arm."

"No shit? Well, Buck, if that's the case, you better try right now because I'll be walking her tomorrow so why waste time? Or do you want to go home and get your baseball bat first?"

"Don't crowd me, Wilcox."

"You shit-head, I'm calling you—fight or run."

For a second he hesitated—he couldn't believe a guy my size could be so cocky bare-handed. Then he came at me in a rush with both hands forward to grab before I could swing. I snatched his wrist, stepped inside while turning, slammed my butt into his upper thighs and ducked. He flipped so beautifully I was tempted to let go and watch him fly but he might have landed without serious damage and figuring he was too big and mean to fight all night, I kept a firm hold and slammed him down solid, removing all the starch with one rinse.

After a combination "Ungh!" and "whoosh!" as he hit,

Buck was all out of comment and for several seconds I
squatted at his side while he worked at getting air back in his
balloon. Pretty soon he figured he was going to live but it
didn't give him too much pleasure.

"You must've stumbled on the way to breaking my arm,"
I said. "Want to try it again?"

He wheezed some, tried to get up, fell back and lay there,
his eyes wide open and his chest heaving. After a few seconds he rolled to his side, pulled up his legs and managed to
get from his knees to his feet.

"Nothing busted?" I asked, trying not to sound too hope-
ful. I kept enough distance so he couldn't get his gorilla
mitts on me if he turned ambitious again.

"There'll be another time," he croaked.

"No time like the present," I offered. "You almost got to
me before, maybe you can manage on the second try. Of
course you could get your shoulder busted, but I don't
mind."

He swayed, big and mean as a drunken grizzly, then
turned and stomped off. I let him go. It didn't seem likely
he'd answer any questions if I asked them.

# * Chapter *
# VIII

I went from Larson's place back to city hall and told Joey what'd happened. He scowled at me.

"Since when'd you start rassling guys instead of punching them?"

"Well, he caught me in a cuddly mood. Why do you figure Buck was at the house?"

"Why not? He's been like part of the family most of his life."

"Go on—he was Fin's drinking buddy. The women hated him."

"So maybe he feels orphaned. Or figures he owes it to Fin to watch out for his family now he's gone."

"Uh-huh. And maybe he's sticking around to keep track of what's going on. He also might have the hots for Cora."

"She's kinda skinny for him."

"Her kind of skinny is okay for any guy under forty."

"Uh-huh, so that leaves me out. What're you gettin' at?"

I rolled a cigaret, lit up and leaned against the wall.

"I'm trying to figure the guy, that's all. He's been walked on all his life by Fin, he can handle a pitchfork—and if he's hot for Cora and she's been Fin's and Buck wanted her— that business the other night could've been just the thing to trip his spring."

"Huh?"

"Cora controlled Fin that night—the guy that's been king

in Buck's life. It surprised the hell out of me, think what it did to Buck."

Joey shook his head slowly. "I can see what you mean, but I can't see murder coming from that."

"Okay. Let's back off and try another run. How about this: Cora comes to take care of her aunt, they get to be friends, Cora sees her aunt takes a lot of crap from Fin—who's only related to Cora by marriage, not blood. Then Fin makes things worse by trying to move in on Cora."

"You got no proof he tried that."

"I got some hints besides from what I saw. Did you know he talked about turning over the theater management to Cora?"

"No. But that oughtn't to have made her mad—"

"Maybe she figured it was just another move he was making to get in her pants. Maybe she worked up a little arrangement so Fin would visit a barn and there'd be Buck, waiting with a pitchfork and big plans."

"I can't see it," said Joey.

"Good. I just wanted to be sure I hadn't written that off just because she's got those great eyes and is too skinny for old men."

Outside a stout wind had come up, cooling the air, rustling the trees and making the corner sign squeak. The hotel lobby was dark except where the goose neck lamp made a puddle of light on the registration desk.

I smoked my last cigaret while sitting on the bed, listening to the wind moan and the hotel creak and thought about the bottle in my drawer. I don't tell myself I can quit any time—I can't because I don't want to. I used to figure I'd settle down eventually and amount to something and then I realized there wasn't anything I wanted to amount to that was worth the trouble.

I decided what I had to do was figure who Fin went to see at the fairgrounds. After putting my cigaret out I thought about it for a good fifteen seconds before I went to sleep.

Tuesday was cool. I gathered my crew at 8:00 and we finished the number one barn (which everybody called Fin's now) by noon. At first everybody was wasting time looking for something unusual in the hay but nothing came up and before noon they were kidding around like nothing had happened. It would've shocked Ma and maybe most of the oldsters, but I thought it was fine. I'd hate a crew that wallowed in the afterward of finding Fin's carcass.

Pop Tucker showed after lunch, riding a mower behind a mottled mare old enough to vote. When he came by the second shed where we were working he pulled up the mare, dropped the reins and sat side saddle on the iron seat facing us while he cut a plug of tobacco.

"Which barn'd you find him in?" he asked.

I pointed.

Pop stuck the plug in his right cheek and moved his jaw slowly.

"Must've been pretty ripe."

"He was. These aren't ice barns, you know."

He nodded and grinned at Clayt's sober face.

"Why do you chew?" asked Chip.

"Why do you smoke?"

Chip looked at his cigaret for a second and said damned if he knew. Pop said it was the same with him.

I rolled a cigaret and hunkered down, leaning against the barn wall. "I seem to remember you did some work for Fin a few years back."

"Now and again."

"How was he—to work for, I mean?"

"Generally a son-of-a-bitch, that's how."

"What way?"

"Ever-way. Coming, going, up and down."

Then I remembered. Pop had a daughter—maybe three —and one of them had been messing with Fin about ten years back. It hadn't lasted long but the word went around that he got her in trouble. She ran off and never came back. She'd been tall, dark and goofy about movies.

I shooed the crew back to work, telling them I'd be along in a couple minutes. Hank gave me a lifted eyebrow but drifted off and his sidekicks went along.

I moved closer to the mower and leaned against the iron wheel.

"You got any notions who Fin was fooling with last?"

Pop squinted at me, turned his head and spit. "Why'n hell'd I care who he was fooling with—first or last?"

It isn't easy for a man with a plug in his mouth to look innocent but he nearly made it.

"Well, you're a fella that moves around a lot, listens good, keeps his eyes open—I wouldn't be surprised but what you know most of what goes on in Corden."

"Don't crap me, you're remembering Emma. You figure I kept track of old Fin. I don't. Not no more."

"You mean since he's dead?"

He grinned, showing healthy gums and stained teeth.

"I'd guess you wouldn't exactly rate as Fin's head mourner," I said.

"If I was a drinking man," he said, "I'd've downed a barrel celebrating when I heard about it."

"You still spry enough to stick a pitchfork in him your-self?"

"If I'd had the chance—you damn betcha."

We grinned at each other as I shredded my dead butt and let the ashes and paper flutter into the wind.

"The way I figure," I said, "somebody got him out here by letting him think there was a gal waiting. The trouble is, the only girl I know about that'd draw him, is living right in his own house so why come here?"

"Why do you care who killed him?"

"Self defense. I got a record—if nobody shows up as a better ringer—there's too good a chance I'll get elected."

He thought that over, shifted his plug and finally said, "How about Sophie?"

"Who?"

"Oldest Markson girl. Works at the café."

"Hell, she can't be old enough—"

"You ain't seen her lately. She's seventeen—looks twenty. Regular spitfire. Just your style."

"I'll be damned. Guess I'd better go to the café."

"I don't think it'll do you any good. She don't like old men unless they got money."

"Hell, I'm not courting. I'm looking for a killer."

"Nobody gives a damn who forked Fin—except a few that'd like to pin a medal on him. Forget about it."

He picked up the reins, straightened around on his seat, clucked at the horse and moved off. I went back to my crew.

It was near 7:30 that evening when I drifted into the café. Sophie Markson was polishing the fountain spigots and stopped long enough to make a Coke for me. She was generously made in most parts; eyes, mouth, breasts and hips. Her waist was slim and brown hair, clean and light, fell below her shoulders.

I asked how was her ma.

She glanced at me with arched eyebrows. That wasn't the kind of question she'd become used to.

"She's okay."

"How many kids did she have—four?"

"Five," she said, and kept polishing the spigots with large hands that were soap reddened.

"Yeah. And there's an older brother—went to Aberdeen."

"He came back."

She was bored and a little suspicious. I grinned.

"Okay. So I don't really give a damn about your family. I'm after something else."

"I'd never've guessed."

"Fact is, I'm after real information—like when was the last time you saw Fin Larson alive?"

For the first time I had her full attention. Her blue eyes stared at me, clear and steady.

"Fin Larson?"

"Yeh you know—fella ran the theater—owned property —got himself murdered—"

She frowned impatiently. "Yes, I know who he was. But what's he got to do with me?"

"That's the question, Sophie, exactly."

She looked past me toward the kitchen, then around the empty café. "I don't know what you're getting at."

"I'm getting at murder. Was he in here last week?"

She put down the polishing rag and folded her white arms under her round breasts.

"Yeah, I guess so."

"You're not sure?"

"Lots of people come in here—"

"I know, but not very damn many of 'em got murdered. Was he in here Thursday night?"

"Yeah."

"Was he drunk?"

She shrugged. "You could say that."

"What time was it?"

"Just before the show let out."

"Did he talk to you?"

"What do you think? Everybody talks to me."

"Did he ask you to meet him after work?"

She turned red and looked around again. "Don't be silly, he was a married man. I wouldn't fool around with a married man."

"I hear you met with him."

"That's a lie!" Her voice rose and the sound frightened her. She moved toward me with wild eyes but spoke just above a whisper. "You're crazy—get out of here—go rob a bank or something—"

Four high school kids came chattering through the door and blundered into a booth across from us. Sophie, her face suddenly transformed back into the beaming flirt, hurried over to serve them. I finished my Coke and went out.

Back at the hotel I jawed with Elihu until he went to bed just before the movie let out. At eleven I turned off all but the counter light and sat in the semi-dark, smoking until the crowd began drifting out of the café. It was just after midnight when Sophie came down the street heading home. She was alone.

She saw me coming out of the hotel and walked faster but I caught up and said I wanted to talk with her.

"Keep away from me," she said. "You got nothing to say I want to hear."

"You rather talk with Joey over at city hall?"

She kept walking. "What's that supposed to mean?"

"You know damned well. You think you could mess around with a man like Fin and not have everybody know?"

"No, I don't—and I never did and I sure don't want anybody talking about me messing with any ex-cons so kindly go to hell, will you?"

"I'm not quite ready yet. Look, I'm not figuring you had anything to do with him being killed—not directly—but maybe you were used by somebody—"

"You're crazy. I had nothing to do with him."

"He came to the café every damned day. You saying he never spoke to you?"

"He gimme his order, I brought it and he thanked me and when he left a tip I thanked him. That's not talking."

"He tip good?"

"Sure."

"But he never flirted with you?"

"Everybody flirts with me."

"And you flirt back—if they're not ex-cons?"

"Not with him."

"Why not him?"

"He was too old—and too drunk."

"Was he always drunk?"

"Mostly."

"He ever ask you to meet him someplace?"

She shook her head, turned right and started up the walk to a small white house set back on a deep lot.

"Did he ever have anybody with him when he came to the café?"

She shook her head.

"You real sure?"

As we reached the step to the front porch she grabbed for the door handle but I leaned past her and held it shut.

"Listen, I'm not gonna bother you but a minute more. Just try to think a little about what I'm asking. I want to know if somebody might've thought Fin was hot for you."

"Get away from that door," she said, "before I scream."

"Damnit, Sophie, you're just making me more sure you're lying—"

She took a quick breath which I figured was cocking the screamer so I jerked my hand from the door and stepped back. She pulled the screen open and gasped as a guy stepped down and blocked her. I recognized Rick, her older brother.

"He won't leave me alone," yelled Sophie, "sock him!"

"I heard," he said.

I stepped back to give myself room. He looked wide as a fullback in pads but instead of moving on me he took hold of Sophie's arm with his right hand and told her to sit on the stoop. She started to argue but gave up when he leaned toward her. When they were seated side by side, he looked up at me.

"What's this about Sophie and Fin Larson?"

"I don't know it's anything—I got word that Fin was interested and I've been trying to figure who could've been used to sucker Fin out to the fairgrounds. Sophie's the prettiest thing around and Fin had a weakness for that—I've been trying to find out if she'd been getting his rush, and if so, who saw it."

Rick looked at Sophie. "Did he make a play?"

"Why're you listening to this old con?" she demanded.

"I'm wanting to listen to my kid sister. Did Larson make a play?"

Sophie glared at him and winced when he squeezed her arm.

"Yes!"

"When?"

"Whenever he came in the café."

"Was it him gave you the stockings?"

"Yes!" she cried, and tried to break loose. It was like a cat fighting a bear trap.

"Where'd he give 'em to you?"

"In the café."

"You didn't meet him someplace?"

"He tried—I wouldn't."

"Why not?"

"Because he gimme the creeps—just like old creepie Wilcox here. If you was a decent brother, you'd sock him."

He stared at her. "You let him see those stockings on you?"

"Why not? He paid for 'em."

He shook his head and tightened his grip on her arm. Her lips went thin and she glared back at him but made no effort to get away. "You're hurting me."

He shook his head and let go.

She stood up with dignity and when he moved out of the way, opened the door and went inside.

"That's a hell of a good-looking young lady," I said.

"Yeah, and a cock-teaser. It's gonna get her killed one night. That's why I stick around. Try to be on the porch when she comes home in case there's a guy along. Some of 'em get so worked up they're about half crazy."

He lifted a cigaret pack from his shirt pocket, shook one loose and offered it to me. I took it. When we both had a light he gave me a long squint.

"You figure somebody made Fin figure she'd be at the fairgrounds, then bushwhacked him eh?"

"Could be. She's the only girl I know of he was interested in lately, outside of what he had at home."

"Why couldn't it have been his cousin?"

"I figure if he had something going with her they'd have been at it long enough to have a better set-up than a fairgrounds barn. Fin was no high school kid. He'd only have gone out there for something new. Sophie seems a natural."

He nodded. "I figured there was somebody with dough when I seen the silk stockings. Sophie pays board to Ma— and the job don't pay enough for silk."

We smoked for a few seconds before he glanced up at me again.

"You're really trying to find out who got him, aren't you?" When I nodded he said, "Okay, I guess you'll want to know where I was that night, huh?"

"Yeah."

"I was right here. And Sophie came home from work, just like to-night, only alone. And we sat on the porch and shot the breeze and she went to bed and then I did too and nobody went to the fairgrounds or anyplace else. They just slept."

He wasn't belligerent. I wondered why he was so tolerant—and why he accepted the idea of an ex-con hanging around at midnight, asking questions like a cop?

"What'd you and Sophie talk about?" I asked.

"Them stockings. She claimed she bought 'em with tip money. She don't lie often enough for me to expect it. She's not really bad, you know—she's just new at being pretty and knowing what it does to guys and she has to use it some. That don't make her bad."

He didn't ask for agreement but that was what he was after and I gave it to him. Didn't cost me a thing.

I didn't learn any more so after a little while I thanked him for the smoke and went home to bed. Rick was a lovely suspect—plenty hefty enough for the pitchforking and cool enough to plan. But was he cold enough to use his sister as bait? Of course he might just have followed them and done it on impulse. That'd explain better why Sophie was so scared.

The trouble was, I didn't want another suspect. I wanted Buck to be the killer—he was the only guy in town I liked less than Fin Larson and that made him the perfect goat. It was a hell of a way to go at solving a mystery—just putting the finger on my pet peeve.

I sat on the edge of my bed and worried about it clear through a cigaret before I stretched out and slept.

# \* Chapter \*

# IX

After supper the next day, I dropped in on Joey at City Hall and told about my visit with the Marksons. He lit a cigar and stared at the fresh ash like it was a crystal ball that would tell him something.

"You figure Rick could've done it?"

"He *could* have. But I don't think he did."

We sat a few minutes, clouding up the little room and finally his face brightened up a little. "Oh, I forgot to tell you—Pop Tucker found the murder weapon."

"Where?"

"North end of the fairgrounds, where he was mowing. It's an old fork. Hand grip's been broke off a long time ago. Tines're all rusty. It was probably left in the barn after the last fair."

"No help, huh?"

"Well, I figure it means the killer headed north."

"More likely he just tossed it that way and then headed back to town."

"I don't know, you'd think he'd have left it in the barn or carried it all the way off—"

"Maybe he saw somebody coming and felt like he had to get rid of it quick."

It was all too much for Joey and he dug out another cigar and lit up. He looked miserable.

"How'd Doc say he got it?" I asked, "I mean, what was the angle?"

"Almost straight on, maybe a shade to the right. Two tines went clean through—one of 'em through the juggler. Took a hell of a jab."

"It'd take some heft to pull it out too, wouldn't it?"

"That's what Doc says. Whoever done it, he put his foot on Fin's face to jerk the fork free. Smashed his nose flat, busted two front teeth."

"How'd Doc know it was done after the stabbing?"

"He don't. It just makes sense because it looks like a foot was shoved straight on. Like he was flat and stomped. There's no knob on the top or back of Fin's head—and one thing's sure—the fork did the killing."

We sat in silence for a while as he puffed on the cigar and clouded up the room.

"You gonna talk with Rick?" I asked.

"Uh-huh."

I offered to go along but he nixed it, which suited me. I didn't think Rick would spill anything and I wasn't eager to have him think I sicced the law on him.

Besides, it was getting on toward dark and I was thinking about Cora.

She was sitting on the front stoop when I climbed the stone steps and didn't move to meet me. I sat down fairly close and said hi. She nodded.

"I guess you're feeling down," I said.

She nodded again.

"What're you going to do now?"

She sighed. "I guess I'll stay on for a while. Aunt Iris asked me to—and I haven't much choice."

"How's she doing?"

She shook her head slowly. "It's amazing—when she first heard she seemed stunned—I couldn't see any reaction at all. Then she slept. When she woke she was calm and—maybe I shouldn't say this—but I thought she was relieved. This afternoon she got out of bed and walked around—spent several minutes just standing by the front window, looking out. When she went back to her bed and was all settled, she looked at me, smiled and said, 'He won't be back again.

Ever.' Then she began to cry, very quietly. I was positive she was *glad* he'd never be back—so why did she cry?"

"Maybe she was thinking how great it'd been if he'd died fifteen years ago."

"That's awful. But I think you're right."

"How's Angie handling it?"

"I can't tell—she's hardly been out of her room. I'd guess she's having terrible guilt feelings—the last time they spoke it was pretty bad."

"That Thursday night?"

"Yes."

"I thought you told me she came in and went straight to bed."

"Well, she almost did, but they had words first."

"What'd they say?"

"It doesn't seem like I should tell you—but I will—all I really heard was Angie screaming at him, 'I hate you!' That was the last thing she said to him before he was killed."

"Uh-huh. And she knows you heard."

"She probably thinks the whole town did."

We were both quiet for a while. I was trying to think about the killing but my mind was busy working on approaches to Cora. I leaned back and rested my elbows on the top step.

"They're lucky to have you here," I said.

She glanced at me—I thought with suspicion.

"You're a fine, understanding woman."

She looked away. "Let's not get personal."

"Okay. Had Fin been drinking regular since you came to Corden?"

"From what I hear, he always drank."

"But he slacked off when you first came to stay, didn't he?"

She glanced at me, looked down toward the street and leaned forward.

"I don't remember noticing him drinking at first—but maybe I was just naive."

"You noticed it lately, though, didn't you?"

"Of course."

"He ever tell you it was your fault he went prowling?"

I got her direct stare again. "That's *very* personal."

"Not at all. Personal is when I talk about you and me. Now I'm just trying to get straight what was happening with Fin before he stopped the pitchfork. Did he ever try to blame you for his running around?"

"Not exactly—"

"Uh-huh. But he let you know—and made you feel guilty, even when you knew it was dumb to swallow that."

She stared silently off toward the pines below.

"How strong a pass did he make?"

She took a deep breath and straightened up. "I don't know. It makes me terribly uncomfortable to be talking about him now—"

"So suffer a little. We're trying to figure out who killed him."

She gave me an arch look. "You're not a detective."

"Maybe not, but I don't guess it'll take Sherlock Holmes to solve a killing in Corden. Tell me about Fin's pass."

She folded her hands on her knees and stared at them as she spoke.

"All right. He came to my room one night—late. It must have been two months ago. He wasn't very drunk, but he was very melancholy. He talked about loneliness and said he thought I must understand a lot about that. I told him he should get out of my room and he said he just had to talk to me. He was married to a woman who was too sick to be a wife and had a daughter who hated him and that his life was wasted on unworthy endeavors. That's exactly the way he put it. He said he'd married Iris thinking she'd inspire him but she always felt superior and mocked his ambition. It was all very sad."

It sounded more like pitiful but I kept it shut.

"Pretty soon he asked me to let him lay beside me, on top of the covers, and let him just put his arm around me for a while. I wouldn't let him, of course, and I got terrible upset with him and finally he went out of the house and didn't come back for two days."

"Was it after that he talked about teaching you to run the theater?"

She nodded. "He invited me to come down there at night.

This was—oh, about a week or so later. He said I should come down after the last show. I said no, and suggested we go in the afternoon some time but he said that was impossible, everybody in town would talk about it and Eddie, his man, would make a lot of fuss—"

"Did you believe he gave a damn about Eddie's fuss?"

"No. But he didn't want talk. I believed that."

I didn't tell her that wouldn't bother Fin any more than the eclipse of the moon on a cloudy night.

There was some more conversation but I learned nothing more about the murder and it was obvious romance was headed nowhere so I said good-night and walked back downtown, trying to decide if I was going to the café or to visit Boswell's shack. The more I thought about Boswell's smooth moonshine, the more I loved the idea and then I figured maybe it was a little too Irish to drink while Larsons were in mourning. So at 10:45 I sat sober but proud, stirring ice cream into a mug of root beer at the café counter. Old Bjorkman, the owner, was busy washing soda glasses off to my right and I asked him where Sophie was.

"Went home sick," he said. His tone was not sympathetic.

"What's her trouble?"

"What's always the trouble with women?" he demanded.

That was way too profound for me to answer. I finished my float and went out. A stroll past the Markson house didn't tell me anything except there weren't any lights on. I went back to the hotel and sacked out.

# * Chapter *
# X

Thursday morning I woke stark naked on the sheet with my throat dry and the hot sun shafting through the wide open window. I rolled out, went down the hall in my shorts and took a cold shower. By the time I reached out and got my towel I was damned near dry. Down in the kitchen Bertha's face was red as the bottom ball on a thermometer and she was moving at about half her usual speed between the hot stove and the serving table. Hank was already bailing in the groceries.

Nobody had pep enough to make a wise crack or even offer greetings. Hank finished eating and ambled off toward the relatively cool lobby. Bertha served scrambled eggs, toast and coffee. I shoveled and poured everything down, burped at Bertha and fled to the lobby for a quick smoke before hiking to the fairgrounds.

I was about half through the smoke when Joey pulled open the screen door and stepped inside.

"Gonna be hot," he announced.

"I'd never've guessed it."

He lowered his carcass into a groaning rocker, tilted back and squinted at me.

"Guess who's showed up missing now," he said.

I lifted one eyebrow. "Sophie?"

He sat up straight, making the chair squeal. "How'd you guess that?"

"She left work early yesterday. I figured she was bad rattled by my questions."

He slumped back in the rocker. "Well, I got a visit from her brother, Rick, this morning. She never went home last night. I talked with Bjorkman and he said she left about nine. Claimed she felt bad. Went out the back door and ain't been seen since."

"So now you wait—what?—forty-eight hours before you look around? Or are you looking for her here?"

He scowled and said he wanted me to go over everything with him that I'd found out about Sophie.

"I'm due at the fairgrounds."

"That's okay. I'll mosey along with you."

"You figuring on another body out there?"

"You know a better place to look?"

"I can hardly think of a worse one. A man'd have to be crazy to leave two bodies in the same place, one after the other."

"Well, we don't know we got a sane killer, do we? Come on, let's go."

All the crew joined in the search with more energy and enthusiasm than I'd noticed on the job but all they turned up was a scared rat and a lot of grasshoppers. We even made a little swing around the nearby fields just beyond the fairground bounderies. It was nearly ten when Joey called it off and we all sat down in the shade under the grandstand roof and swigged water from the big thermos.

"Maybe she just ran off with some guy," suggested Hank.

"Like who?" asked Joey.

"Well, lotsa fellas'd go with her. Find out who else is missing."

"Check out Eddie Langer," said Chip.

We all looked at him and he gave us an innocent grin.

"You think he's been messing with Sophie?" asked Joey.

Chip spread his hands. "All I know is he goes by the café every night she works and a few times he's walked her home. He lives just a ways beyond her place, you know."

"How long's this been going on?"

Chip shrugged. "Ever since I been working the popcorn machine."

"He didn't walk her home night before last," I said.

"Oh, he didn't do it every night. Only when he figured nobody'd notice."

It seemed to me that was something that'd get noticed every time, but decided to wait until I could talk with Rick before asking any more.

Joey shook his head. "I can't picture Eddie having the nerve—he's scared to death of his wife, Doris." He stood up, pulled his hat down to shade his eyes and squinted across the oval dirt track before us. There wasn't a breath of air. I could've heard grasshoppers chewing if I'd been alone. After a while Joey drifted off to town and we went to work.

We got through the morning quick but the afternoon stretched out like a Sunday sermon in the Congregational Church. When five o'clock crawled around we trooped back to town, stopped at the creamery and inhaled a quart of chocolate milk apiece. Hank topped that off with a malted. At supper we both picked at our meals and Ma complained bitterly about how murders and people disappearing were spoiling everybody's appetite and family life. I allowed it was blamed selfish of Fin to get himself murdered and for Sophie to disappear but if it turned cooler I'd be back on my feed even if the whole town was done in.

After dusk there was a half-ass breeze now and again—almost strong enough to stir a dandelion seed but not enough to pull one free. I sat in a wooden chair out front where I had a good view of the near-deserted mainstreet and the bug carnival around the corner light. Boswell hove into sight from the south and inch-wormed his way to the chair beside me.

"Ain't seen you in a while," he said, "been on the wagon?"

"Giving it a try."

"Feel better for it?"

"Mostly feel numb."

"Beats the shakes," he said, without conviction.

"If you had to hide a body, where'd you put it?"

"Depend on where I started with it."

"Say it was out back of the cafe."

He thought for a moment, rubbed his nose and lifted his head a little.

"Well, if it was a small enough body, I'd work it into a railroad car if there happened to be one on the siding there beside the grain elevator."

The fact he could accept the notion of hiding a body was enough to give me a start, but I was really jolted that he came up with the only notion that seemed perfect.

"How the hell come you thought of that?" I demanded.

"Moonshiners just naturally think about places to hide stuff," he said.

I got up and Boswell trailed along across the street, then south a half block to the tracks. We followed the rails at a northeast angle between the elevator and the buildings facing north on Main.

"It'd be about perfect," said Boswell, "if the body went into a car just before it was filled with wheat."

"They're not loading wheat this early."

"Didn't say they were—said it'd be perfect if they were."

Big elms edged the alley and it was dark as a killer could want behind the cafe. The railroad tracks were about thirty paces from the cafe's back door and we found two box cars on the siding. One was sealed, the other was open on one side and there was no corpse inside. We came out of the car and stood there a moment, looking up at the peaked elevator top. It seemed tall as a skyscraper and still as a tombstone. The peak still caught a hint of light from the gone sun.

We walked around the elevator but it was locked up tight and I figured it wouldn't have been any easier for the killer than for me to get in, although he would've had stronger reasons for trying.

"What's a second choice?" I asked Boswell.

He didn't have any. One idea a week was about his limit. We walked back to the hotel and I sorted out my ideas.

"I figure this killer's cute but not too ambitious. I mean, if he'd taken the trouble to dig a good hole and put Fin in deep, chances are nobody'd ever have found the body. But he liked the hay because the barns were closed up and there was no reason to think anybody'd poke around for years, especially if he made it tough to get in."

"Maybe he just didn't have time to dig in hard ground."

"Maybe. But he took time to barricade the doors, he climbed out and hiked into a field to toss the fork away—"

"Mebbe he took off in that direction. You come to something after a while no matter which way you go."

I wasn't too sure about that in South Dakota.

"What I figure," I said, "is this guy planned his setting when he got Fin, and he did the same for Sophie—got her to a handy place—how's a sandpit strike you?"

"It don't seem a likely place for Sophie to meet a fella."

"How much do you know about her?" I asked. "Was she in school while you were janitor?"

"Uh-huh. Sophomore, I think, last year I was there. She read movie magazines and didn't have any girl friends. Wanted to be in the movies."

"Yeah? Did she tell you that?"

"Naw. She never talked to me. She told it once to Miz Hendrickson though. Right in class, in front of everybody. She was a sassy kid—got mad when ol' Hendrickson told her she'd never amount to anything. How can you be so sure Sophie's dead?"

"I got a feeling, that's all. She wasn't romancing with anybody we know about, she had big ideas, and all of a sudden, right after I've talked to her about a murder, she disappears. Her brother says she didn't have any money so she couldn't have gone off alone. I think she figured out from our talk who did do in old Fin, and she thought she'd cash in on it. Either that, or she actually was a decoy to get Fin to the barn."

Boswell pulled a half pint flask from his rear pocket and offered it to me. I thought it over and shook my head.

"I'm trying to work," I apologized.

He nodded solemnly, gave himself a medicinal shot, and put the flask away.

"Let's go by the park," I said.

Boswell's pace slowed me considerable but we managed to make it before midnight and walked all around the park which was almost two blocks long and one wide. Young elms planted in even rows cover all but the north corner where soft ball diamonds are laid out and there's a little clearing on the southwest corner there the World War Monument stands with its bronzed doughboy holding a rifle at ready, looking reverently noble and alert. A plaque on the base lists all of Corden's soldiers with stars beside the ones that died in service. Everybody likes to think the dead got that way being shot in bloody battle but Abe Rufert was the only one in the bunch who saw action and he died of mustard gas. Flue killed the others. Even mothers are ashamed of the ones that didn't get killed honestly.

We walked through the park and stopped at the water fountain near the monument.

"This is no good," I said. "It's too open for a killing, let alone any burying. He might have met her here, but I even doubt that—I figure he was waiting behind the café, got her in a car and took her to one of the sandpits."

"I knew you'd get back to the sandpit."

We were still standing there when Joey swung by in his Model T and pulled over. He expected us to be hitting a bottle and looked let down when he stood close, trying to get a whiff, and came up dry.

I laid out my theory about where we'd find Sophie. He agreed it made sense but then complained it'd take a posse of a hundred men with shovels to search for a body in those places and it was still too early for so much work.

He wanted to find a killer considerate enough to leave a body where a one-man search would find it without digging.

I asked what had he learned from Eddie. He said Eddie denied messing with Sophie.

I was disgusted but instead of popping off I said goodnight to the pair and went back to the hotel, found Hank in his room and talked it all over with him. He thought my ideas made sense and so the next day, Friday, we went over it with the fairgrounds crew and to my surprise, even Clayt agreed to help out. Hank was so enthusiastic he talked us all into starting the search at 7:00 a.m. on Saturday.

The morning was fresh and cool as dew wet lettuce when we gathered in front of the hotel.

"We'll try to make it easy," I explained. "First we'll start at the nearest pit, the one next to Peterson's place on the north side. If we don't have any luck there"—bad word choice but only Clayt winced—"we'll try a far-away place, like beyond Whittaker's farm way northeast."

I didn't go beyond that in outlining my plans; no point in discouraging them early. We had probes I'd made of heavy clothesline wire, each about three feet long and twisted around small wooden pegs which served as handles.

The in-town pit was roughly G-shaped with a high ridge at the center that Hank told me they'd called the Tonto Rim when they played cowboy a few years earlier. His tone suggested those were the good old days. He'd been a great one for playing out stories he'd read and naming things for them. The deepest section of the pit, on the south side, he'd called Dead Man's Gulch.

The entrance area was too shallow to seem promising but there were steep walls in the southeast and northeast corners so I sent Hank with Chip to probe the north side and took Clayt south with me. We hadn't been working the probes long before I noticed that Clayt was poking around so delicately he wouldn't have disturbed an ant an inch under.

"Look," I told him, "if we're gonna find her, she'll be buried, not dusted, and you're not gonna hurt her because she'll sure as hell be dead."

He gave me an agonized look. "I keep thinking I might poke her in the face—"

"If she was murdered, whoever did it probably put her face down, so she wouldn't be looking at him."

I don't think he swallowed that but as long as I kept scowling at him, he poked a little deeper.

Most of Corden has a top soil about a foot deep or less and then you hit yellow or maybe red clay. That goes down from three to four feet and then, at least where the sandpits are, there's fine sand and under that, gravel. The pits outer walls had a firm crust of clay that held its edge firmly but below those three to four foot cliffs, the sand slanted away. I figured the killer might have picked a loose slope, put the body near the bottom and worked the sand just enough to make a good pile sift over it.

By 9:30 the sky had a bleached look, as if the blue had been faded by too much sun. In the pit there wasn't enough shade to shelter a red ant and it was like working in an ungreased pan over a high flame. By 11:30 we'd covered everything that looked even slightly promising and we were all ready for basting.

"I don't figure she's here," said Chip as he fished out a cigaret.

I admitted that the same notion had occurred to me.

"You don't even know she's dead." He sounded resentful.

"I never guaranteed it."

"Well, I'm tired of poking around. I'm going swimming —how about you guys?"

It didn't take a vote to know how the others felt so I grinned and said, "Why not?"

Hank talked his grandfather into loaning us the Dodge, then decided to add girls to the party and I sailed along with it all. Nancy offered to bring sandwiches.

It was nearly 1:30 by the time we drove up the hill for Angie. I parked in front and got out to stroll up the walk with Clayt who'd already called Angie and told her we were coming.

As we approached the front steps, Cora rose from the porch swing and came to stand just inside the screen. Her face seemed unnaturally white in its frame of black hair. She wore a plain black dress. Clayt stopped on the first step, struggled for a polite opening, then blurted "Where's Angie?"

"In her room," said Cora. "She's not going."

Clayt's mouth dropped open and he turned to me.

"How's Iris?" I asked.

"Why? Did you plan to invite her swimming?"

"It might do her good, but no. How is she?"

"She's a new widow—upset, depressed, lonely."

"But up and around?"

She nodded. It was a big concession.

"So she's okay. What about Angie—she told Clayt she'd come."

"She agreed before she thought."

"Before she thought? Or before somebody talked to her?"

"I don't think that makes any difference. She's not going and that's the end of it. Go have a nice time."

"Thanks. We will."

* * *

The water wasn't cold enough to cool the steam I'd built from six hours of sun and a few seconds of Cora's scorn. I swam and dove and swam some more until I was about winded and then sat alone on the beach near the parking area where there was shade from the cottonwoods. The sky was still pale blue and there wasn't enough breeze to feel it even sitting there wet. But in spite of that I went from sopping to dry in a few minutes.

After a while, Clayt drifted my way and sat down.

I offered to roll him a weed but he shook his head and kept squirming around, first hugging his knees, then stretching out his legs and now and again poking his straw-dry hair off his forehead.

"What do you figure that meant at the Larson's house?"

"I think it meant somebody figured it was bad form to ask a girl swimming right after her pa's been forked."

"She acted like it was more than that. Like she hated me."

"That's a little strong. And anyway, I'd guess it was me she really put the frost on."

Clayt shook his head. "She kept looking at me. Like everything was my fault."

"Well, that just goes to show you we all figure the world centers on us. I was sure I got all the nasty."

He stayed quiet for a few seconds, staring across the road at a windmill and a watering tank where a few scrawny cows milled around in the muddy spill.

"Angie says her mother has taken this very well," he told me. "She says she even looks better and has been up out of bed ever since. Maybe, for her, it was a good thing, huh?"

"Uh-huh. The Lord moves in strange ways—"

He looked at me sideways and I grinned. A little of his tightness eased off and he turned toward me, crossing his long legs tailor fashion.

"Maybe Cora was mad because you didn't invite her."

"What makes you think she'd want me to?"

"Oh, well, Angie says you two hit it off big. Nobody else has been able to talk to her like you—except maybe Fin—and he doesn't count now."

"I guess she can tell I'm harmless."

He shook his head. "I don't think that's what girls want."

"Yeah? What do you figure they want?"

He shifted uncomfortably. Feeling was his long suit, not thinking, and he was never able to express himself. He was sensitive enough to understand more than he could know.

"My pa says that Cora's a gold-digger—that she planned to hook Fin as soon as his wife died. Ma asked if that was so, why was Cora making eyes at you now and pa said she was just keeping her hand in."

"You swallow all that?"

"No. I think it's like Hank says. She's interested because you've had lots of experience, being married and divorced, traveling all over, having lots of girls—"

I'd been married for about six months and only spent a month or so with the bride. It'd been my crowning practical joke on Ma and Pa when I brought this New York vaudeville peroxide blonde to Corden.

"How many women have you had?" asked Clayt.

"As many as I could get and less than I wanted."

"Do many say no?" he asked.

"I never asked."

"You mean you just went ahead and—"

"If you gotta ask you ain't gonna get."

He squirmed over that and leaned forward. "Well, how do you go at it?"

"Not by being shy. But if she's scared—just lay off."

"Well, sure, but what do you say?"

"As little as possible."

He didn't think much of that. There had to be a formula.

"How long've you been going with Angie?" I asked.

"Since last fall. Why?"

"I just want to know how well you know her—like how'd she really feel about her old man, Fin?"

He stretched his legs out straight and leaned back on his hands. "It was sort of mixed up. He made her awful mad sometimes, you know, but it never meant anything. I don't think she ever thought he counted, you know?"

"You mean she was indifferent? That all the yelling and the things he did—none of that meant anything?"

"Well, she wouldn't do anything to hurt him."

"Not even by accident?"

"No. Look, I'm hot—think I'll go swimming."

When we got back to town just before supper, Rick Markson was standing in front of the hotel, waiting for me. He had a mournful-Jesus look—or as close to that as a square-jawed flathead could get—and he was sour.

"Been having fun?" he demanded.

"Some. What's on your mind?"

"Joey says you figure Sophie's in the sandpit. I hear you searched one with that bunch of kids. Why didn't you call me?"

"I didn't figure there was any percentage in letting Sophie's brother know I thought there wasn't a chance for her."

"And you gave up after poking around a little in one pit?"

"We spent six· hours at it and my crew was ready for mutiny."

"The hell with them. You and me can look."

"Okay. If you want. But first I'm gonna have dinner, okay?"

He stepped so close he was nearly on my toes. I put my hand on his chest and he paid no attention to the pressure. He shoved his face forward and his voice was a choked whisper.

"Listen, Wilcox, I got to *know!* I don't want her laying in some Goddamned sandpit while people are swimming and stuffing their faces and having a Goddamned ball—"

I couldn't see it'd make that much difference to her any more but since it meant plenty to him I sympathized, apologized, said I'd be with him in twenty minutes and went in to eat.

# * Chapter *
# XI

I took about fifteen minutes to eat and found Rick out front waiting for me in his Model A at 6:30. We took off straight to the second nearest sandpit about a quarter mile east. It was thirty feet deep, a block long and about three quarters of a block wide. A ten foot high cottonwood grew near its center. We went around to the north end and parked beside a pile of trash blocking the old entry road. I carried the probes, Rick brought the shovel. Slowly we walked around the pit rim, staring down, trying to spot signs of recent sand slides. The bowl bottom was filled with shadows, our trail was weed covered, uneven and dusty. There were no grass-hoppers.

"This doesn't seem too likely," I told Rick. "It's too close to town, too hard to get into and too damned popular with kids playing cowboy."

He glared into the shadows, nodded and said, "Okay, let's go out to the west pit."

"Rick, that's two miles away and damned near big as the badlands. We could hunt there for days."

"So we might's well start now."

"Damn it, man, we need a crew—"

"You coming with me or you want to go back to town and get drunk?"

"I'd a hell of a lot rather get drunk."

"So go ahead."

"No, Goddamnit, I'll stick with you—but you're crazy."

"I ain't begging."

We glared at each other for about two seconds, then both turned and hiked for the car.

The west pit looked like two moon craters, just barely overlapping to make a squat figure eight. It'd been a fair sized hill before the digging which left a rim high enough to spot from half a mile off. We pulled into the entry road on the northeast rim and looked across a hole about a quarter of a mile wide and from forty to fifty feet deep. It'd been abandoned for two or three years—maybe more—so the truck ruts had worn away and the small cliff edges had smoothed down enough to leave the place looking almost nature-made.

Rick got out of the car, hunkered down and peered at the ground.

"Tire tracks, fairly new. Somebody's been here lately."

"Probably neckers, or somebody dumping garbage."

He stood up and stared down the road which angled right and followed the pit rim in a counterclockwise curve to the shadowed center below.

"You see any garbage?" he asked.

"About all I see are shadows. It's gonna be dark before long."

"Well then, we'd better get started, huh?"

We followed the tracks down the sloping road. They became vague after a few rods. We'd had no rain but steady winds had sifted sand across the trail and made it spotty. About half way down Rick found a bare stretch of clay where tracks were clear and his eyes bulged as he bent low to study them. I expected his nose to quiver.

"Same tread," he told me, "came all the way."

We found a clay mound at the pit's center and the tracks circled it once and then ran west toward the other half of the twin holes. Rick climbed the mound, straightened his back and looked all around. There was nothing but shadows and silence; no wind, no crickets. I could hear my breath in my nose.

Rick's head jerked suddenly and he raised his hand.

"You hear that?"

"No."

"I heard something—back there—"

"Down here you could hear a flea fart, but I don't think there're any around."

He scowled and climbed down beside me. "Why'd anybody drive around this point and then go on?"

He didn't expect an answer and I had none. We walked in a wide circle along the bottom slope and then he said we might as well give the second half a look and we went over there. It wasn't much different—maybe deeper since there was no clay center—except over on the southeast corner we found a big fresh slide. It started at the top rim and came all the way down in a widening trail that spread into the deepest hole.

"Oh shit," said Rick.

I couldn't tell from his tone whether he was upset by the size of the job or the realization that my theory was right and we were about to prove it. At that time I figured he was about as sentimental as a black widow spider after mating. Which only proves how wrong you can be just watching a guy before a crisis.

We messed around with the probes for fifteen minutes or so and it was a hell of a job because the sand was damned near liquid and kept sliding when we moved in it and came up to our knees in seconds. We floundered and cussed and finally took a break. Pretty soon Rick was up again only this time he grabbed the shovel and started digging. For every load he tossed, two more flowed down and it struck me about as sensible as trying to bail out the bottom of Niagra.

He was so carried away I thought he'd kill himself and pretty soon I was helping him on the stupid job. We took turns, working stripped to the waist as the shadows turned gray and finally went black. Rick swung the shovel into the slide and it'd go "chunk!" and sand would slide with a whisper, piling around the handle, and then he'd grunt with effort as he jerked each load up and tossed it aside. He'd stay at it until he was too pooped to lift and then I'd move in and take over. The shovel handle became slippery and hot.

I worked steadily, using more science than heft, but it was a killing job and I didn't fight it when Rick took over again.

On my sixth or eight hundredth shift I found her. The

moon was up by then, turning the pit into a half-glowing bowl filled with black shadows. I had just lifted a healthy scoop and was swinging it to my right when another little sandslide broke a yard up and I saw a shadow widen as the sand flowed away from an uneven ridge.

I glanced back at Rick. He was sitting on the ground, staring between his feet but his head jerked up when he caught the break in my rhythm. I pointed at the ridge.

"Oh, Jesus," he whispered. He jumped up and moved past me. For a moment he stood, staring, then he reached back and I handed him the shovel. Gently he scraped sand below the ridge which stirred slowly until sand began to run and finally a white bare arm gleamed in the moonlight.

Rick carefully pulled her clear of the slide and began pawing at the sand over her white face.

"Want me to get the car?" I asked.

He shook his head.

"Maybe we'd best not move her until Doc's had a look and we've let Joey see the lay out."

"I'm not leaving her here," he said. His jaw was so stiff I could barely understand.

"Okay. Let me bring the car down."

He took a last dab at the white face, bowed his head a second and slowly stood up.

"You stay with her. I'll get the car."

I was trying to convince him I could handle it fine when he exploded.

"No, Goddamnit. If I stay here alone I'll bust. I'll get the car, you wait!"

He moved off in the stiff, almost stumbling gait of a punchy fighter. By the time he reached the narrow gully to the eastern pit, I'd lost him in the black shadows.

I didn't want to look at Sophie so I sat on the ground a few feet away from the pale corpse and stared at the half moon and stars. I could feel my heart beat and hear my breathing. All around me the sand reflected pale moonlight and silence seemed thicker than oil.

I built a cigaret, put it in my mouth, felt for matches and changed my mind without knowing why. Ten minutes passed slow as a winter month without a sound from Rick or the car. After another five minutes I was so edgy I jumped when a bat swooped by and then I was on my feet, moving away from the corpse and into the shadows below the pit rim to my left.

Suddenly, a long way off, I heard the Model A engine start. It was such a relief I grinned to myself, got out my matches and lit the cigaret. It seemed obvious what'd happened—Rick went off alone to bawl and didn't start the car until he figured he was under control. I ambled back into the moonlight and waited near dead Sophie.

Car lights flickered along in the distance, reflecting around the pit like casual heat lightning in a cloudbank on the horizon. Soon they became direct and bright as the model A jounced into the west end and approached. I turned my head to avoid the glare. He was coming too fast, I thought. So it *was* late, there was no point in charging around like a drunk. Even when I heard the engine rev up, it didn't dawn on me he was planning to run me down until he'd damned near done it. At the last second I threw myself at the slope over Sophie. I landed hard enough to start a fresh slide and found myself moving down toward the body. The lights were a glare that blotted out everything as the motor roared, tires crunched into the sand, the car bounced, slammed Sophie into me and suddenly I was buried.

# * Chapter *

# XII

Half stunned by the body thrown against me and the burying sand, I lay still, holding my breath. The car door slammed, that much I was sure of, but I'd no notion of what else might be happening. I held my hands cupped over my face where I'd slapped them when the slide began and kept holding my breath. I felt sure there wasn't enough weight over me to prevent getting up if I tried.

When I was about to bust for air I heaved up and struggled clear of the body and sand. The lights were blinding. I threw myself to the right, rolled, somersaulted to my feet and bounded clear of the light where I promptly tripped over a rock and went tumbling into a small trench. For several seconds I lay there, panting and listening. There was only silence. It was so damned still I rubbed my thumb and forefinger beside my ear to be sure I wasn't deaf. Finally I lifted my head. I could see the car with its front end buried in sand up to the headlights which threw their bright beam up the slope and glared at the body now resting less than a yard from the buried bumper.

After a long wait I moved slowly toward the car. I froze when I made out a figure inside, behind the wheel. He didn't stir. I went forward again, humped like a stalking cat, reached the car and straightened up by the driver's seat.

"Rick?" I whispered.

He didn't move.

I reached through the open window, touched his cheek and found it cool. Slowly I moved my hand to his temple, felt for the pulse and couldn't find any. I pulled my hand back and looked all around at the black shadows while I listened. A dog barked a long ways off—the most cheerful sound I'd heard in hours.

The hike to town was long. I was too spooked to go straight up the road and exited by the ravine I'd seen earlier, circled the pit's north end and cut south to town.

Joey wasn't at city hall when I arrived and I waited half an hour before he pulled up in the Model T and popped his eyes at the sight of me.

"You been toward the west in the last hour?" I asked.

"I been in all directions. Where've you been?"

"At the sandpit two miles west. I found Sophie. Rick and I found her. Come on—"

His long face twisted and he shook his head sorrowfully.

"Damn!"

"We'd better get Doc . . . and Joey. We got two bodies—not just one."

"Two?"

I told him about Rick as we drove over to Doc's. It took a little time to roust the old man but finally we crowded into Joey's coupe and Doc sat clutching his black bag and blinking at the road ahead as I told my story again.

I half-expected to find the sandpit empty since the whole night had seemed like a bad dream but everything was exactly as I'd left it, including the burning headlights.

Doc examined Rick after we pulled him from the car and laid him out in the light.

"Looks like the crash might have thrown his head against the steering wheel's top rim—caught him right over the eyes," said Doc. "Why in the pluperfect hell would he try to run you down?"

"I don't think he did."

They both stared at me.

"I don't believe he was driving. I heard the car door slam right after I was buried."

Joey's eyes roamed the scene; the shadows made by the

headlights, the pit rim which seemed to be hanging over us on three sides, and the still bodies in the cold light.

"I dunno, Carl," said Joey, "considering how things went —you might've heard Gabriel's horn."

"Even under sand I'd know the difference between a toot and a slam. Besides, Rick wouldn't have rammed the body of his sister to hit me—even if he'd got the notion I killed her."

"He makes sense," said Doc.

Joey shook his head. "You're taking it for granted Rick wasn't crazy. He could've gone over, you know, from all the worry and then the shock. Why else wouldn't he stay with the body of his own sister?"

"He couldn't just sit and wait," I said, "He had to *do* something."

Joey sighed. "He was unnatural fond of that kid." He turned and walked slowly over to stare at Sophie's body.

Doc got up with a grunt, went over and began examining her. He kept muttering angrily about her being struck by the car so a man couldn't tell what the hell had happened but after a while he guessed she had been strangled. All the while Doc was poking around, Joey snooped around the car and took notes in a raggedy little pad.

I smoked and watched until they were finished and then Joey asked what did I figure had happened.

"The killer heard we were coming out here—it wasn't any secret. He followed along, watched till we found the body and waited by the car when Rick went back. Maybe he waited in the back of the car, maybe down beside it. When Rick started to open the door, he belted him with something like a hunk of pipe—right across the eyebrows. Then he got him inside, drove into the pit, took his shot at me, got out, pulled Rick behind the wheel, slammed the door and took off."

"And didn't bother to see if he'd done you in?"

"Well, I was buried. He didn't see anything move so he figured everything was fine. What the hell, everything's gone his way—and he was in a hurry to get the hell away and fix an alibi in case he needed one."

Joey sat on the Model A running board, leaned back and adjusted his hat.

"Let's go over this a little. We got to cover all the angles, right? Tell me why I shouldn't wonder if maybe you and Rick had a little difference when the body was found. I mean, it wouldn't be too surprising if he went a little wild about then. He might've got the notion you killed her—maybe he at least figured it was your fault because you went and asked her questions that made the killer think she was dangerous. You know, he was some mad at you when you two set off searching. You told me that yourself."

"Goddamnit, Joey, he was worried mad, not fighting mad. And I went along with him and worked my ass off helping. And besides, you don't have any call to figure Rick was anything but steady—and on top of all that, why the hell would I drive this car down here and bury myself and—"

"We only got your story on that, Carl. You could've made it all up."

"Oh, crap."

"Mebbe. There's another angle too. Maybe Rick did kill Fin. Maybe he got Sophie to play bait and sirened Fin to the fairground. Or maybe he found them there and lost his head. You been figuring all along that Fin's death was planned . . . but it didn't have to be. That fork was in the barn for sure. Rick could've picked it up, done Fin in and chased Sophie out. Later, when she got scared because of you, she might've threatened to spill the works and he lost his head and killed her—"

"And then hauled her out here, buried her, and after that got me to come out and help him find her?"

"Oh, no," he shook his head, "he didn't talk you into that. He heard you guessed where she might be and he probably felt guilty about leaving her there and figured you'd find her sooner or later so he figured to throw us off by pushing the search himself."

"So when he found her he started a fight with me and—Jesus, Joey, that's all bullshit."

"Yeah," he agreed glumly, "it does sound like it."

Doc cleared his throat impatiently and asked, "How're we going to get these bodies back to town?"

Joey grunted, stood and arched his back.

"Carl, will you take Doc back in my car and get Bill Gates out of bed—have him bring his panel truck?"

I did and Gates went and I hit the sack.

# * Chapter *

# XIII

Church bells woke me. I laid there a while on the sheet, thinking if that's the way the last call comes, I won't answer. Let everybody else go to hell or heaven, I'll stay here and hope the bells and bugles follow the people and leave me to sleep. But sleep, like a lay, is only important when you haven't had any and pretty soon I was sitting up, staring at Dutton's garage across the back lot. It gave me no inspiration.

So who'd tried to retire me in the prime of life, full of sins and hopes for more? I enjoy no insights at wake up time and decided that although I'd showered the night before to wash out sand and sores, I could probably survive a second wetting in eight hours and went to try it.

Everybody wanted to ask about the night before after I'd finished breakfast and moved out into company and I decided to hell with that, got into my truck, drove to the lake and stayed till dark, swimming some and fishing a lot. I didn't get anything but tired and didn't care because it felt good just sunning and swimming and letting the float bob on the blue water. A little after dusk I drove back to Corden and went up the hill to visit Cora.

When I knocked on the front porch door, Angie came to the screen and stared at me sullenly.

"How's your ma?" I asked.

"You didn't come to see her," she told me.

"I didn't ask to see her, I asked how she was."

"She's all right."

"Fine. You mind telling Cora I'm here?"

She disappeared and a moment later Cora came down the stairs, hurried through the inner door and pulled the screen open.

"Are you all right?" she asked.

"Finer than frog hair—"

"Can I get you something?"

"Like what?"

"Well, coffee, iced tea—"

I said coffee'd be fine, she said follow me, and I did. In the kitchen light she looked me over so close it made me uncomfortable and I thought she was a little disappointed not to find any bruises or scars. She put a kettle of water on the stove, waved at a chair and told me to sit.

"You seem," she said, "indestructible."

"Don't bet on it. Was Angie home last night?"

She looked at me with narrowed eyes. "Angie? Why, yes, she was. She and Clayt were on the porch most of the evening."

"How late?"

"I'm not sure. It must've been past midnight."

"When did Clayt come over?"

"Right after dinner. He was terribly depressed—and Angie's just as bad. It worries me but I can't say or do a thing because Angie acts as if her father's death were my fault."

"She's jealous. You're better looking than she is and her father didn't yell at you."

Her cheeks flushed and she turned to the counter, opened a yellow Butternut coffee can and scooped out four tablespoons into a pot.

"Why are you asking about Clayt?" she asked.

"Just nosey."

She shook her head. "You want to know if he could've been at the sandpit, don't you?"

I shrugged.

"I don't think he could have—actually he was here pretty late."

"What's pretty late?"

"Well, I'm not sure. I kept thinking it was my responsibility to check on the clock and finally I heard Iris get up and go downstairs and speak to them. Clayt left right after that."

"You don't know the hour, though?"

"No."

I asked if it was okay to smoke, she nodded and I rolled one and got it fired up.

"You don't honestly think that boy would kill, do you?"

"I guess not," I said, and wondered why I wasn't sure.

She poured boiling water into the coffee pot, stirred the mess, added a spoonful of cold water and a couple minutes later poured. I took a sip and it tasted as good as it smelled.

"Where'd you learn to make tramp coffee?" I asked.

She laughed. "Angie showed me. It's the way Iris taught her." She sat down across from me, hunched her shoulders and sighed. "I'm glad you weren't killed."

"That makes two of us."

She put her chin in her hands and gave me her big, brown-eyed gaze.

"You know, I think last night changed you. You suddenly seem very purposeful."

"Is that what I am? I just thought I was mad because somebody tried to do me in."

"Well, whoever he is, he's in trouble."

"He'd be in a hell of a lot more if I knew who he was."

"What're you going to do next?"

"I'm gonna ask you to go for a walk."

"Oh? Why? Do you think the walls have ears?"

I nodded. She gave me a slow smile, sipped her coffee and leaned back.

"You don't just want to get me alone?"

"Never dreamed of such a thing."

"It seems a shame to waste the coffee."

"It's not *that* good."

We went out the kitchen door, through the back porch and across the back lawn. It was dark, warm and still except for crickets.

"You probably shouldn't be wandering around at night," she said.

I said I figured I was safe with her. She laughed, took my arm and we set off.

We wound up on the high school steps. That put us at the top of a long slope where I had a view in all directions and my rear was covered. Not that I seriously figured I'd be followed, but it was a fairly safe place to sit with a girl if you didn't think there was any chance of going the whole way. When I thought about that as we sat down, I decided the night before must have changed me. I don't ordinarily take it for granted I'm not going to make it with a girl. This damned killer was murdering my technique.

She asked what was it like, being on the bum and I asked where she got the notion I'd know about that. She said she'd learned a lot about me from Iris but she wanted to hear from me directly. I said bumming was a lousy life, hungry, dirty and cold.

"Why'd you do it then?"

"Well, it was that or cowboying, which is hungry, cold and full of callouses—"

"Couldn't you have just stayed home?"

"Mostly no."

"Didn't you get along with your parents?"

"Didn't Iris tell you?"

She laughed. "All right. But tell me about them—how long have they had the hotel?"

"Oh, about twenty years now. I was near fifteen when we came to Corden from Michigan."

"What was it like then? Was it a new building?"

"Hell, no. It was just the east wing. The old man brought in two frame houses and hooked them up—that's why the halls are crooked and the floors are different levels. It was all rats, bedbugs and cockroaches. We turned old mattresses, washed walls with kerosene, hunted rats . . . It was a damned war—no truce, no prisoners. Work, work and sweat. They loved it."

"Your parents?"

"Yeah. And Sis too. Ma and Pa went at it all grim and righteous. You know, the bugs and rats were evil and they were doing it in. Sis was more like a joyful crusader—glorifying God, not attacking his enemies. For Pa, work is penance, for Sis it's celebration and Ma—well, there's just nothing she likes better than working everybody's tail off, including her own."

"Do you like your sister?"

"Everybody likes her—she wouldn't allow it to be any other way."

"How long was she living at the hotel?"

"Only a couple of years. Then she got married—deserted us and had Hank."

"And when she left you did too?"

"No, I'd run off before that."

"Why'd you come back?"

"Well, that time, Sis talked me into it."

"Did she think they needed you?"

"I suppose—or that I needed them. Mostly she was trying to make up for leaving them herself."

"Did they make her feel guilt for that?"

"Sure, Pa did, anyway. Ma figured it was right."

"So all of your aimlessness is like a revolt against your parents' Puritanism and the hard work, huh?"

"I'm no more aimless than you are."

"Well, you're older than I am."

I didn't have a come back for that so I kissed her. I made it pretty casual. When she pulled away I let her go and she looked at me thoughtfully for several seconds so I kissed her again, this time a little longer before she pushed her head forward, then turned her face aside.

"That's no answer," she said.

"It's more fun than talk."

"It's not going to go anywhere—"

"Why not?"

"You're not serious enough." She pulled free and stood up.

I've known a lot of girls that just liked to wrestle a little, but Cora didn't strike me that way so when I stood up beside her I kept my hands to myself and we went down the hill and headed back toward the house.

"You ever let Fin kiss you?" I asked.

"No."

"He ever try?"

"He tried to work up to it. I told you enough, why do you keep asking?"

"I was just trying to find out how serious he was."

"He was very serious. He was frightening."

"You're pretty hard to please—he was too serious and I'm not serious enough. What do you want?"

"I don't want to be just lusted after . . . for fun, or whatever. I want to be important to a man, not just something he wants to satisfy his appetite or ego."

"You're too damned complicated."

"Yes," she said, "for you, I think I am."

I took her home and walked back to the hotel in a perfect mood for a fight but luckily didn't run into anybody to work it off on and just hit the sack.

Monday was another scorcher and Clayt didn't show for work. When I called his ma at noon she said he'd had an upset stomach but would be back on Tuesday. Later I asked Hank if Clayt ever boozed.

"Naw, he won't even try a beer. Why—has he been sick to his stomach again?"

"That's what his ma said. Does it happen often?"

"Sure. He can heave if you look at him cross-eyed."

After supper I drifted over to city hall and found Joey sitting at his desk looking as thoughtful as a man with his face can.

"You see any clay spots where you and Rick was diggin' Saturday night?" he asked.

"It was all sand."

"That's the way it looked to me. I went back and checked it today. Everywhere you fellas worked, just sand."

"I guess you're gonna tell me something before the week's out?"

He nodded. "There was clay on Rick's britches."

"So somebody knocked him on his ass by the car, like I told you?"

"Looks like. Of course he might've sat on clay a week ago—there's not much of any way you can be sure how long he had it on those pants. But with things so dry, I figure it'd come off fairly soon. Besides, Doc's not sure Rick hit the steering wheel—he thinks a smack like that would've cracked the wheel—and there should be blood on it. But the clincher's the fact that there's blood on the seat—under where we found the body. And there's a spot on Rick's britches near the crotch on his wallet side."

"So he got belted outside the car, was put inside and propped up behind the wheel after the killer tried to finish me."

"Mebbe. But we still don't know who done all that."

"Well, it took a guy with some heft to heist Rick off the ground and shove him in there—he was no feather pillow. And I'd guess this guy knew Sophie pretty well—good enough to get her playing bait for Fin. Then he had to kill her because she knew the score and tried to cash in on it—"

"So why'd he try for you?"

"Because I'm getting close—or he thinks I am."

"And Rick?"

"He was hot to find who'd killed his sister. And besides the killer figured somebody might be dumb enough to think Rick had done it himself. You were ready to."

"I was just studying all the possibilities. That was only one of 'em."

I'd hurt his feelings and pretty soon he decided he'd ought to go drive his rounds so he left and I went back to the hotel where I found Hank in the lobby reading a Saint novel.

"Let's go see how Clayt's doing," I said.

He gave me a wise look and asked how come I was so worried—had the judge promised a bonus if we finished the fairgrounds early?

"If he had, I'd have been riding you guys with a buggy whip."

Clayt lived a block and a half northeast of the Larsons. The front porch was open and the white house stood naked on a treeless lot that sloped toward the road on the east side. Clayt was sitting on the front stoop with Angie and they looked about as gay as bloodhounds that'd lost the trail.

"Well," I said to Clayt, "you're drawing visitors like a dying millionaire. How do you feel?"

"Okay. I'll be back tomorrow."

"Great, how's Angie?"

She said she was great but she wasn't cheerful about it. Something was wrong between them and as usual, when a couple has a row, the fellow was glad to have company postpone the showdown while the girl was impatient to finish it.

I gave them my understanding uncle smile, got out fixings and sat down beside Angie to build a cigaret.

"What made you sick?" I asked Clayt.

"Nothing special, I don't think." He leaned forward to watch me around his girl. "I get that way like other folks catch colds. Maybe heat does it."

"Probably need more salt."

Angie stood up. "I hate to miss any of this fascinating talk, but I've got to get home."

Clayt jumped up and reached for her arm which she jerked away and his face turned so red and anguished I thought he might get sick again. Later, after she'd flounced off, Clayt stood with his hand still half-reaching for her, then he dropped it and turned away with his head down like a heartbroken girl in a movie serial.

"What was that all about?" I asked.

"Nothing."

"It usually is with women. But what'd she think it was all about?"

He brought his head up and gave me a straight look. "It doesn't concern you."

I grinned. "If it bothers my crew, it concerns me."

"Don't worry, I'll be at work tomorrow. Now I'm going to bed."

"Gee," said Hank as we headed down toward the hotel, "old Clayt really surprised me."

"How?"

"Well, he practically told you to mind your own business —that's not his way—he's always respectful toward older folks."

That made me wince but I didn't let on.

"So he's feeling owly. Sometimes that makes guys more honest."

"I don't think that's it. I think it's because he's in love."

"I thought that was supposed to make people happy."

"It hasn't made any guys I know happy. At least not for long."

"That's only the way with young people. It gets better when you get older."

"Is it better for you?"

"I don't know. I'm not that old yet."

He didn't even smile. He just said he guessed he'd go see Nancy and I went on down the hill alone, considering the wisdom of youth.

# * Chapter *

# XIV

Joey pulled up beside me in his Model T as I was approaching the hotel and suggested I stop at city hall and chin with him. I said fine and a few minutes later he'd settled down in the captain's chair, leaned back and asked, "Well, where do we go next?"

I shrugged. "The last guy I picked is dead."

"We got to find somebody. Hell, at the rate things are going we'll run out of citizens before Christmas."

"Okay—I figure it was a man—no woman around here, except Bertha, is strong enough to lift bodies and slam pitchforks into a guy Fin's size. So that leaves us Pop Tucker, Buck Dover and Eddie Langer—if you won't take Clayt."

"Why Buck? Why'd he kill his favorite cousin?"

"Maybe he was sore that Fin got all the women—maybe they hassled once too often and Fin yelled too loud—"

A flying beetle landed on Joey's knee and he stared at the bug until it began crawling toward his crotch.

"You treat 'em right and the first thing you know, they get personal," I said, as he flipped the beetle off. It landed on its back, flopped over and stayed there, thinking.

"It seems like to me," said Joey, "that if Buck done it, he'd have stuck Fin with the fork, walked out and left the doors open and the fork still in his neck. And it ain't like him to pull all that cute stuff at the sandpit neither."

I wasn't convinced. He was a hell of a ways from a criminal genius, but he was loaded with animal cunning.

"One thing's sure," said Joey as he crossed his legs, leaned back and closed his eyes, "you'd better watch your ass. Just because you got missed Saturday night don't mean this fella's through. You hadn't ought to be walking down dark streets alone—and you'd best keep off the sauce."

He sneaked a peek to see how I took that and I glared at him.

"I'm thinking of your own good, Carl. You got to be careful."

He said it like he was really worried. I had to grin because it was so different from Ma who says be careful in a way that makes you feel being careless is sinful and might embarrass the family.

Tuesday the judge showed up to check on progress and I was glad that Clayt was back on the job. The judge didn't break his arm patting me on the back but he didn't accuse us of dogging it either so I guessed he was satisfied. Then he asked to borrow Chip since he wanted somebody to ride around the county with him, putting up posters advertising the fair. Chip was tickled silly. He loved getting close to important people.

All of the barns were clean by then and we started on the grandstand. It should have been scraped, sanded and sealed but of course nobody wanted to pay for all that so what we did was hardly a whitewash job. I replaced a couple broken boards and pounded in nails sprung by warping and freezing while the guys made with paint brushes.

During lunch break I asked Clayt to tell me what he knew about Sophie. He said he didn't know anything.

"Come on, she lived in this town all your life, she was in the same school—"

"Yeah, but she's two years older than me, we weren't in the same class—"

"Well for Christ's sake, that didn't put her on the moon. Didn't you ever see her, hear anything about her?"

"Oh sure, now and again I saw her—she was pretty, you know—but I don't think she went with any special crowd at school. It seemed to me she mostly dated older fellas."

"She pals with any girls?"

"None I ever knew of."

"Name a guy."

"Well, there was Swede—he's a farmer with a place near Sophie's grandfolks over west a ways. I heard he wanted to marry her. He gave her a ring when she was a junior."

He couldn't come up with anybody else and after work and supper I talked with Joey and he agreed to drive out to Swede's place. He knew the family, there'd been two uncles —quite old—who adopted Swede when his parents were killed by a tornado in West Corden County.

We found him cultivating corn in a field about three miles north of town. He was stripped to the waist and wore a battered straw hat well back on a head of curly hair. When Joey hailed him he climbed off the tractor and shook hands with us. I'd guess he stood about five-seven and went 160, all knotty muscles and leathery skin.

"I suppose you heard about Sophie," said Joey.

Swede gave us a squint and a nod.

"I'm trying to get a lead on who done it. I hear you was once pretty good friends with her. Mind helping out?"

"How?"

"Tell us a little about her. When'd you see her last?"

Swede lifted his hat, tousled his hair and put the hat back on. Finally he shrugged. "Maybe this spring."

"You talked to her then?"

"No."

"When'd you last talk?"

He leaned against the back wheel of the tractor and scowled. "Must've been a year or more. You break up with a girl—you don't chase her no more."

"Mind telling me who broke it up?"

"What difference does that make?"

"Maybe none. Then again, maybe a lot. I wanna know what she was like, how she treated folks."

"She got on fine with me."

"So why'd you break up?"

He looked sulky. "I guess she figured she could do better. She was always going to movies and they give her a lot of crazy ideas."

"Did Fin Larson have anything to do with your bust-up?"

"Naw." He said it with indifference and Joey stared at him before deciding it was real.

"Somebody else?"

Swede looked disgusted. "That's what everybody's got to think, ain't it? I'll tell you plain and simple—she didn't want to be a farmer's wife. She said we'd marry if I'd sell the place when it was mine and went to the city. What the hell'd I do in the city? And where in hell'd I get a price for the farm that'd set me up for more'n a week? And what the hell's wrong with being a farmer where you can stand up and never kiss anybody's ass?"

"So you told her you wouldn't do it, eh?"

"That's right. And she wouldn't go with me no more."

"And that was all there was to it?"

"It was good and plenty." He scowled at the dusty earth for a few seconds and then gave us each a look in turn. "I'll tell you one more thing—if you promise to keep shut about it."

"Shoot."

He looked at the ground again. "I crawled back. I said I'd do whatever she wanted. But she knew I didn't mean it. Sophie was real bright—she figured it out that I'd *say* it— that I'd sell the place when the time came, but she knew I wouldn't. She was right, you know. I wouldn't've. I didn't plan it like that when I was trying to get her back but when I thought about it later I knew she was right. Sophie was a real smart girl."

"When was it you tried to get her back?"

"Christmas time. I took her presents: a nice muff and a little manicure set. For her fingernails. She worried about her hands a lot. She didn't think much of the muff—it wasn't fur—but she liked the manicure set. I thought when she opened that maybe I'd pulled it off. She was really keen on that little case with the red trim inside and the scissors and things so silvery—"

He looked at Joey a second, then back at the ground, took a deep breath and talked in a rush. "I guess we talked about half the night—about all the good times we'd had. She was real sweet and she kissed me good-bye and we parted good

friends. She said I was a grand fella but we just had to go
different ways."

I glanced at Joey but he was too embarrassed for Swede
to meet my eye. The young man was clear as washed glass
when he lied and neither one of us wanted to poke his dream
bubble.

"Didn't you ever hear that Sophie was messing around
with Fin Larson?" asked Joey.

Swede's face reddened. "No, I never heard no such thing.
I don't believe it. You shouldn't say stuff like that and her
dead."

"I didn't say it was a fact. I asked did you hear?"

He shook his head.

"You know any other fellas she was seeing?"

"Naw."

"Where were you last Saturday night?"

The switch rattled him a little. The sulky look went and
he was suddenly watchful.

"Why's that matter?"

Joey scowled. "Some reason you don't want to answer
where you were Saturday night?"

"No, course not. I went to the Willow Forks dance."

"You take some gal home?"

He shook his head.

"Did you ask anybody?"

"What's that got to do with anything?"

Joey leaned forward. "I'll ask the questions. You just answer 'em."

Swede squirmed, got redder than ever and said yes, he
asked a girl named Rosie Caswell but she was already spoke
for so he went home alone.

"Straight?"

"Yes!"

"Can you prove it?"

"Shit no. I was alone."

Joey's scowl eased off and he straightened up. "How's
the corn coming?"

It took Swede a couple seconds to get his gears shifted
but finally he looked around and said it was barely coming.

"Needs more rain and less grasshoppers."

"Uh-huh. I'll put in your order but don't bank on any-thing. Does this Caswell girl live in Willow Forks?"

Swede nodded and we left him standing beside his trac-tor, gazing after us.

Rose, a slim girl with a big warm mouth and wide eyes, didn't remember Swede until Joey said we'd been told he asked to take her home from the dance. Right away she got indignant.

"Yeah, sure. That dumb farmer. Imagine a fella you never saw before asking to walk you home practically at the end of the night—and him hardly able to dance at all!"

"So he was there till the last note?"

"Yeah, sure. I saw him go out right after he asked. I remember because I pointed him out to Freddie, my date."

"Was he drunk?"

"Oh, sure. Not falling down, you know, but lurchy. Did he do something bad?"

"Not that we know of. Just wanted to make sure."

She looked disappointed but smiled brightly when Joey thanked her and even threw me a warmer.

Joey sighed as we climbed into his jalopy. "I don't guess he could've been the one. In the first place he just don't seem right, and in the second he wouldn't have had time to get from that dance to the sandpit even if he'd known you guys were gonna be there when he left Willow Forks. And how'd he know?"

Back in town we made a little tour around and stopped by the park where a few kids were playing softball in the fading light. Buck Dover was sitting on the south end of the small bleachers with his elbows on his knees and his chin in his hands. If he was enjoying the game he meant to keep it a secret. We got out of the car and walked toward him. His eyes shifted to take us in and then went back to the game. When Joey sat beside him he grunted acknowledgement of the cop's greeting and said, "Your company don't do you no credit, you know."

"I don't worry about credit," said Joey, "don't spend enough for it to matter. How's your ribs?"

"There's nothing wrong with me, but if your peckerhead friend messes around again, I'll break his neck."

"I'll warn him," said Joey. "Was you at the dance last Saturday night?"

"I went around for a while, sure."

"What time?"

"About ten or so. Why?"

"Talk to anybody?"

"Talked to everybody. I got lots of friends."

Sure, I thought, he could count them on his index finger and it'd take him all afternoon.

"Where'd you go from the Playhouse?"

"Pool hall."

"How long there?"

"Till closing."

"Where'd you go from there?"

"Well, if I'd known what was up, I'd have gone out to the sandpit and helped somebody run over Wilcox."

"Even if it was the fella that killed your cousin?"

"Oh, for God's sake, Joey, don't be an asshole—there was nobody in that pit but Wilcox and Markson."

"Oh? How'd you know that if you wasn't there?"

Buck dropped his hands from his chin, rested his meaty forearms across his thighs and glared at Joey.

"You really swallow that cock and bull story of his?"

"Right now I'm trying to get a story from you. Where'd you go when you left the pool hall?"

"Are you accusing me of killing my own kin? Is that what this's all about?"

"I haven't accused you of a thing. I asked a question, now how about you gimme an answer?"

"Okay. When I left the pool hall Wilt Bowman walked with me. He had a bottle and we had a few belts and talked some—"

"What about?"

"Hell, I don't remember—"

"You didn't maybe talk about Carl and Rick being at the sandpit?"

"We didn't know nothing about that, not till morning."

"How can you be sure Wilt didn't know?"

"Okay, *I* didn't know—and he didn't tell me. Is that better?"

"How long was Wilt with you?"

"He walked back to my place with me. I don't know the time. Must've been pretty late—one or so—maybe more."

"Since when have you been pals with Bowman?" I asked.

Buck gave me a look that'd wilt a Russian thistle, then turned to Joey.

"I got to answer that peckerhead's questions too?"

"Why not?"

"I don't like the son-of-a-bitch."

I'm way too old to get excited about being called names but that one had me up before I thought and then three of us were standing with Joey in the middle and some kid hollered "Fight!" and everybody was watching us.

"All right," said Joey, "everybody cool down. Carl, you maybe better take a little walk—"

Buck made the mistake of trying to push Joey aside and the next thing he knew Joey'd snapped him around into a hammerlock that made him yell, probably more in surprise than pain.

"Let him go," I said, "you take the walk and we'll get squared away in short order."

"No, you go on now, Carl . . ."

He was asking a favor so I said. "Okay—but Buck, you cretin asshole, we'll have a party you won't forget."

Buck made a move and Joey pulled him up so sharp he yelled again and started cussing about why was the town cop protecting a crook like Wilcox. Joey told him only a damned fool would think the man getting protected was Wilcox and that sent me back to the hotel happy.

# * Chapter *
# XV

I ambled back along Main Street after leaving Joey and Buck to their waltz and leaned against the wall beside Chip who was running the popcorn machine under the theater marquee.

"You put in a long day," I said, "Don't your feet get tired?"

"Not much. I don't weigh enough to trouble 'em. I guess the fairgrounds job won't last much longer, huh?"

"Nope."

"I hate to see that job end. We've been having fun."

"It beats breaking rocks in a chain gang," I agreed, "but not much."

I looked inside and saw Wilt Bowman was working the ticket booth so I told Chip I'd see him later and went in.

"How the show?" I asked.

"Just fine," he said, reaching for the tickets.

I told him to never mind them, I wasn't buying in.

"Oh," he said and for a second his small eyes met mine. Then he looked down at the ticket roll, patted it and took a deep breath. When I didn't say anything he fidgeted and finally asked well then, why'd I come to the theater?

"To see you."

"Well," he laughed nervously, "you see me."

I leaned on the shelf and grinned at him. "I hear you played a little pool Saturday night."

His head bobbed. "That's right. Play some just about every Saturday night."

"Who'd you play with?"

"Oh, lotsa fellas—Howie, Jim, Buck."

"Beat 'em all?"

"About half and half."

"Who beats you?"

"Howie—most of the time."

"How about Buck?"

He looked at me briefly and gave a little grin. "I lose to him now and again—but Saturday I whipped him good. I suppose he had Fin on his mind—put his game off."

"What'd you do when the pool hall closed?"

"Well, Buck was so down, I walked along to his place."

"That was nice. I hear you even shared your pint with him."

I got the small eyes again.

"Why not?"

"Where'd you go?"

"I told you—to his place. We sat on them side steps and talked."

"What about?"

"Oh, old Fin, mostly. They were real close, you know. Buck just thought the world of Fin."

"I always heard Fin was pretty snotty to Buck. Did he say anything about that?"

"Sure did," his head was bobbing again. "He said Fin just only hollered at folks that were important to him—like his wife and Angie."

"He ever holler at Cora?"

"I dunno. He never said nothing about Cora."

"You two guys sat boozing on the side step for a couple hours and never said anything about that girl living in Fin's house?"

Wilt made a face and took a deep breath. "It sounds funny when you say it, but that's right. Buck didn't want to talk about her. When I tried to, you know, get some idea what was going on there, he got real huffy and said I should mind my own business. You have to be careful talking with

Buck—he flies off the handle quicker'n a squirrel can scratch fleas."

"How long did it take you two to finish your pint?"

He shrugged. "Maybe a couple hours."

"To finish one pint?"

"Well, we wasn't drinkin' that much—and we talked some after it was gone."

"So what time did you go home?"

"I got no idea. Must've been past one or so."

"Uh-huh, you got no idea—except it was enough to give that red-faced ape an alibi. In all that gab you guys had over one little pint, did he ever mention how come he quit going up to see Lil?"

"Not exactly. I sorta got the notion he had something better but he wouldn't tell so I didn't ask. You won't tell Buck I said anything, will you?"

"Not likely." I took my elbows off the ticket window shelf and looked over toward the door that led to the projection booth.

"Excuse me," I told Wilt, "I'm going up to visit Eddie."

His eyes widened and he began shaking his head. "You can't go up there—"

"What'll you bet?" I asked as I opened the door marked KEEP OUT and started up the steps.

The booth was bigger than I'd expected with room for the two projectors, an easy chair, and small table and about a million magazines piled all across one wall in stacks from one to three feet high. Eddie was in the easy chair reading Film Fun when I looked in. For a second he seemed shocked speechless by my invasion and then, more in resignation than anger, he said, "I might've guessed you wouldn't believe in signs."

"Don't hardly believe anything I read," I admitted. "How come you have to have two projectors?"

"Because film comes in more than one reel and people can't wait between."

I started to reach for my makings and he raised his hand.

"You can't smoke up here, film's too inflammable."

I shoved my tobacco bag back in my shirt pocket and hunkered down in front of his chair.

"Who's paying the help now?" I asked.

"Mrs. Larson."

"You talked with her?"

"No. The cousin—Cora—called right after Fin turned up dead. She said I was to carry on as usual, Mrs. Larson'd see I got what was coming to me. She said I should pass the word on to Chip and Wilt."

I nodded, stood up and looked around.

"Where do you keep the stag films?"

His head jerked just a little, but his expression didn't change. "Stag films?"

"Yeah. Fin ran 'em for years. Everybody in town knows it, for God's sake."

He shook his head stiffly. "They just think they do—they like to think things are going on, they don't know what they're talking about."

"Uh-huh." I wandered the little room and it was plain there wasn't a spot in the place where anything could be squirreled away unless it was under movie and pulp magazines. "How long's you work for Fin?"

"Five years—short a week or so."

"You must've run a lot of movies in that time. Ever get sick of 'em?"

"I suppose I ran over seven hundred shows, all good family stuff. No, I didn't get sick of them."

"How come so many magazines? Don't you watch the shows?"

"Sure, but once is enough for most."

The projector hummed and we could hear music and dialogue from the speakers behind the screen, distant and muffled. I tried to decide whether Eddie was nervous because of my questions or just because he couldn't adjust to the notion of somebody intruding on his cocoon.

I walked to the door, leaned against the jamb and stared at him a few seconds. He squirmed and waited.

"I suppose if old Fin had felt like it, he could've come down here and run the stag films himself, couldn't he?"

"Of course. It's his place. But I don't think he did."

"You think you'd know if he'd been up here when you weren't around?"

He hesitated enough so I didn't believe him when he shook his head. I grinned to let him know I figured he was lying, and went down the steps.

Outside Chip was handing a fresh box of popcorn to a young man. I waited until change had been made and asked if Chip remembered any of the guys Fin brought around occasionally from the cities.

"Sure."

"What were they like?"

"Well, they weren't popcorn eaters, I can tell you that."

"That mean something special?"

"Sure. Regular folks eat popcorn. These were steak and wine guys."

"White shirts and silk ties?"

"And shiny shoes. You want some popcorn?"

"You giving it away now?"

"For ten cents a box."

I gave him ten cents and took a box to keep from getting classed with Fin's city friends. I didn't own a white shirt, silk tie or shiny shoes, but kids Chip's age don't draw fine distinctions.

"When's the last time any of these dudes came around?"

"Couple months ago."

"He ever take them up to the house?"

"Damnfiknow. You think Fin got in bad with those guys and they hired a job on him?"

"I'd like the notion. But I have a tough time putting together Chicago hoods with a rusty pitchfork."

"Maybe they sent a guy from Minneapolis."

It was later and heat lightning flickered across the western horizon as Cora and I reached the hill top well beyond the Larson house. The clouds where the lightning played were so low and vague they only showed when there were flashes. Overhead the stars were high and bright. The air was still as God in church.

"Want to go swimming?" I asked.

"I don't think I should."

"Why not?"

"You might get ideas."

"I've always got ideas."

"I'm sure you do—"

"You afraid of me?"

She glanced up soberly. "Yes—a little."

"I won't harm you."

She smiled. "Iris thinks you've already ruined me."

"How?"

"Well, my reputation. People are saying I encourage you."

"I've been encouraged?"

"I haven't turned you away."

We walked a ways in silence before I asked, "Does Iris say you should keep me off?"

"No, she's never been that direct, but she's hinted at it in roundabout ways. I think she's just a little bit jealous. I don't mean she has romantic ideas about you, but she rather feels you belong to her family because she was so close to your sister and all that shared childhood business. You know what I'm trying to say?"

I wasn't too sure but I nodded.

"I mean, I've intruded so much on her life here, on so many of her relationships—"

"What'd she say that made you think she figured I was bad news?"

"Nothing direct—really—she's very fond of you. And you like her, don't you?"

"Sure. I always liked older women before you showed up."

She laughed and pretty soon linked her arm through mine. I watched her profile as we went along and she lifted her chin, decided that was showing off and lowered her head a second before turning to smile at me.

"Don't stare at me—it makes me self-conscious. Tell me, why were you sent to prison?"

"Because I didn't make the people lay on the floor."

"What?" She stopped dead and faced me.

"I was sticking up this jewelry store and the people put their hands in the air and a passing cop saw them and caught me."

"Why, in heaven's name, were you robbing a jewelry store?"

"Well, it had money and was easier than a bank."

"Were you drunk?"

"Of course—why'd I stick up a place if I was sober?"

"You wanted money for more liquor?"

"No, I was drunk enough. Fact is, I was going with a widow woman who had a kid and needed money and I didn't have any so I robbed the store—or tried to."

She shook her head. "That's crazy—what if you'd killed someone?"

"The gun wasn't loaded. It wasn't even big enough to scare anybody much. I don't think the cop even saw it before I laid it on the display counter when he charged in."

She slowly took my arm and we walked on. Every now and then she'd shake her head and mutter, "Incredible!"

We reached the school grounds, walked up the slope and sat down on the front steps. Before us was the empty lot, across the street the silver water tower rose higher than Jack's beanstalk, all ghostly in the starlight.

"You are," she said, "the most unusual man I've ever met."

"I wouldn't be surprised."

She leaned back, rested her elbows on the step behind her and looked up at the sky. Light from the water tower peak formed a silvery halo that erased stars above it.

"What do you think of Buck?" I asked.

"Buck? I hardly think of him at all."

"Did he come to the house often when Fin was around?"

"No. Fin went over to his place—normally when he'd been drinking quite a bit. I don't think he enjoyed him much unless he'd been drinking."

"Fin ever say anything to give you that idea?"

"Well, he called him 'muscle-head' sometimes. It was obvious he didn't respect him."

"So why'd he bother with him?"

She leaned forward and hugged her knees. "I don't know. I guess he needed someone to talk to, someone he could trust and he only believed he could trust relatives. I suppose he was sure Buck would look up to him, no matter what he did."

"Like Old Dog Tray."

"That's not very kind, but yes, very like that."

"Has he been around since Fin died?"

She nodded. "He delivers meat about every other day, and asks if there's anything else we want."

"Does Iris like him?"

"No, she associates him with Fin's drinking. She knows it wasn't his fault, but he was part of the pattern she hated and she can't forgive him for that. She's been much more kind to him lately, though. Why are you so curious about him?"

"I want to know if I should be jealous."

She laughed and shook her head. "I'm afraid you're devious. You don't seriously believe Buck would murder Fin, do you?"

"Yup. If you hadn't shown up at the right time a week or so back, all he'd have needed to kill me was a little better aim."

"With rocks? But that wasn't sneaky or planned. . . ."

"Well, Fin's death didn't have to have been either."

She thought about that for a few seconds and decided not to argue. Then she turned until her knees were touching my thigh and stared straight at me.

"Let me ask *you* some questions. I don't really know anything about you."

"You figure I might be the killer?"

"No. What did you do in your free time when you were in prison?"

"Learned some Spanish and taught some English."

"You had a Spanish cellmate?"

"Mex."

"What had he done?"

"About three years by the time I left."

"No, silly. I meant what sent him to prison?"

"You wouldn't want to know."

"Please. Tell me."

"Well, he stabbed his daughter."

"His own *daughter?*"

"Uh-huh. It was kind of complicated—he was going

after his wife because she'd burned the tortillas and the daughter got in the way."

"I wish you wouldn't make fun of me."

"I'm telling you what happened—or what the man told me."

"All right, I've heard enough. What does a man do when he comes out of prison? Do they just open the door and let him out?"

"They give him a suit and ten bucks and a lot of talk about sinning no more."

"What did you do?"

"I set out looking for sin."

She nodded. "I can imagine that. What was it like when you reached home, I mean, how did people treat you?"

"Well, I don't remember any ticker tape parade."

She shook her head slowly, leaned back to rest her elbows against the step again and asked, "So what are you going to do next—with your life, I mean."

"I'm open for suggestions."

"I'd think you'd want to go to the cities, where there are more opportunities."

"Uh-huh—for almost anything. I think I'd rather stick around Corden and see what happens with you."

"Don't worry about me."

"I don't mind worrying about you."

"All right, go ahead, I don't mind that. But there's no future in it."

We grinned at each other and then she looked away.

"You're not smoking to-night. It doesn't seem natural."

"I don't want anything in my way if I decide you want to be kissed."

"That doesn't bother most men."

"Maybe not. But I'm neat."

When I edged closer she didn't move, not even to look at me. As I touched her chin she turned her head and tilted it just enough for us to meet. We stayed with it for quite a while before she slowly pulled back and lowered her head to my shoulder. When I reached for her chin again she took my hand and squeezed it.

"Wait," she said. "I want to think about it a while."

"It was pretty short. You might forget how it was."

"No, I won't."

"I can do better, I think."

"I'm not sure I could handle anything better. It was very all right."

It had been good enough for a starter but I was afraid she'd let me talk it to death if that chatter went on so I tried once more and when she held off I got untangled and made a smoke. She hugged her knees and watched.

"You're very good with your hands," she said. "Is that why you roll your own—to show off?"

"I roll 'em because it's cheaper."

"I think you do it because you enjoy it. It's very independent and masculine. I think that sort of thing is terribly important to you—that's why you fight so much—and always against bigger men, isn't it?"

"It's tough to find smaller men."

"You're not that small, you don't fool me. I think you'd like to be a pirate but you aren't cruel or greedy enough for that. I think maybe you should have been an explorer; that's how I see you."

I don't suppose anything in this world boosts the ego like having your character analyzed by a good looking woman—especially if she doesn't know anything about you. She doesn't have to be right or even all that flattering—just the interest does it. It's almost like an orgasm without a letdown.

"What're you after?" I asked.

She tilted her head and looked solemn.

"What makes you think I'm after anything?"

"I get this notion I'm being played like a trout on a fly line, not for the catching but just for the sheer hell of it."

She grinned. "Are you hooked a little?"

"I think it's right through the jaw."

"Tell me about it."

"I don't think I will. You don't need any encouragement."

"I do too. Go on, what do you think of me?"

"I think you're too young, too good-looking—and maybe too smart."

She squeezed her knees and rocked. "Tell me."

"You've got eyes I want to look into, a mouth I want to kiss and a nose I'd like to rub with—"

She laughed, jumped to her feet and pulled me up against her. "You're crazy," she said, and kissed me.

We went into a good clinch and after quite a while she pulled her head back and told me not to crack her ribs. Then we were back at it so fierce if I'd had any sense I'd have worried about my own ribs. Finally we came up for air, I looked around and started leading her down the steps.

"Where're we going?" she asked, trying to smooth her hair with one hand.

"I'll show you—"

"We can't go back to the hotel—"

"Sure can. There's an empty apartment in the west wing. We'll go in the back."

She was trotting at my side as I charged along with my arm tight around her waist. "No," she said, "really, I can't . . ."

"The hell you can't. We've had an appointment since the first time we spoke. Hell, I felt it when I heard you call old Fin at the swimming hole."

She didn't stop trotting but she put on more drag.

"You think that about every girl you meet, I'll bet."

"No, not like this. I've never known anyone like you. . . ."

I was damned glad Corden was a dinky town, if the hotel had been another block away I'd never have been able to keep her with me. We circled around west of the brick city hall and hurried along the dirt road to the back of the hotel. The lot with its four box elders was dark and still. There were two apartments downstairs in the west wing, each with front and back entries. The empty one was on the end. I guided Cora up on the back porch, pussy-footed over the squeaking floor and slipped her inside.

We kissed again and by then I was so damned hopped up my knees were shaking like a high school freshman at his first big dance.

"Is the apartment furnished?" she whispered.

"Some."

"With a bed?"

"Uh-huh."

"I wouldn't do it without a bed."

"We got it, we got it," I told her. At that point she'd have had to go through with it if there wasn't anyplace but the toilet seat.

We moved into the kitchen, through a tiny hall dividing a walk-in closet and the bathroom, then through the living room and to the bedroom on the right.

I don't know what told me someone was in the bed— maybe I heard a creak, or the movement of sheets, even a gasp—I'm not sure because being so damned worked up it was mortal hard to believe anything could spoil that un-believable chance with Cora. Something stopped me inside the door and I froze there, holding her with my left arm, my mind shifting from desire to fear and then rage. I pushed Cora behind me, slipped out my matches and struck one.

The sudden flare revealed the couple, white-faced, with a sheet pulled to two chins.

"Well," I said to Clayt, "I'm sure as hell glad you two made up."

Even before I shook the match out, Angie disappeared under the sheet.

"You won't tell, will you, Carl?" begged Clayt.

"Tell what? I don't know a damned thing—but next time lemme know in advance—it'll save us both embarrass-ment."

I followed Cora back through the apartment and out on the porch.

"Damn!" I said.

She kept still until we were in the back yard and then she began to laugh very softly.

"I'm gonna kick Hank's ass," I said.

She stopped laughing. "Why pick on Hank?"

"Because he had to be the one that told Clayt about the apartment. That kid would never have found one on his own."

Cora laughed again.

"Come on," I said, and headed toward the garage. I was going to have her in the old man's Dodge.

"No," she said, pulling up.

"Cora, come on, for Christ's sake—"

"I'm sorry—I can't now. I'm really sorry, but it was never a smart idea . . . I just got carried away."

I didn't beg or coax; I've been around too long not to know when the moment's shot and God knows that one had been blasted as far as they can go.

"Well, shit," I said before I could think and she laughed out loud this time, grabbed my hand and started to run. We ran a block down the back alley and only slowed when we reached 2nd Street and turned north toward the Larson house.

"It's just as well," she told me, panting. "I'd have been awful—I was too scared—"

"Of what?"

"*You* know."

"You think I'd be rough?"

"You might. But mostly I'd be afraid of a baby."

"I wouldn't do it in you."

"Uh-huh."

I should have been sore that she let me know flat out she figured me for a liar, but it tickled me she was so smart.

"How about if I get some rubbers?"

"Sometimes they break. I think you'd break one."

"You make it sound like they were made of glass. It's rubber—that doesn't break."

"Well, tear, then."

"How come you know so damned much?"

"I'm not a child. I've talked with girls and heard fellows talking—"

I shook my head. "It's getting so a man can't teach a girl a damned thing unless he starts with her straight from the cradle."

She let me kiss her good-night but kept it cool and short. It taught me more about the meaning of anti-climax than seemed healthy.

# Chapter
# XVI

I half expected Clayt would be too embarrassed to show the next day but he was there. I decided he was more afraid of being talked about if he was missing than of being teased if he showed. I was dying to know how things had gone but decided he might get sick if pressed so I just casualed it and asked Chip about things at the theater when we took our morning break.

"How about Doris. Does she come to movies much?"

"Only every time the feature changes."

"Ever see her talking with Fin—before or after a show?"

"Naw. He never hung around the lobby that much."

"Didn't he watch movies?"

"I don't think so. I never saw him in the auditorium but he could've watched from the booth."

"What does Doris do beside cook bad and go to movies?"

"Well, she drives around in Eddie's car sometimes."

"She drives?"

"She'd have a tough time riding around alone if she didn't."

"Where does she go?"

"Hell, all over. I even saw her in Aquatown last summer once."

That roused me enough to make my ears wiggle but I tried to stay easy and let maybe a tenth of a second pass before I asked where he saw her in town.

"Well, I was sitting in the Cozy Café, on Main Street,

across from the White Hotel. I was drinking a cherry Coke, looking out the front window, and there she came, big as life and all gussied up so great I hardly knew her at first. Man, she was cinched in the middle and popping out the top. Everybody on the street got goggle-eyed.''

"Where'd she go?"

"Into the hotel."

"You positive it was Doris?"

"Abso-tively."

"When was that? You know the date?"

"Sure. It was the Fourth of July weekend. Saturday."

A little after dark I went up to the Larson house. It was the coolest evening for a month and no one was sitting on the front porch. A couple raps brought Cora to the inner door. I thought her eyes should show a little extra glow considering what had almost happened the night before but she looked about as fired up as a waitress approaching a new diner.

"Every time I see you," I said, "you look better."

That brought a smile, but no glow.

"I'd like to see Iris, if she's up," I said.

Her eyebrows climbed a notch, then dropped to normal as she opened the door. I followed her into the living room.

"You've a visitor," announced Cora.

Iris was sitting in Fin's favorite easy chair with her small feet on the stool and a Good Housekeeping magazine in her lap. "How nice," she said with a smile, "would you like coffee? Cora—please?"

Cora bowed and walked a little stiffly toward the kitchen. I asked polite questions about Iris's health and we exchanged remarks about the weather before I finally got down to cases.

"You mind talking about Fin?"

Iris placed her magazine on the floor, folded her hands in her lap and asked what did I want to know.

"About a year ago, the weekend before the Fourth, was Fin out of town?"

She looked at the floor and frowned thoughtfully for a second before nodding. "I remember being annoyed with him—everyone else puts off business things just before a holiday but he never did. Holidays never meant much to him. He took days off when he pleased, not when others did." She smiled. "He said a day off was no fun when everybody did it."

"Where'd he go?"

"Oh, that's hard to say. Aquatown, perhaps the cities."

"Where'd he stay when he went to Aquatown?"

"Why, the White Hotel, where else?"

"I thought maybe he had friends there. Do you think he was meeting film distributors that weekend?"

"I assumed it."

Angie came in the front door and stopped to stare at me silently. Iris, who was turned at an angle didn't see or hear her.

I went on. "You got any idea why the distributors Fin worked with never stayed overnight in Corden?"

Iris seemed a little flustered by that question and before she could make up an answer, Angie stuck her oar in.

"He wasn't crazy enough about the Wilcox Hotel to have his bigshot friends stay there, that's why."

Iris jerked around and turned red. "Angie! What a thing to say!"

"That's all right," I said, grinning at Angie. "If it weren't for the family rates I wouldn't stay there myself."

"It's a fine, clean hotel," said Iris. "Everybody says that."

"Yeah," I said, "and nobody says it more often than Ma."

"And it doesn't allow tomcatting—except by family," said Angie. She was glaring at me so hard you could smell the hate. I'd caught her in bed with her guy and she'd never get over it.

Iris had had enough, she sat up and frowned firmly.

"Angie, you obviously didn't come in to be sociable, was there something you wanted?"

"Why's he asking questions about Daddy? Why are you answering him?"

"He's interested, that's why. Now, child, don't ask silly questions and for heaven's sake, show some manners. Why don't you help Cora with the coffee?"

"Cora doesn't need any help with anything. And you

don't need any more servants." With that, she jerked her head and flounced out.

Iris shook her head sadly. "Poor child. She's horribly upset about her father. You know, they quarreled the last night of his life. I'm afraid she'll never get over that."

The talk turned general when Cora brought coffee in and it took me a while to get back on track. I was on my second cup before I asked Iris if they'd ever had Eddie Langer and his wife to their house.

"Why, no . . . no . . ." She was trying to think why and the reason was so simple it didn't occur to her. You just don't invite social inferiors into your home in Corden. Nobody ever had. It wasn't a rule—it was a fact.

"Ever meet Eddie's wife?" I asked.

"No, I don't believe so. I might have seen her in the theater lobby once or twice. She's rather plump, isn't she? Let herself go, I hear . . ."

"You mean she looked pretty good once?"

"Well," she shrugged, "some men like that type."

"Did Fin?"

She tried to laugh, couldn't pull it off and made a face. "He did have a coarse streak."

"Like carousing with Buck when he'd had a few drinks?"

She nodded, as if she thought a silent agreement wouldn't slander the dead.

"How'd Fin act when he came home from a trip?"

"What do you mean?"

"Well, was he tired and grouchy, or glad to be home—?"

"Oh, he didn't act any different. Sometimes he'd sleep more than usual, now and again he'd talk a lot—sometimes not at all. He wasn't predictable."

"Do you remember how he was after the Fourth?"

She frowned a few seconds and then said, "Tired. Very tired. He went to bed and just slept the clock around."

That was all I got. He hadn't talked about his trip, she didn't even remember if he said where he'd been. I thanked her for the coffee and when I went out Cora came along to the front step.

"What are you after?" she asked.

"Anything at all. You gonna walk me home?"

"That isn't the way it's done. Fellows walk girls home."

"I'd be glad to if I could get you away from it."

"Not tonight."

"Don't tell me—you've got a headache."

She smiled. "No, that's not it."

"So what are you afraid of?"

"You know good and well."

"Come on, you aren't going to get in trouble talking—or even walking."

"It can start that way."

"Only to weak characters. You're a strong character."

She shook her head. "Until last night, I might've believed that. Not any more. Don't crowd me, okay?"

"Right," I said and took her hand and solemnly shook it. She smiled, pulled me to her and gave as good as she got for a few seconds kiss, then faded away.

High-toned women, I told myself as I went down the walk, are usually a pain in the ass and all a bum ever gets from them is a hard-on ache for company.

The night was cool and still, the sky was so clear the stars hardly left room for dark. I decided it was a perfect night to visit Eddie Langer's wife, Doris.

Their house sat well back on the lot and in the dark looked white and almost trim. A lamp was on in the front window behind the porch and while the shades were up, I couldn't see anyone inside. I rapped on the screen door. It rattled. I tapped again, harder. When nothing happened I backed off and strolled around to the back. A cigaret glowed at one end of the hammock.

"Doris?"

The light tip moved as she took the cigaret from her mouth. "Yeah?"

I walked slowly to her side.

"Nice night."

"If it doesn't rain."

I almost stumbled over a folding chair near the hammock, sat down on it, got out my fixings and built a cigaret.

"Don't mind me," she said, "make yourself to home."

"What am I supposed to do—stand 'til you invite me to sit?"

"I wouldn't ask you to sit."

"So I didn't ask. When's Eddie get home?"

"Any time now."

"Doesn't he stay at the theater kind of late now and then?"

"No. He comes straight home. He can't wait."

"I heard he worked late a lot."

"You heard wrong. Now you better just haul off before he shows up. He don't appreciate men visiting his wife when he's working."

"Jealous, huh?"

"You bet your ass he is. Crazy."

"But you don't ever give him any cause, do you?"

"Never have, ain't starting. So why don't you get?"

I leaned back and crossed my legs.

"I always took Eddie for the easy-going type—live and let live. He even lets you drive his car sometimes on trips around, isn't that right?"

Her cigaret tip glowed bright for a moment, then smoke floated up like a small ghost.

"He knows he can trust me."

"Uh-huh. Typical of the jealous husband. He know where you were on the Fourth of July last year?"

"He always knows where I am." She said it very quickly.

"That's a good trick with him busy every night of the week and then some. You must have a lot of time alone—when you're not at the movies."

"What's it to you?"

"I'm not real sure. I guess having somebody try to knock me off has made me nosey. All of a sudden I see a hell of a lot goes on around town that might be damned interesting if a guy could sort it all out—like how come you went into the White Hotel on the same afternoon Fin Larson was staying there just before the Fourth. You want to tell me about that?"

"You're talking rot. I was never there—"

"No? Fella says you were. Just about lunch time. He was in the Cozy Café, you know, right across the street from that front lobby door. You got out of that green Chevvie and sailed in wearing a white dress with a low front and high heels and your hair all done up for fair."

"Your fella's a Goddamned liar."

"I wouldn't be surprised," I said. "You don't strike me as Fin's type."

I wished I could see her face. For several seconds she didn't say a word, I doubt she breathed. Then smoke rose from her cigaret and drifted away.

"You're really cute, aren't you. No wonder your nose has been stomped flat. Now I'm supposed to say, 'a lot *you* know.' Isn't that it?"

"I wouldn't have been awful surprised."

"Well, it don't make any difference whose type I am. I never did any messing around with Fin Larson or anybody else—not in Corden or the city or any damn place else, so stick that in your pipe and smoke it."

"How about with Buck?"

Her legs came over the side of the hammock as she sat up.

"I'll thank you to get the hell out of my yard."

"Sure," I said, getting up. "If you're right about Eddie I should meet him along the way. I really wanted to talk to him anyway."

She dropped her cigaret on the ground, got to her feet and stepped on it.

"Okay, if you wanna talk with Eddie, hang around. You got a cigaret?"

"I can roll you one."

"I don't want your spit on it."

"So you can give it your own lick."

She squirmed at the notion but finally wanted one too bad to say no and I built it. Her warm tongue touched my finger when she moistened the paper I held out and she flinched. I lit it for her and she took a slow drag while tipping her head back.

"It tastes funny," she said.

"Needs my spit."

She laughed, short and hard, like a dog's bark. "You really are a nut, you know that?"

"Yeah."

"You wanna cuppa coffee?"

"Okay."

"I might need a quarter for the gas meter."

"I haven't got a quarter."

"That figures."

She led the way to the back door and pulled on the light —a naked bulb hanging from the kitchen ceiling center. Dinner dishes were stacked clean on the sideboard but the sink was full of pots and pans soaking in greasy water. She turned on the gas and lit it with a wooden match. The flame came on blue and steady as Doris put the kettle over it.

I sat on a frail chair at the kitchen table and watched her. As a kid she'd been round, pink and bouncy with curly hair and dimpled knees. Some had called her Betty Boop even though her hair was too blond and she pretended to get mad when they did it. She hadn't changed much—the chin sagged a little and there were crowsfeet around the eyes and a bit of bagging under them. She wore a pink house dress with ruffles in the front and little white polka dots all over the place.

"Well," she said, leaning back against the sink, "you've looked me over. What do you think? Am I going to pot?"

"Not a bit. Right now you look tasty as a hot cross bun. Now the other day—"

She touched her hair. "I hadn't had a chance to do up yet. No girl looks good without she's done up some."

"This fella I mentioned, he said you looked done up to the nines in the city last summer. *He* was impressed."

"My God," she groaned, raising her hands and eyes. "Are you gonna keep harping on that?"

"It's hard not to, Doris. He was positive. Did Eddie ever talk about Fin much?"

She sighed and folded her arms under her breasts. "I'll tell you what, Eddie's notion of big news was to tell me the boss was out of town. Eddie lived for when the boss was out of town and he didn't have to take any crap off him. I'm damned if I know what's left for him now Fin's dead— there'll never be anything special to look forward to."

"What kind of crap did Eddie take?"

"*All* kinds, horse, pig and bull. He loved to keep Eddie in

a sweat. He was always telling somebody—a girl or a new
boy—that he was gonna teach 'em to run the movie machine. Every time he'd let that get back to Eddie so he'd be
scared he was gonna get canned. I told him, why the hell
would Fin can him? He did everything he was asked, right
down to running them movies after the regular show—"

"Eddie ran the stag films?"

"As if you didn't know!"

"Where'd Fin get them?"

"How the hell would I know?"

"Didn't Eddie say?"

"No."

"How'd you find out about them?"

"Because I asked Eddie why he got home so darned late
every now and then. He didn't wanta say but I made him."

"Why'd you believe him?"

"Because he can't lie worth a damn, and he told me what
they did in them movies. Eddie couldn't ever make up stuff
like that. Hell, he couldn't believe what he saw. He thought
they faked things."

"Like what?"

She gave me a leering grin. "Wouldn't you like to
know?"

I said yes and leered back.

She told me with a straight face that a lady didn't talk
about stuff like that.

"Did Eddie ever think about quitting?"

"Sure, he talked about it, but what the hell else would he
do?"

"He could move someplace else. Other towns got
movies."

"Not for Eddie. He wouldn't drive to the swimming hole
and that's only three miles. Going to the cemetery's a trip to
the moon for him."

For a moment we were silent, just sipping coffee. I
thought about poking her on the subject of her travels but
decided that wouldn't go anywhere and picked a new line.

"Did Eddie ever tell you that Fin brought in women when
he showed stag films?"

"Huh?" She scowled. "Whatdya mean?"

"When he ran those movies, he invited friends from the city and they brought women with 'em."

For a second I thought she looked relieved and then she straightened up and shoved her head toward me. "You trying to tell me there was a woman for Eddie?"

"I'm not trying to tell you anything. I just wondered how much Eddie told you."

She pulled back her head and sneered. "Eddie wouldn't have anything to do with 'em. He'd be scared. He don't travel to other towns, he don't try other women. Eddie wouldn't bet on the sun coming up, never took a chance on nothing . . ."

"He ever say anything at all about the guys from the city?"

"I never asked. I never heard about any women."

The front door opened and Doris didn't so much as turn her head as steps came down the hall and Eddie stopped in the open doorway. He was wearing a white shirt with the sleeves rolled tightly to the center of his upper arm. His skin was white under black hair that was thick as fur around his wrists and down the backs of his bony hands. For a skinny guy he had big forearms—they reminded me of Popeye.

"Carl here thinks you're a killer," said Doris cheerfully.

That jolted me some, but Eddie didn't even blink. "Yeah? Got any coffee left?"

Doris took a cup from the cupboard, filled it and set it on the table across from me. Eddie sat down, used cream and sugar, took a sip, sighed and leaned back. He hadn't looked at me yet.

"You look tired," I said.

"I was born tired."

"Have trouble sleeping?"

He nodded.

"You probably keep the wrong hours. Ever had a day job?"

"That was worse. I had to get up mornings."

"Huh," grunted Doris, "he comes home in the middle of the night, swills coffee and wonders why he can't sleep. He's too dumb to sleep."

"It's all right, though," said Eddie. "I got an understanding wife to stick by me."

"Maybe I understand more than you figure. How come you never told me about them whores Fin Larson brought in when he showed them dirty movies?"

Eddie gave me his first look and it wasn't exactly loaded with gratitude.

"You weren't ever interested in who was watching, just in what was going on."

"Well, I'm interested now. Tell me about them whores."

"They weren't anybody you know."

"Well, damn, I sure know that, but what'd they look like?"

"They looked like hookers. What'd you expect—movie stars?"

She turned red and for a second I thought she was going to throw her cup at him. Then she turned sideways, put the cup down with a sharp clunk and turned back to glare at him.

"I guess that was supposed to mean something, eh?"

Eddie deflated a little under her glare. "It just meant they weren't anything special. I never even saw them close. They were down in the auditorium while I was up in my booth. I didn't get introduced; I was part of the machinery."

"How'd you feel about Fin?" I asked.

He glanced at me again, this time with indifference.

"I hated him and you know it."

"Yeah, I just wondered if *you* knew it."

Doris gave her barking laugh and moved over beside me.

"Roll me a cigaret," she said.

Eddie's head jerked a little but he didn't look at her. His face was tighter than dried leather. I shook tobacco into a paper, started the roll and offered Doris the lick.

"Go ahead, you do it."

I didn't look at Eddie and a second later handed her the cigaret. She bent down for a light, took her drag, smiled at me and let the smoke out slowly.

"You're right," she said, "it tastes better when you lick it."

"Want one?" I asked Eddie.

"I don't smoke," he said, "it's a filthy habit."

He went to the sink, dumped his coffee and went out.

"Nighty-night," said Doris, "don't wait up."

"You two always been such good friends?" I asked.

"Not always. Now and again we fight."

"You mean he hits you?"

*"Him?* Hit *me?"*

"Stupid question," I agreed. "You hit him, huh?"

"How'd you think he got so punchy?"

"I'd been wondering." I got up and thanked her for the coffee.

"Don't go. We're just getting acquainted."

I paused at the doorway and looked at her. "Thanks, but I think I already know you better than I ever wanted to."

She laughed when I went out. She might even have thought it was funny.

# * Chapter *

# XVII

Two days passed with hot afternoons, still nights and no progress except in the fairgrounds cleanup. Friday afternoon we got a storm. One minute before 4:00 p.m. it was hotter than a moth's ass in a lamp chimney and the next minute I looked up to see this wall of black and blue moving in from the northwest like the final curtain. We scrambled into what the guys now called Fin's Barn and watched. It was really a dandy with roiling clouds, winds that flattened the fields and shook trees 'til you couldn't believe they'd keep a leaf or limb. The barn creaked under the first blast and we felt the chill just before hammering rain hit and thunder crashed.

Half an hour later a few straggling clouds were scudding after the passing mob and the rest of the sky was pale blue to forever. We found new gullies in the dirt track and along the fairgrounds road and I knew that all around the nearby farms' good top soil had been gouged out and carried off to ditches and sloughs, leaving clay and maybe some gravel.

I decided the hell with work the remaining half hour, called it a day and led the crew back to town. By the time we reached the creamery the sun had the sky to itself and the air was as close to steamy as it ever gets in South Dakota.

We stopped for our ritual malts and when I was almost through I looked up to see Iris Larson entering the front door.

"Well," I said, "look what the rain flushed out."

She looked almost apologetic and smiled.

"Cora drove me down as soon as the rain stopped," she said. "We were just going out when the storm hit."

"Where'd Cora go?" I asked.

"She's at the grocers. I needed some whipping cream here and then I'm going over to buy meat."

"Mind if I tag along?"

"Of course not. I'd be delighted."

Buck gave me a look when we entered his shop and then pretended I wasn't there. As soon as he and Iris got talking about the roast she wanted, I think he really forgot me. You'd have thought he was waiting on the Queen of England. She turned him so polite and proper nobody'd ever guess he was normally a total ass-hole.

Back out under the sun I asked Iris if Buck was still hanging around the house.

"No. I saw it upset Cora and I told him it'd be better if he stayed away a while. He took it very nicely."

"He thinks a lot of you."

"Well, I've always been a very good customer and of course he was terribly attached to Fin. More like dependent, actually. He hardly did a thing without talking it over first with Fin."

"They seemed like a strange pair—"

"Oh, I suppose so. Buck isn't very bright and he did get on Fin's nerves now and then. But the truth is, Fin had a wide streak of roughneck in him—they had more in common than most would think. And Fin liked being looked up to or was comfortable looking down—I'm not sure which it was but it went on all their lives. Did you know that about a year ago, Fin talked Buck into taking a helper so he could go off on a vacation? Buck hadn't had more than a day off in his life until then. Fin found a man in Chicago, paid for his room and board, made all the arrangements."

"Like over the Fourth of July?"

"Why, yes. How did you know?"

"It seemed likely. Where'd Buck take this vacation?"

"I don't know as I ever heard. I suppose he went fishing or something. I believe he left town—"

"To where?"

"Goodness, Carl, I don't know."

"Didn't he maybe go to Aquatown with Fin?"

She frowned. "What's so special about that weekend? What're you trying to get at?"

"I'm not real sure, but something happened there and I'm pretty certain it was connected with Fin's murder."

She stopped still and frowned at me. "What happened?"

"If I knew, I guess I wouldn't be asking, Iris. Listen, try to think back—if not right now, sometime when you're alone. Just kind of run over things that went on that month, before and after the Fourth."

She said she'd try but I didn't believe she took it very seriously and before I could work on her any more, Cora drove up in the big Buick. I told her she was prettier than Dolores Del Rio and she smiled real friendly and asked if I would ride with them. I knew it wasn't the compliment that made me accepted, it was just that natural perversity of women that makes them one day cut you dead and the next turn flirty as a cat in heat. It makes me mad but I'm not one to shun a chance on poor old principle so I climbed in beside her after handing Iris into the back seat.

When Iris invited me for dinner I telephoned the hotel to let Ma know. She was impressed. Fin's getting murdered had only temporarily damaged the Larson's social status and I think, if anything, his exit had upped Iris's standing one full step on the ladder.

We had a fine beef roast with potatoes and gravy so brown, smooth and rich I could drool the next day just remembering it. The big red tomatoes had been peeled and were served in thick slices on a white plate with chopped chives. The fresh peas were bright green and cooked so easy there wasn't a wrinkle in the lot and tasted like you'd just popped them out of the pod. I made a polite hog of myself, sitting there with three handsome women (Angie had come down out of hibernation when she smelled food) and thought how a few months earlier I'd been sharing gluey beans in a tin plate with a mob of scruffy men, and now, here I was eating the best grub in Corden or maybe all of South Dakota.

It was almost enough to make a man grow ambitious.

Angie sat directly across from me and barely glanced up. I avoided a direct study of her because I know how kids hate that but now and then I copped a peek and could see she wasn't in our world. She looked more like her old man than seemed possible for a pretty girl and the sullenness had dropped away. She looked dreamy sad. I couldn't help wondering what was going on nights with Clayt and what sort of a partner she might be on the horizontal.

Iris was full of talk about my sister and old times and Cora didn't have much to offer short of asking did anybody want more to eat or drink. When we started the meal I could see her checking out my style with the knife and fork. That didn't worry me; I'd operated under the eye of Ma all my life and critics don't come any tougher.

"How do you like working with the boys?" asked Iris in a sudden switch of topic.

"It's kind of fun."

"Does the judge come out often?"

"No."

"I'd expect him to be a hard taskmaster."

The judge had been some put out when we quit working to report finding the body our first day but I didn't think I needed to mention that in this company.

Iris looked at Angie and decided she'd ought to be in the social circle so she smiled and said, "Does Clayton ever talk about Carl as a boss?"

It took Angie a second to realize she'd been spoken to and then she had to have the question repeated. It flustered her, being caught like that, but she finally looked at me and nodded.

"Well," said Iris, "what does he say?"

"Oh, Clay likes everybody—"

Iris was only a little embarrassed. She laughed and said, well, she was foolish to ask in front of me. Angie kept looking my way but her eyes didn't see me.

"Tell me something, Angie," I said. "The last time you saw your Dad—were you really hating him? Enough to want to kill?"

She went rigid.

"Sure you did," I said, "and that doesn't mean a damned thing, you know that? Your pa was a man who stirred people up—lots of them—and every kid alive has hated the old man somewhere along the line, even when they didn't earn it. And I'd guess Fin did regular—so quit kidding yourself that you're some kind of monster or have some goofy guilt thing stuck on you. And try to remember your Ma's still around and deserves some consideration."

For a couple seconds she just glared at me, then she took a deep breath and let go.

"You don't know a thing—you're just a bum and a jail-bird. You don't know anything about Daddy and you won't—"

Iris tried to cut her off but didn't make any impression until she got to her feet and then Angie jumped up and ran to her room.

I was so damned disgusted with myself for trying to pull a Dutch uncle act that I had trouble soothing Iris out of her bad manners reaction. She could barely talk it hit her so bad. I worked her around enough to learn that the fellow Fin brought in to spell Buck had stayed at Bertelson's a few blocks to the southeast.

When I left, Iris walked me to the front door and Cora came along to the steps down to the public sidewalk. It was like they both figured Angie had cut me up so deep I'd bleed to death if I was left alone. When I told Cora I was going to the Bertelson's I got the feeling she was a little offended that I was so insensitive I could still function after what had been said.

Ernie Bertelson is a short, balding man with a gray fringe of hair, a neat paunch and no secrets.

"Sure, I remember the fella. Name was Dodd—real slim, wiry, quicker'n a snake's tongue. Come from Minneapolis—didn't talk much but he was civil enough. I asked how he liked working for Buck and he said it was fine, he never saw the fella. He wasn't crazy about Corden—not enough movie houses or pulp magazines. Wouldn't eat chicken. Said no butcher would. Said I wouldn't either if I knew what he knew but he never said what he knew about 'em."

"Did he ever say why he came to Corden?"

"Never said. I never asked. Figured it was for money—what else?"

"Can you imagine Buck paying a butcher what he'd make in the city?"

Ernie allowed it wasn't likely. We both knew Buck was so tight he farted in high C.

"I figure he was paid by Fin Larson," said Ernie. "Fin made all the arrangements. Came right here to the house, knocked on our front door and said he heard I had a room and he had a fella wanted one for four weeks. I offered to show him but he said no, he knew it'd be okay—I was no hog and the Mrs. was clean so it'd do and what did I want? I said five dollars a week and he said he'd gimme four and I said that ain't with meals and he said I was a robber but he grinned and gave me four one dollar bills and said the fella'd be here July first. And he was. Fin brought him in that big Buick. I just naturally figured he was going to be working for Fin but instead he went to the butcher shop."

"Buck ever come over to visit him?"

"Never. Fella never had no visitors, no mail, no telephone calls. Minded his own business, paid the first of the week and the first of August he was gone. Didn't say goodbye or nothing. He'd paid in advance and he left in the night."

"Maybe Fin picked him up."

"If he did, I didn't see. All I know is the man was with us Friday night and Saturday morning he was gone. Took a towel. It wasn't new but it was good enough for a long while yet. I called Fin on it and he said sue the bastard and I said where is he and he said he might be in hell for all he knew and that was the end of it. Why you want to know all this?"

"Oh, I'm working with Joey a little. He still hasn't a notion of who killed Fin. I thought maybe I'd find a lead."

"You figure it could've been Dodd?"

"Well, it had to be somebody—you weren't mad enough about that towel to hit old Fin with a pitchfork, were you?"

He gave me a gummy grin and said no, he guessed not.

"I didn't think so. I bet you wouldn't pitchfork a man if he stole your wife."

"No. Not unless he brought her back."

# * Chapter *

# XVIII

Joey was sitting at his desk, staring glumly across Main Street when I came into city hall and sat down in a straight chair against the wall.

"Did you know the fella named Dodd that worked in Buck's butcher shop last summer?" I asked.

Joey scowled. "I saw him when I bought meat a couple times. Why?"

"Buck didn't hire him. Fin did. Now why'd Fin want Buck free over the Fourth of July? I figure it was connected with Doris being in the city that weekend—the three of them were together."

Joey nodded slowly and his forehead puckered. "You figure they was playing games?"

"Uh-huh. With dirty movies. Making them."

"Aww—"

"Fin liked to work people—he liked dirty movies—and he knew people he could get to do the job. I think what happened in that hotel got Fin killed. Now what we'd ought to do, is go to the White Hotel and find out just who was there over the Fourth and what went on. Maybe the clerk will remember something."

"If he does, he ain't likely to tell us."

"Well, we won't know 'til we ask, huh?"

"Don't gimme that Lindbergh stuff. *I'm* not going on any wild goose chase."

"Okay, I'll go."

"I ain't deputizing you either. I got no jurisdiction outside Corden County."

"I don't figure you've got jurisdiction beyond the front walk—and I don't need a badge, only a little per diem."

"Uh-uh. I'm fresh out."

So I went on my own. It would've been nice to borrow the old man's Dodge for the trip but I didn't feel up to answering questions half the night and as was, it was nearly nine when I took off in the truck.

The South Dakota sun had turned the White Hotel gray and it looked more like a rest home for the aged than a setting for a blue movie. I parked the truck a half block down the street from the front entrance and moseyed along the street, looking around. Directly across from the hotel I saw a couple of old parties behind the window of the Cozy Café where Chip had probably watched Doris a year before. The street itself was dead—not so much as a stray dog in sight. I climbed two steps, entered the cool lobby and walked across a worn carpet to the registration desk tucked under a balcony spanning the north wall which was all Spanish style arches and big dusty plants.

There wasn't a soul in sight. I leaned over the register and stared at the column of scribbled names. There were just five for that day, Friday, August 19th.

A girl appeared in the doorway of an office behind the registration counter. She was slim with streaked blond hair, a wide mouth and full lips that couldn't quite seem to cover white, even teeth.

"Hi," she smiled. I started thinking seriously of staying the night.

"You wouldn't be a Woodford, would you?" I asked.

"No."

"You're a dead ringer for a family I met in Wisconsin— women were all knock-outs."

"Really? Did you want a room?"

"I'm thinking about it. What've you got?"

"Well, since you've already looked over the register, you can tell we've got most of the hotel. What did you want—a single?"

"That's right. Something modest—even humble. You got anything like that?"

"Can you handle up to two dollars?"

"I usually fondle it." I didn't mention that was damned near a day's pay. "The truth is, I'm more like trying to get some information."

Her full lips almost met and her eyes became less friendly. "I can give you information about rooms."

"Could you tell me who'd stayed in a couple of them about a year ago?"

"Why?"

"Because I'm trying to find out about something that happened a year ago that's important to friends of mine."

"Like who?"

"Like officer Joey Paxton, in Corden, and Mrs. Fin Larson—"

She frowned—or tried to. It wasn't easy to erase the natural smile in her mouth. "Fin Larson—he was the man murdered in Corden, wasn't he?"

"That's right. You know him?"

"Oh, well, I didn't really *know* him. I saw him here about a year ago. After he was killed, Max showed me his picture in the paper."

"Who's Max?"

"Max White, my great uncle, he owns the hotel."

"Oh, yeah, that figures. Is he around?"

"No, he's in Minneapolis."

"When'll he be back?"

"I don't know. He's in the hospital there. We don't know if he'll ever be back." I was afraid she was going to cry and hurried to tell her I was real sorry and would she mind letting me look at the register for the weekend of the Fourth a year ago? It took her a few seconds to stop thinking about the tragedy of Max and she went after the register in a daze. A few moments later she was back and watched as I located the right page and ran my finger down the column until I came to the scrawled signatures of Fin Larson, Tom Smith, Dick Smith, Harry Smith and J. Stanley Doe.

"Two of the fellows that signed as Smith were older men,"

she said. "One was gray haired—the other almost bald, and they were both, well, sort of portly."

"How about fat?"

She uncovered her smile again. "Okay, but sort of stylish fat. The other Smith was real tall and a lot younger."

"How about J. Stanley Doe. What was he like?"

She shuddered. "Big, mean looking—"

"Like a peeled ape with a red face?"

She laughed and nodded. "That's him, all right."

"He's a butcher in Corden. A cousin to Fin Larson."

"Really? I'd never have guessed. They weren't anything alike."

"How long were they here?"

"Over the weekend."

"Was there a woman from Corden in the group—kind of plump, with curly hair, maybe a little taller than you?"

She nodded. "They called her Mae. I don't think that was her name, though, they were calling her after Mae West—"

"But she didn't sign the register," I said, examining the list again.

"No, none of the ladies did." The way she said that she didn't figure any of them were ladies.

"How come?"

"Well," she said, looking a little embarrassed, "none of them were supposed to be spending the night."

"How many were there?"

"I'm not sure—they came and went. There must have been at least five."

"Including Mae?"

She nodded.

"Listen, would you mind taking me up so I can get a look at where all this went on?"

"What good will that do?"

"Probably none. But it can't harm, can it? I just want to get as familiar as I can with everything involved. It might give me an idea. Wouldn't you like to help?"

Max was forgotten. I got her big smile and then she took a key from the wall rack and we headed for the elevator. It was a wire cage in a wrought iron shaft and moved as slow as a sun rise.

"How come a pretty girl like you's working in an old hotel like this?" I asked as we creaked upward.

"Well, Uncle Max likes to have relatives working for him, and there weren't any boys in the family old enough so he offered me the job and I took it."

"Still in high school?"

"Of course not," she laughed.

"Come on. How long since?"

"A year."

"So you're what—eighteen? And you're in charge of the White Hotel. He must think you're quite a girl."

"Well, I'm not alone. There's lots of experienced help."

We finally reached the fourth level and she jockeyed the cage to get it even with the floor before opening the doors. She led me down the hall to the extreme south end, stopped in front of Room 421, unlocked the door and pushed it open. I entered a small vestibule flanked by a bathroom on the right and a closet on the left. Beyond was a large living room with a couch and day bed, four easy chairs with striped upholstery in red and gold, and a library table in the center of a worn red carpet. The red and gold wallpaper was faded and grimy. I walked around the center table and looked into the bedrooms. Both were good-sized, one in blue, the other all yellow. They had double beds, fancy bureaus, and thick, persian-style carpets in a few million colors. Double windows overlooked Main Street and flat roofs of lesser buildings on each side. I could smell old cigars and just a hint of mothballs.

I turned to the girl. "What's your name?"

"Jessica. Everybody calls me Jessie."

"Okay, Jessica. How many people were at this party—do you know?"

"About ten. Five fellas and five women—not counting me."

"*You* were at the party?"

She giggled. "Not for long. Max made me go when Mr. Larson offered me a drink."

"Did you want to stay?"

"Well, it looked pretty interesting, with all the cameras and stuff."

"What cameras?"

She looked innocent. "Didn't I mention them? They had movie cameras and lights on stands—"

I shook my head and sat down on one of the easy chairs.

"Is something wrong?" she asked, looking worried.

"No, nothing. Did you see them bring these cameras and things inside?"

"Oh sure. And if I hadn't, Rudy'd have told me."

"Who's Rudy?"

"The bellhop. He was mad because they had so much stuff for him to carry and then they only tipped him a quarter, as if he'd only carried a couple suitcases. Of course Rudy's always mad because nobody's ever tipped him more than a quarter. Usually he just gets a dime. He doesn't smile. I tell him if he'd smile he'd get bigger tips but he considers that would make people feel superior and he'd rather not get tips than admit anybody's better than he is."

Rudy sounded like my kind of man.

"Did they take any pictures while you were in the room?" I asked.

She shook her head.

"You got any notion of what kind of movies they were planning to make?"

She walked slowly over to a chair across from me and ran her slim fingers along the seat back. "I wouldn't guess they were anything very serious—I mean—they were all acting pretty silly."

"Like maybe drunk?"

"Uh-huh," she admitted.

"Did all ten of these people spend the night in this suite?"

"Well, a couple of the fellows had a room across the hall. Mutt and Jeff did."

"Mutt and Jeff?"

She laughed. "That's what I called the tall one with the hair and the short bald man. They had the cameras."

I got up and wandered over to the yellow bedroom door.

"When you were in the room—who else was here?"

"Uncle Max, and the Smith fellows, Mr. Larson and the butcher. Then there was a peroxide blond, a red-haired girl,

real tall, and a little brunette. I remember, Mr. Larson said
they had something for every taste."

"I thought you said there were five girls."

"Well, that was all together, through the night. The one
they called Mae West came in later and then there was another woman—I never saw her—Rudy did—said she was
real young—"

"Where were you when the Mae West one came in?"

"At the desk downstairs."

"What'd she do?"

"She just walked over to the elevator and told Rudy to
take her up to four."

"Is that the way things operate in the White Hotel?"

"Oh no," she said, shaking her head so hard her hair
flopped. "She told Rudy she was visiting the party in Mr.
Larson's room. Rudy knew Mr. White was up there so there
couldn't be anything wrong with taking her up."

I made a cigaret, lit up and stared at her through the
smoke.

"If the girl named Mae showed up after you'd left the
party, how come you knew they called her that?"

"Uncle Max told me."

"What else did he tell you about the party?"

"Nothing much—I think he was embarrassed about
knowing those people." She twisted around and glanced at
the open door behind her. "Look, I think maybe I'd ought to
be getting back downstairs—"

I said fine, went into the hall and waited while she locked
the door before we walked back to the waiting elevator.

"If Max didn't talk about the party, how'd the nickname
come up?"

"Well, I asked him if this woman had come up there and
he said yes and the first thing he'd thought was, this is Mae
West and then one of the fellows called her that and he knew
it wasn't really her and it struck him funny so he told me."

"Did Fin ask you to be in his movie?"

She glanced at me with a raised eyebrow. "How'd you
guess that?"

"Well, you're young, pretty—"

She blushed, lowered her head and gave a short laugh.

"Well, I don't know about that—but yes, he did ask. That's when Uncle Max told me to go downstairs."

"I thought that happened when he offered you a drink?"

"He offered both at the same time."

"Was Max mad at Larson about that?"

"Oh boy—I'll say! He told Mr. Larson I was family and when that only made him laugh, Uncle Max was just furious—he told him he could take his whole crowd and their junk and get out of the hotel but the red-faced one—the butcher—he came over close and didn't say a word, just stood there, scowling, and Max was afraid of him but he still wouldn't let me stay."

"So then what?"

"I went back down to the desk."

"How long'd the party last?"

"I don't know for sure—Ellie—she's a maid—said it was still going on when she started doing rooms at 7:00 a.m."

"Was Max up there all that time?"

"I don't think so—he doesn't like late hours—but he was still up there when I went to bed at 11:00."

"Well, how long did the crowd stay?"

"Until Monday night."

"Including Mae?"

"Uh-huh. She didn't go until Mr. Larson and the butcher fellow left, Monday afternoon."

We'd left the elevator and were talking beside the registration desk by then. Pretty soon she excused herself, went across the lobby and spoke to a dark young man sitting in an easy chair near the windows. He put down his Liberty magazine and answered a question I couldn't hear. After a moment she came back to me.

"If you want to ask Rudy anything," she said, "he'll talk to you."

"He's the bellhop that was on duty that night—or weekend?"

"That's right."

I thanked her and went over toward the young man. He was all black hair, black eyes, and dark skin. His eye raised from the magazine and watched, unblinking, as I approached. I sat down on a chair nearby, turned it to face him and returned his stare.

"I'm Carl Wilcox, from Corden. Miss Jessica said you'd be willing to talk to me a little."

"*Como no?*" he said. His voice was soft.

"Yeah, why not?"

He grinned. His teeth weren't very straight or white.

"*Habla Espanol?*" he asked.

"*Poco*—more like *pocito*."

He laughed and nodded sympathetically. "Where you learn?"

"In stir. You gonna let me ask the questions?"

"You not a cop," he told me, grinning.

"That's right and neither are you. So we talk, okay?"

"Okay." He suddenly looked serious.

"Were you working here through July last year?"

He nodded.

"Did you see any of what was going on up in the suite on four?"

"*Pocito.*" He grinned again. "What you in prison for?"

"A stick-up. How about you?"

"I cut a fella."

"Okay. We're a couple of hard cases. Would you mind telling me what you figured was going on up in that suite a year ago?"

"Big party, man. Way big party. Gorls, booze and wee-man."

"You get in on any of it?"

"Me? A spik? You got to be kidding, man."

"Did you deliver ice or anything while it was going on?"

"Oh, sure. But they never let me inside. Always someone come to the door. I stuck around once, after the man closed it, I even tried peeking the key hole but they left the key in the door. Real bastards."

"You listen a little?"

"Not much to hear. They got victrola on. Lotsa laugh."

"Everybody friendly?"

"Why not? Plenty weemon, booze for ever'body."

"You figure Max had a good time?"

"No. Max, he mad. Mad as hell. Come down before 12.00."

"What was he mad about?"

He shrugged.

"Didn't he say anything?"

"Jus only cuss words."

"How long had you been working here then?"

"Not long—since Spring."

"Had any of those people ever stayed at the hotel before that you knew of?"

"Not while I was around. Before, I think."

"This Uncle Max—how old is he?"

"Sixty, maybe more."

"You like him?"

"He's okay."

"What kind of a guy is he? I mean, friendly, tough?"

"*Caballeroso*—a proud man."

"You hear where he came from, what he did before he opened this hotel?"

He didn't know. I asked him some more questions but only learned that Max had usually been decent to Rudy and was alternately worshipful and despairing about his grand niece. I thanked Rudy and went back to the registration desk.

"You got him to smile," she said, "he must have liked you."

"We got a lot in common—can you tell me what hospital your Uncle Max is in?"

"I think they call it Emergency Hospital—it's right in downtown Minneapolis. But it won't do you any good to call. He can't talk. All he can do is blink his eyes."

Her voice tightened as she spoke.

"When did it happen?"

"Couple days ago—Tuesday."

"Well," I said, "I'm sorry."

She was fighting tears and it made her angry.

"Why should you be sorry—you've never even met him."

"That's right ... but I've met you."

"Just barely."

"Well a guy doesn't have to grow up with people to feel for them."

She took a deep breath, tilted her head back and released a slow sigh.

"No, you're being nice. Thank you. Now I guess there's nothing more, is there?"

I still wanted to get better acquainted with her but it was a lousy time for promotions so I thanked her, waved at Rudy as I went out and drove back to Corden.

# * Chapter *

# XIX

Saturday morning, after nearly an hour of badgering by me, Joey called the General Hospital in Minneapolis and learned that Max White was there, totally paralyzed and dumb.

"Everything the girl told me fits into my notion of what happened," I told Joey. "Fin was making stag films—and he got Buck and Eddie's wife into the act and to keep anybody from knowing about that, either one of 'em would kill."

Joey shook his head. "Even if we knew all that for certain—how the hell you gonna prove it?"

"Well, sure as hell not by sitting on my ass here. Come on, let's go talk to Buck."

He didn't like it much but he finally sighed, got up and set off with me. It wasn't noon yet and walking down the deserted street it was hard to believe that in a few hours people would be thicker than bees at swarming time as they showed up for Saturday night.

"Well," said Buck, giving us a wary eye as we came into his shop, "if it ain't the law and the outlaw. You figure the best way to keep order in town is by keeping Wilcox on a leash?"

Joey let that sail past.

"I hear that you went to a party over the Fourth last year," he said.

Buck's face went wooden a second before he pushed it into a grin.

"Now where'd you hear that?"

"Is it true?"

"It might be. I like a party now and then."

"I hear this one lasted a while, and there was some gals from the cities there with some of Fin's rich city friends."

"Yeah? Sounds good. Tell me about it."

"It was in Aquatown, at the White Hotel. There was a camera crew and a lot of action, and you had to lean a little on Max White to keep him from trying to throw the crowd out."

"Hey, I wouldn't bully an old man."

"How'd you know White was an old man?"

"Well, you said—"

"I didn't say a damn thing to tell you his age. You were there—and I know you were—and I'm gonna find out what it was all about, see?"

"Well, for Christ's sake, why get excited about a little party? Sure I was there. Never said I wasn't, but I don't remember much." He grinned. "I got drunk."

"So what happened?"

"I don't remember that much. There were picture fellas Fin knew from the cities. One from the coast, I think. They were on their way someplace to make some movies—"

"Didn't they take pictures at the hotel?"

"In the White Hotel? Why'n hell'd they take pictures there for?"

"I don't much give a damn *why*, I want to know just now *what*. Now are you trying to tell me they had a room full of people, hauled in a mess of cameras and stuff and didn't take any pictures?"

"That's right. You expect they was gonna leave that stuff out on the street?"

"You're saying they absolutely didn't take pictures?"

"I don't remember they did, no."

"What do you remember?"

He grinned again. "I got drunk."

"How about Doris Langer. Did she get drunk too?"

Buck swallowed his grin, choked on it a little and leaned on the butcher's counter with both hands.

"Doris. You mean Eddie's wife?"

"That's who I meant."

"Well now, that's funny. I don't remember her bein' there at all. Where'd you get that notion?"

"We've talked to people at the hotel, Buck. We *know* she was there. We know they took pictures, we know Fin used to show blue movies at the theater for his friends and you knew it too—don't you? We know you left the White Hotel on a Monday morning after the party and picture taking and you left with Doris. You been anyplace with her since?"

Buck drew himself up, threw a glare at me and then scowled at Joey.

"Listen now, that's a hell of a way to talk to a man with his own shop and lots of friends. You wouldn't talk like that if Fin was alive—not in front of that Goddamned jailbird you got with you. What's all this 'we' shit? What the hell—"

"That's enough of that talk," Joey told him.

"All right. But I ain't saying another word with that peckerhead here."

Joey glowered at him for a moment, then glanced my way and said maybe I'd best drift. That burned me some but I didn't really blame either one of them and I gave a wave and strolled outside.

I decided to visit Doris.

The house stood small and baking under the prairie sun as I went up the long walk and knocked at the rattly door. The shades were drawn but I could see through the hall clear to the back screen. I pressed my knee against the front screen and knocked harder.

"Come in," called Doris.

I pulled the screen open and went inside. The porch floor, which sloped outward, creaked as I walked to the living room entrance and then I was in a darkened room filled with cluttery furniture and scattered newspapers and magazines. Doris was stretched out on the couch.

"Well," she said, "if it ain't the poor man's private eye."

A glass stood on the floor beside her and I guessed she had been drinking although her voice sounded clear enough.

I leaned against the door jamb and built a cigaret.

"There's another witness," I said after I'd lit up.

She watched me for a moment, shifted to lift her head and said, "To what?"

"Your visit to the White Hotel last summer."

She dropped her head back. "My God, you still harping on that?"

"Uh-huh. Right now Joey's having a little talk with Buck."

"So what?" She sat up slowly and leaned on her knees. "You gonna make a smoke for me?"

I took mine from my mouth and stuck it in hers. There was no smell of alcohol and it dawned on me she was drinking iced tea. She stood up, gave me a short smile and said stick around, she'd be right back. I watched the back of her baggy housecoat that was too short to hide a gray nightdress. Her long hair straggled down between her shoulders.

I sat down in a sagging easy chair, built another cigaret, lit up and stared at the mess around me. Upstairs Doris moved briskly, a little water ran, the toilet flushed, the floor creaked back and forth and then she was on the steps and made an entry.

"Well," I said.

She'd brushed her hair, put on the cincher, stockings, high heels and a white dress. She touched her hair carefully with both hands.

"It looks better when I curl it. But I didn't think it'd be polite to take that much time."

"I'm impressed," I admitted.

"Living in this dump, a girl gets to letting herself go."

"Is that the outfit you wore in Aquatown last year?"

She put her hands on her round hips and glared at me. "You got a hell of a one-track mind."

"I'm sorry, Doris, but what you got on is what the fella described. To a T."

She sighed, half turned to give me a good squint at her jutting breasts and said, "Make another cigaret, Carl, while I build us a drink."

"We gonna have a party?"

"What the hell. It's Saturday, isn't it?"

"Where's Eddie?"

"The hell with Eddie, he can make his own drink."

She was swaying toward the kitchen door as I got up.

"Is he running the matinee?"

"That's right, we got lotsa time."

"Tell you what—skip the drink for me—I'm on the wagon."

She arched her eyebrows and then grinned. "Whatsamatter—you figure I'm gonna hand you a Mickey?"

"Never dreamed it. Where'd you get hold of the mix?"

"That's right. Okay, you mind if I buy myself one—?"

"Go ahead. You going to admit you were in Aquatown last Fourth?"

"Are you gonna make us a smoke?"

"Okay."

"Okay, so I been to the city lotsa times. That's where I shop—there's nothing a girl can find in this Goddamned town that's decent to wear."

"You're telling me you went shopping on the Fourth of July weekend?"

She took the cigaret I'd made, accepted a light and gave me a long, pouty look. I guessed she'd practiced it in the mirror and figured it was sexy. She was almost right.

"No, big boy, I'm not tellin' you nothin'."

"Oh yeah," I grinned, "you're telling me a whole lot. Did you do the Mae West act for the cameras that weekend?"

She was so exasperated she pitched the whole role and flounced out to the kitchen. I strolled behind her and stopped in the doorway to watch as she poured a drink for herself.

"About now," I said, "I figure Buck is admitting to Joey what went on in the White Hotel last year."

Doris took a swig of her drink and held the glass with both hands. "I'll tell you what, Buster, I don't give a *damn* what Buck's telling that dumb cop. And right now I'll thank you to get the hell out of my house."

"You gonna throw me out after I made you a cigaret?"

"If you're not out in ten seconds—I'm gonna start screaming."

"Will it make any difference if I accept a drink?"

She took a deep breath, and I said, "Okay. Save yourself . . . and enjoy the smoke."

She told me to do the impossible and I went outside, into the sunshine and slowly walked back toward city hall.

As I passed in front of the hotel, Hank bounced out of the lobby and greeted me as if I were a long lost rich uncle in poor health.

"Hey Carl! You gonna be around tonight?"

"If the goblins don't get me, I suppose so. Why?"

"Well, the folks are going to Aquatown for the Old Guard Club meeting and they'll be staying the night and I'm going to the Spider Palace for the dance with Nancy and I hoped maybe you'd watch the hotel."

"Watch it do what?"

"Come on. Will you?"

"You think I'm too decrepit for a social life of my own?"

"No, course not—but it's just this one night. Come on, Carl!"

I kept him worried for a respectable time before agreeing and as usual he was so damned grateful it made me feel like a prince.

"How soon I got to take over my duties?"

"Well, the folks'll be leaving about five—and I'm going at six—"

"So I got about an hour."

"Well, yeah. Say, it's really great of you . . ."

"Uh-huh. Now don't slop all over me, I got a weak stomach. I'll be back by 5:30."

He slapped me on the shoulder and darted back into the hotel.

Joey was alone at his desk and gave me a mournful look as I came in and plunked down on his extra chair.

"He wouldn't admit anything," said Joey. "Oh, he allowed he was at the hotel with Fin—but he says Doris was never there and there wasn't any movies made and if there was he was too drunk to know but he knows there wasn't."

"I'm not surprised. I went and talked to Doris and she wouldn't admit anything either—which just convinces me that what went on there was something they wouldn't admit if we could put 'em on the rack."

Joey sat back and twiddled his thumbs. He's the only guy

I've ever known that honest to God did that—and in slow motion.

"I'll tell you one thing," said Joey, "don't ever turn your back on Buck."

"He's not too crazy about me, huh?"

"All I know is if you turn up missing there'd be no question for me about who done it."

"You figure knowing that would do you any good?"

"It probably wouldn't do either one of us any good. I sure wish to hell none of this mess had ever started. I'm sick of it."

"Murder's tough on the survivors," I agreed. "What'd Buck say that made him sound sore at me?"

"He wouldn't've had to say anything after the look he gave when you went. But then he asked me, real innocent, why I was letting you try to hang him for a killing that you done. Then he told me all about you, Carl. He knows a good deal—I come near being convinced. You really been a heller all your life, you know that?"

"Uh-huh, I've some notion, having spent most of it—but somewhere along the line I must've missed a couple years. I keep hearing about things I don't remember a thing about. But let me tell you something interesting about Buck, okay?"

"Shoot. I'm drop-jawed."

"The real reason he hates my guts is Cora."

He raised his eyebrows but he wasn't anywhere near as good at it as Doris had been. "Fin's cousin?"

"That's right."

He mulled that over and finally nodded his head. He was thinking so hard his thumbs came to a whoa, stiff as a wood carving. He stared at me.

"So, how you making out with the young lady?"

"I'm not."

He grunted and looked a little relieved. "Just as well. She looks like a gypsy but I figure she's quality at bottom. You'd only give her grief."

"What the hell do you know about what I give a woman?"

"Oh, I know a little something about women—and a lot

more about you. They like things in order, and you're just pure the opposite."

I couldn't think of a polite comment for that and decided I was due back at the hotel. He didn't coax me to stay.

Since everyone else was gone or going, Bertha fixed dinner for just the two of us and we ate in the kitchen. Next to liver my pet hate is lamb chops and she fixed them with creamed potatoes which I'd rather eat than toadstools but not much. Naturally that led to words, none of which are used in polite society and I got out of the kitchen before she made up her mind whether she was going to lay into me with the rolling pin or the cleaver.

The lobby was quieter than dead Coolidge so I went out front, parked in one of the captain's chairs and leaned back to smoke and watch the Saturday night mob. It was hot enough to make people move slow and easy and a good many of the fellows had their coats off and sleeves rolled up a couple turns but only the early drunks had their shirt collars unbuttoned and there weren't many of them. Watching all the orderly, law-abiding, God-fearing, mostly woman-bridled folks, it was hard to believe that three people had been murdered in our town and the killer was still loose and maybe primed for another job.

At dusk what little breeze we'd had curled up and died.

The street lights came on and about the time bugs began gathering around the glow, people started forming a little group in front of the Playhouse. Inside somebody tootled through the scales on a tenor sax and I heard the bass drum thump a couple times and then there was a riffle on the traps. A woman laughed. It drifted across the street, all intimate and happy, leaving me lonely.

I got up, stepped on my cigaret butt and went inside to the telephone on the wall outside Elihu's bedroom. After twisting the crank I asked the operator for the Larson's number. Cora answered on the third ring.

"Would you like to hear what Joey said about you today?" I asked.

"Sure."

"He said you looked like a gypsy but he figured you were really quality folk."

"You think that's a compliment?"

"Well, it's about as flowery as Joey's gonna get."

"Did you call just to tell me that?"

"No—there's more. He figures I'm not good enough for you."

There was a moment's silence. "What brought all this conversation on?"

"We'd been talking about Buck. You came in sort of round-about. Has Buck been coming around lately?"

"Not since Aunt Iris talked to him."

"Why'd she talk to him?"

"I told her he made me nervous. I don't trust him."

"You've got good judgement. Look—did Fin ever ask you to Aquatown for a weekend?"

"Certainly not."

"Don't go getting hot—I'm trying to find something out. Why was it so certain he wouldn't ask?"

"Only a fool asks a woman to do something she won't have any part of. What are you getting at?"

"I'm not real sure. Fin had something going on at the White Hotel there. Buck was in on it and so was a local housewife along with some people from the Cities or Chicago—maybe both. I wondered if he ever tried to work you in."

"What sort of thing are you talking about?"

I told her what I'd picked up at the White Hotel. For several seconds she thought that over and then she said, "You think they were making blue movies, is that it?"

"Yeah."

"And you actually thought I might have been asked to get involved with something like that?"

"I know damned well you wouldn't go into it wide-eyed. But somebody got mad enough to kill Fin like he was a rat and I think it had to be pretty special because people been putting up with his crap for years without murdering him"

"That doesn't have to follow. From what I read, people kill over some very little thing that comes after a lot of big things piled up."

We were both silent for a few seconds and I could hear the band across the street playing "Marie."

"You think Buck did it, don't you?" said Cora.

"Uh-huh. With maybe some help from Doris Langer."

"Eddie's wife? Why her?"

"I figure she was one of Fin's rejected ladies. I think she's a very good hater and she was at the hotel that week-end."

"You think *she* performed in a blue movie?"

"Yup."

"Well, Fin never asked me to go anywhere for a weekend —he never so much as asked if he could take a snapshot of me."

"I'd like a picture of you."

"Well, bring a camera next time you're around. Which reminds me—how come you're telephoning and not visiting?"

"I'm baby-sitting the hotel. Folks went to a club meeting and Hank's gone to the lake."

"Oh."

"Why don't you come down and visit me?"

"I don't think that'd be wise."

"Don't worry I'm not alone—Bertha's around."

"I've heard she never gets closer to the lobby than the dining room."

"Well, what do you want—her sitting between us like a spik chaperone?"

She laughed in a way that made me think she really wanted to come. I waited a moment, trying to figure what might persuade her.

"Tell you what," I coaxed, "you come down here and we'll sort things out 'til we solve this murder business—I'll bet between us we can do it."

"Are you serious?"

"Hell, yes. I think it's already clear—the only problem's coming up with proof. Maybe woman's intuition can find a way."

We waltzed it around a while longer before she decided she'd come.

I didn't really expect her to show. It was too unnatural a thing for a woman to do in our town and if anybody saw her enter the hotel there'd be talk until the whole earth was dead as the moon.

A few minutes after ten she slipped in the side door next to the parlor. Across the street the dance was in full swing and a block east on Main traffic was thinning out as stores closed and farmers finished loading up and wheeled for home. Cora was in gray, which was practically a disguise since I'd never seen her in anything but black or white before. She entered with her head high but her face turned away from the street. I led her into the parlor and she stopped at the center of the room and took in the furnishings, making a complete turn to catch it all.

"I suppose your mother picked all of these pieces?"

"Uh-huh."

She looked at the marble-topped black walnut table between the front windows and smiled faintly at the brightly colored cloth with long tassles that hung over the curved edging.

"It's very Victorian," she said. I nodded. She looked at the bookshelf with glass doors and asked if anyone ever opened it.

"Sure. Hank does—even I have."

"I can't imagine you reading. Do you actually sit still and read a book—ever?"

"I have."

"I picture you always being on the move, doing things."

"Yeah, but I haven't always been free for it."

She thought that over, decided it might lead too far if continued, and sat down on the couch. She didn't perch, she sat back comfortably and watched me. I went over and sat down beside her, about two feet away.

"I almost didn't come," she said, "not for reasons you probably think of—but because of things you said about these murders—that something had happened, very special, to trip them. You implied that Buck might've gone berserk because Uncle Fin tried to get me involved with one of those movies and I thought, if you're right, if he *is* jealous and that dangerous, won't my coming to visit you make him upset if he finds out?"

"It might."

"Is that why you invited me here? To sort of force his hand?"

"Is that why you came?"

Her smooth forehead wrinkled in a small frown. "I don't know—I guess I felt it was too far-fetched—and I didn't want you to think I was one of these ninnies scared of her reputation." She stood up and walked toward the front windows. "Maybe I was just restless. It *was* foolish to come. I suppose."

"Not at all—you wanted to solve a murder, right?"

She turned and gave me a long look. "Is that all you want—really?"

"No, not all."

"I think it's all you really want. You'll just take anything else you can get along the way."

"I might at that."

"I think I'd better go back up to the house."

I stayed on the couch and smiled at her. "Don't get skittery, I'm not going to pounce. And the way you're talking, I'm gonna start thinking you're sore because I haven't turned all buttery—that's not why you're about to take off, is it?"

"Oh, don't try to work me," she said impatiently. "That's too transparent."

"Okay, so let's talk about you. When Fin gave you the pitch to come to Corden, what'd you think would happen in the long run?"

"What do you mean?"

"Well, he must've told you his wife was dying—he'd told others he thought so and she'd made everybody believe it. Did you think then, maybe way in the back of your mind, that you'd come to Fin's place, take care of the house and when Iris quietly slipped off, you'd wait a decent time and when old Fin popped the question, you'd say yes and become the queen of Corden?"

She moved to the northwest corner and sat down in the big easy chair. Her lips were tight for a moment, then relaxed and suddenly she laughed. "You *are* something," she said, shaking her head. "Fin was old enough to be my father."

"Yeah, I know, but you wouldn't be the first girl to marry an older man."

"Especially one with money?"

"That never made a man ugly."

"I thought you liked me. Why are you suddenly being so insulting?"

"I do like you—but I don't take you for a plaster saint. I wouldn't like you if you were and I'm not saying you calculated everything—I'm asking you to be honest and tell me what you really figured on when Fin asked you to his home."

"I didn't figure on anything, he asked me. I thought he honestly needed me—so I came. After all he was my only living relative and he'd been very nice to me."

"Did he promise to take care of you?"

This time she blushed a little. "Yes, he did. I had to have some assurance, after all—"

"Of course. How long did it take to figure out Iris wasn't really sick?"

She shook her head. "You don't miss a thing, do you? I guess it took me a couple weeks. I noticed she was only sick when Fin was around to see. He knew she wasn't really ill too. I mean, in a regular way. You could say *he* made her ill, I suppose it was just as real as something more physical but he never believed she'd die of it."

"So Fin didn't really need you at all—why'd you stay?"

"Well, I never intended to for long. The trouble was, I didn't know what else to do. I didn't have any money and Iris became so dependent and was terribly nice I felt sorry for her. She's much better off now, I think even she knows it."

"If Iris had died and Fin asked you to marry him would you have?"

She frowned at me. "What in the world has that to do with what we're supposed to be talking about?"

I grinned. "Probably not a thing. But I do like you and I thought I'd like to know more. Don't you want to answer that question?"

"I can't. I don't really know. Now it seems silly even to think about. But when he was alive and when you'd been around him and seen how persuasive he could be—I don't know. I hope I'd have said no—I think I would have said no."

I had a strong notion she was leaning over backward to make me think she was honest, but of course there was no telling.

"Doesn't it bother you that Fin was making blue movies and messing with those kind of people?"

"I suppose I should be shocked, but I'm not. It doesn't surprise me much—maybe I'm a little disappointed. It *is* tawdry, isn't it?"

I asked her what kind of a man she thought she wanted and she gave me an arch look and said one that knew what he was doing.

"It'd also help if he didn't suspect me of being a murderer."

"Where'd you get the notion that I suspected you?"

"Because before you couldn't keep your hands off me and now you sit there and measure me and weigh my words and keep asking nasty questions."

"Okay. Come over here and we'll forget about the questions."

"No." She got up, went to the door and looked back at me. "I was an idiot to come down here." Then she left.

I went to the door and watched her walk up the street, very erect and quick with toes pointed straight ahead and hardly enough hip roll to show she had buns. She wasn't my style, I told myself and then wondered what was? The Lil and Doris types with their hot appetites, empty heads and always the danger of clap?

I drifted through the lobby to the east door and stared toward the theater where the show was letting out. People straggled down the walk in all directions, some toward the cafe across the street, but most toward home or cars parked along Main. Fifteen minutes later the street was empty except for cars belonging to people in the cafe and the dance hall. A little before twelve Joey came lumping along the walk, heading for the Playhouse to see they closed at the stroke of midnight before their coaches turned to pumpkins and as he disappeared inside the band started playing Good Night Ladies.

I wondered where old Boswell was hanging out and wished he had a phone so I could give him a call and order up a jug of moonshine. He always had some, along with a thirst and he never talked when I didn't want to listen. I thought about the bottle up in my bureau, hidden under the long johns, and figured there wasn't enough left to do me any real good.

When the dance hall was dark and the street deserted, I turned on the registration desk lamp, a little goose neck that stood on the cigar counter and spotlighted the bell beside the register. Then I turned off the overhead lights and walked over for a last survey of the town. Only the streetlight bugs gave it life.

I went back through the dining room, kitchen and into the dark back shed where I checked on whether Bertha had used the hook lock on the screen. She had and it gave me no comfort—any kid with four inches of wire could open it without a sound. Buck could force it with his eyelashes.

I was just entering the dining room from the kitchen when I heard the front door open.

It might be a traveler, I thought, too tired to finish the thirty miles to the city, but I didn't believe that—the entry had been too quiet. I moved catfoot style, quick and light, to the hall. A woman came from the lobby into the far end of the hall, paused at the stairway bottom, saw or heard me, and started up.

Every instinct in my carcass hollered whoa. I pulled up, swung to my right, skipped between tables to the dining room door on the east which opened into the lobby, and stopped to listen. If there was an ambush it'd probably be someone waiting in the register alcove, expecting me down the hall. Hearing nothing, I crossed the lobby in a crouching run and the floor didn't creak until I was at the counter but there was no one squatting behind it. I looked across the hall toward the old man's bedroom. The door was closed tight, as I'd left it. I scooted around the lobby and glanced into the parlor. It looked empty.

Just as I reached for the bannister and took one step up, I

heard a spattering sound behind me. I've no idea what I thought it might be but I whirled, sidestepped and went into a crouch. Another gust of wind threw heavy drops of rain against the door and I slowly straightened, feeling foolish and shaky. I peered through the streaming window and saw the wind whipping sheets of rain across the gravelled street. The building creaked and the rain began to pound.

I walked down the hall back into the public dining room, took a right through the private diner, opened the door in the alcove on the right far corner and looked up the servants' stairway. The dim hall light reflected feebly above. I eased up slowly along the steps made just wide enough to pass Bertha in two layers of petticoats. The steps emerged on a small open area in front of the bathroom and linen closet. I smelled the mothballs from the closet and felt a slight draft from the open bathroom window, moist and cool. There was a little gate at the top of the steps, to keep drunks and sleep walkers from tumbling down. I leaned over it to look left down the hall toward the front stairway, pushed through and paused for a moment. There were sounds of movement down the south corridor where my room was but I couldn't be certain because the storm confused sound.

I closed the bathroom window to keep water off the floor, then passed from the open area into the corridor running east. There was a light under the door of my room. The rest of the hall was lit only by a fifteen watt bulb over the entrance of room number one on my left.

I hitched up my pants and walked toward my room.

# * Chapter *

# XX

Outside the door I paused to listen but again couldn't be sure of what I heard because of the pounding rain and the wind. Abruptly I turned the knob and threw the door open.

Doris, wearing her white dress, stood between the bureau and my bed, fussing with her hair.

"You don't have a mirror," she said.

"You can find one in the shower room," I said.

"A hotel room should have a mirror."

"I'll take it up with the management."

She smiled and sat down on the bed. I looked back down the hall, stepped inside and closed the door.

"How'd you know this was my room?" I asked.

She smiled cozily. "You'd be surprised how much I know about you, Carl."

"You didn't know I wouldn't have a mirror."

She laughed, patted the bed with her left hand and told me to take a load off my feet. I parked my fanny in the straight chair beside the bureau and faced her.

"What the hell are you after?"

She crossed her legs, leaned back on her hands and arched her back. I stared at her jutting breasts and shook my head.

"Doris, you're really weird. Can't you figure that once Buck's killed everybody who just might know something dangerous, he's not going to leave you running loose to blow the whistle on him?"

She kept smiling. "You think I'm decoying you? That I've come here to let you make love to me so he can catch you too busy to fight? Is that it?"

"Just like it happened with old Fin."

"Don't be silly—he was stabbed from the front."

"Tell me about it."

Her grin broadened. "You know what's the matter with you, Carl? You haven't been getting any. You were in jail all that time and since you've been out you've only chased that gypsy up at the Larsons and she isn't going to give you anything but a palm reading. What's happened, Carl, is you've lost your nerve with girls."

She leaned forward until her head was only three feet away and the naked bulb overhead showed her skin was coarse and pale under its bright rouge and powder; her painted lips looked sticky. I stared and listened, hearing the rain patter on the flat roof but there was something else—a creak down the hall. I stood up. So did Doris.

"How about it, big boy, we gonna have a drink and some fun?"

I looked back at her and heard another creak outside, this time closer.

"You must have something," coaxed Doris. "I never heard of Carl Wilcox being a temperance man—"

"Yeah," I said, "why not?" Gently I pushed her back toward the bed and when she resisted I was less gentle. She bounced and said, "Hey!" and I apologized, saying it was too small a room and then I was rummaging in the bureau for my bottle. I found it, grasped the neck and was almost to the door before Doris realized what I was planning and bounded up.

It didn't seem like a time for high chivalry so I jerked my elbow back, figuring to plant it in her belly and flatten her out—only she came low and it caught her in the shoulder. She grunted and latched onto my left arm. Knowing the bottle might not be good for more than one swat, I couldn't waste it on her which meant that for a second I was fighting her one-handed and that wasn't effective with less than two square feet of maneuvering room. I threw my whole weight into her, she hung on, tripped onto the bed and dragged me

with her. I let go of the bottle and tried to jerk back but she'd
become an octopus and I couldn't get clear enough to swing
a punch and the bed squeaked and groaned so loud I couldn't
have heard a battering ram on the door. I came off the bed
carrying Doris with me and the second we were upright,
brought my forehead down in a sharp chop to her nose. She
screamed and collapsed.

One jump and I was against the wall just right of the door
before it crashed open. The blast from the double-barreled
shotgun numbed me for a split second but I saw the twin
muzzle extending into the room, grabbed it and pulled from
the side. Naturally the gunner held on—I shifted my grip as
I leaped forward, snatched his wrist above the trigger, threw
my ass into his middle and jerked him over my shoulder. His
pulling back, trying to keep the gun, took away the momen-
tum needed for a really good throw and he slid over instead
of flipping clean, smashed my chair, cracked his head on the
bureau and riccocheted into Doris on the floor. She
screamed.

I stepped between their tangled legs, got hold of the shotgun, jerked it free and went into the hall for a quick look.
Everything was deserted and still except for the steady patter
of rain and the moaning wind.

Buck groaned and stirred while Doris sobbed. I turned
back to them and asked Doris if she'd been shot. She shook
her head.

"Okay—get up."

She managed to get untangled, staggered up and flopped
on the bed. She kept both hands over her face and I could
see blood between her fingers.

"Put the pillow behind your neck and keep your head
back," I told her. She obeyed. "Now pull your legs over
toward the wall so Buck can sit on the edge there. Buck, get
up."

He shook his head. "You busted something, Jesus!! I
can't move my arm."

"Get up," I said, "before I bust the other arm and then
start on your thick head."

It took him a while but he managed and pretty soon there
they were, side by side on my bunk with Doris still hiding

her face and him cradling his right arm like it was a sick baby.

"Get me the doc," he moaned.

"Like hell," I said, "more like the undertaker. I want to know what's been going on, the whole damned story, and if I don't get it nice and straight, there'll be nothing left to hand Joey but a couple of stiffs. Now, why'd you kill Fin?"

He gave me a haggard look. "I didn't. It was Rick Markson killed Fin. He done it because of Sophie—so I got him. I got 'em both."

"What? Where the hell'd you get that crazy notion?"

"Wasn't crazy at all. Fin was gonna lay Sophie. He was crazy to have her—told me he'd manage because she wanted money for going to the cities and she'd do anything to get it. And Rick knew Fin was trying to get in her pants and told him he'd kill him if he did. Fin told me all about it, said Rick was worse than a jealous husband and might really try. Fin was meeting Sophie that night, that's why he was so Goddamned mad at you—having to chase out to the pond for his daughter put off his lay. Listen, I got to see the doc—"

Before I could threaten him with another dose of the shotgun butt I heard a call from downstairs. I backed into the hall, turned my head and hollered. "Yeah?"

A couple seconds later Joey came loping around the hall corner.

"Somebody heard a shot."

"Yeah—Buck tried to sew things up with a shotgun. Join my party."

At first Joey seemed more upset by the damage I'd done to the pair than he was about what they tried to do to me. He went down and phoned for Doc, came back and fussed over Doris and clucked around like an old hen.

I wanted to get them all out of my room and pretty soon he agreed because he was too prudish to let them be on the three quarter bed even with us there. We went down to the parlor (I only agreed to that because by then Doris had stopped bleeding) and Doris sat in the corner chair that Ma had reupholstered and Buck stretched out on the couch. I was trying to tell Joey what I knew when Doc arrived.

Getting him up at night for anything but delivering babies (and he was only moderately tolerant about that) always put him in a sour mood but he had sense enough to be sore at Buck and Doris, not me.

"What'd you hit her with," he demanded of me while he was examining Doris.

"My head. She had my arms pinned."

"Marvelous—must be the only woman in Corden who ever found a way to keep your hands off her."

"He tried to rape me," she said.

"Really? I suppose he carried you up to his room from your house after he made you get dressed in your Saturday night best?"

She was still fumbling with that when he said her nose wasn't broken and she'd be fine except for puffiness and lots of color for a few days. She told him he was a stupid quack and he said that was okay, she'd get a real doctor's bill and if she didn't pay she'd get some genuine legal collection action.

I'd obviously been hasty in all my work that night. Buck didn't have anything broken either but Doc said he wouldn't be using his right arm for a while and fixed him with a sling made from towels I got from the linen closet.

So finally we sat down in the city hall office with Buck in a corner chair under the light from the desk lamp and Joey and I parked in front of him. Doris was back in the cell behind the fire engine.

"Okay," said Joey, "why don't you just start at the beginning and tell us why you killed your cousin Fin?"

"I can't tell you no such thing because I didn't do it. Rick Markson did."

"You see him do it?"

"Didn't have too. Look, Fin was after Sophie—I mean he just wanted to fu—"

"Keep your Goddamned language clean," demanded Joey.

"What do you want—a sermon or what happened?"

"You can tell me decent—"

"Come on, Joey," I said, "let the man tell it his way, this isn't a church social."

Joey glared at me but settled back as Buck nodded and went on. "Like I was saying, Fin wanted to fuck Sophie. Rick knew it—Rick told Fin if he tried he'd kill him. Well, that night, after we went out and kept Wilcox from screwing Angie—"

That got both Joey and me started and it took a while to get back on track but we managed without bloodshed.

"So anyway, Fin had told me he was meeting Sophie after work and planned to take her to the fairgrounds and I knew him well enough to figure the little business with Carl didn't change his plans any and I knew Markson well enough to know he followed them and did it to Fin. Well, there wasn't any way I could prove what he done, but I knew Sophie'd been in on it since she didn't tell on him—that makes her just as guilty, don't it? I mean, even under the law?"

Joey nodded and said get on.

"Well, I knew Fin had told her he'd fix her with the Chicago guys to be in some movies—that was Fin's favorite line with dumb twitchies—and I knew she wanted out of Corden bad so I gave her a call at work and told her I'd had a talk with them fellas from Chicago and Fin had talked her up so fine they wanted her to come to the Cities for a screen test and if she'd meet me I'd give her the money for a ticket that they'd sent me. She fell for it, I knew she would, and she told her boss she was sick and cut out the back way to meet me by the Lutheran church. Only I was waiting for her in the alley there. Used a little piece of clothes line rope—it worked fine—took longer than I figured though—"

Joey made him tell exactly how but I didn't listen close because it made me mad and sick.

"Why'd you do her first?" I asked when Joey was satisfied.

"I wanted Markson to hurt. He was so Goddamned high and mighty about his tart sister—"

"And then you killed him at the sandpit?" said Joey.

"It was easy. I heard about him and Carl going out to the pits and I just went out there and waited 'til they showed and kept an eye on the whole business. And when old Rick came up to the car, I was waiting. He was all sniffly and head down, dragging his feet. I waited back of the Model A with a little piece of black pipe and when he was opening the car door I stepped around and called his name and he looked up and whop! I give him a backhand across the forehead with that little pipe and he was done by the time he hit the ground. I shoulda used a pitchfork, like he done to Fin, but I didn't have one around and anyway he might've yelled—"

"And then you propped him in the front seat, drove down the hill and tried to finish off Carl. Why him?"

"Well, I figured I could make it look like Rick'd blamed him for Sophie being dead and it'd be all sewed up nice and neat. If he hadn't been so damned lucky and slippried out of there—what would you have figured?"

"The whole damned business was so damned dumb I guess it might've worked," admitted Joey.

"When that sand came down on Wilcox," said Buck, "man, it looked like enough to bury an elephant. I never could've believed he wasn't dead."

Joey took him back over his story a couple times and it never was convincing to me but I couldn't see why except I guess I couldn't swallow the notion of him being quite so deep down vindictive about somebody killing Fin.

"Let's talk about the Fourth of July a year ago," I said.

"That's got nothing to do with anything," said Buck.

"We'll talk about it anyway," Joey told him. "Why'd Fin fix you to have a week off?"

Buck said it was none of Joey's business and he wasn't going to talk about it. "I admitted I killed Sophie and Rick —what the hell more do you want?"

"The whole story, not just parts. Was Sophie in on the Fourth of July business?"

"I don't know what business you're talking about."

"I'm talking about them stag movies you and Doris was in at the White Hotel. Look, Buck, there's no point in lying —I know what was done there—now just fess up and make things easier for all of us."

"If you know so much, how come you got to ask if Sophie was there?"

"I know you and Doris was there and that there was a young girl but I'm not sure who."

"You don't know a damned thing and I'm not talkin' any

more. I killed Rick because he killed Fin and I'd do it again and I'll hang for it and that's all anybody can do to me so go to hell."

"What about tonight? You figured on killing Carl and Doris both, didn't you?"

"You're the Goddamn Sherlock—you know it all—you tell me."

"You tried to kill Carl because he was snooping into the Fourth of July thing and you figured Doris might blab so you planned to kill her too. And I suppose you figured Eddie'd take the rap, huh?"

"It had nothing to do with the Fourth of July thing. Man, when you get a wild hair up your ass you never quit, do you? I was just gonna do Eddie a favor, that's all."

"By killing his wife?"

"I wasn't figuring to kill her—just that ass-hole, Wilcox."

"Whose shotgun were you using?" I asked.

He gave me a crooked grin. "That's Eddie's."

"It figures," I told Joey.

"How'd you know Doris was going to be visiting Carl?" asked Joey.

"I didn't know. Just happened by—saw her go in—knew she'd need help."

"And you were just carrying Eddie's shotgun by chance, huh?"

"That's right. I was hoping to maybe spot a pheasant along Main."

"Are you gonna claim you weren't in Aquatown a year ago Fourth of July?"

"I ain't gonna claim nothing."

"You admit Fin brought in a replacement for you at the butcher shop, don't you?"

"Is that a crime?"

"Not that I know of, but I think it led to one. You went to the city and you spent a week getting drunk and performing in a dirty movie, isn't that right?"

"You're full of shit. I never was in no dirty movie and you can't prove I was and by God you better stop saying—"

"Oh?" said Joey and his voice was soft. "What'll you be doing if I don't stop?"

"You'll see," said Buck as he settled back in his chair.

Joey sat still and watched him for several seconds. Buck squirmed a little but kept quiet and when Joey started questioning him again he just flat out refused to answer.

Finally Joey got disgusted, stood up and said he was going back into the cell.

"Don't let him speak to Doris," I warned.

Joey nodded. "Right, you go back and get her—bring her straight through. I'll take Buck around outside. And listen to me, boy," he told Buck, "if you open your yap, so help me, I'll drop you."

Doris looked scared when she saw me coming. I tried to look business-like as I unlocked the door and told her to come out but she wasn't reassured.

"Where's Joey?" she demanded. "I ain't going anywhere with you."

"He wants you out front. Come on."

She shook her head.

I sighed, stopped inside the cell and reached for her.

"Don't touch me!" she yelled.

"Okay, just walk on your own—if you don't, I'm gonna drag you all the way by your hair."

She got up, slipped past me and half ran toward the front. I walked behind her and heard Joey opening the side door to bring Buck back in. Doris darted to the office, popped in and started back when she found it empty.

Her eyes were bright with terror when I blocked her way and told her to sit down and we'd wait. She saw I was going to keep my distance and after a quick look around, she suddenly sat.

Joey came up, I stepped aside and we both took chairs facing Doris.

"Awright," said Joey, "we got the whole story from Buck. All I want now is to tie up the loose ends, see? If you cooperate, maybe we can keep anybody from knowing about the movies you were in and just stick to murder—okay? You didn't have anything to do with the killings, did you?"

The swelling across her nose and eyes made a mask that

kept us from catching any expression but I thought I sensed
a little relaxing in her body.

"No," she said softly, "I had nothing to do with any killings."

"Fine. We might even forget about tonight's little bait and
bushwhacking party, since it turned out you the bait, was
gonna be one of them bushwacked—you have got that figured out, haven't you?"

She nodded. Her eyes were wet and a tear slopped over
and dribbled down her swollen cheek when she blinked. I
didn't figure she was sentimental about Buck—terror made
her grieve.

"Buck admits he killed the Marksons. He says it was
because Rick killed Fin. Did you know that?"

"No, I don't know anything about any killings,"

"Awright, let's go over what happened tonight."

She swallowed, blinked a couple more tears loose, took a
breath and started talking real low.

"Buck called this afternoon while Eddie was showing the
matinee. He said Carl was on to the—to what happened in
Aquatown last year—he's been there and talked to the hotel
people. He said he had to be stopped. And then he said I
should get Carl to come to the house and invite him upstairs
and, you know, get him to think I was ready to go to bed
with him and then he—Buck—would come with Eddie and
they'd say if Carl didn't quit poking around about the Fourth
of July thing, they'd say he tried to rape me and he'd go
back to prison. I said that was no good, he was leery of me
and wouldn't come. We talked a lot and he kept saying Carl
had to be stopped else everybody'd know what happened
and I'd be stoned like harlots in the Bible if I didn't help
shut him up and I was so scared I agreed and he worked it
out for me to go to the hotel. He said Eddie would follow
me—"

"How'd Eddie get into this?"

"He—Buck—knew Eddie's seen the movie and wouldn't
want anybody to know either."

"What'd he say he was gonna do when he and Eddie
caught Carl with you?"

"He said he'd fix him, that's all. I thought they'd beat him up—I didn't know there'd be a gun."

"So where was Eddie?"

She shook her head.

"Why didn't he come along with Buck?"

"I don't know—he told me he would. I had to ask and explain. I knew he'd seen the movie but he'd never mentioned it and neither did I. He pretended it never happened. It was dumb but I didn't care. He couldn't do anything. I told him if he helped on this I'd never mess around again but I don't suppose he believed me so I guess that's why he didn't come with Buck."

"What'd Fin pay you to be in that movie?"

"Fin didn't pay nothing. Fat Fritz paid—the fellow from Chicago. He paid everybody except Buck. He just done it for fun and booze and of course he got that substitute fellow at the shop for a week."

"Was this Fritz fellow in the movie?"

"No. He just helped Fin run it. He had lots of ideas."

"What'd he pay you?"

"What difference does that make?"

"I'd like to know what a woman'll sell her soul for."

"I don't think I hafta tell you that."

"You admit you got paid?"

"You'd rather I just did it for fun?"

"I'd rather you'd just behave yourself."

"That was never any fun and I was never any good at it."

Joey stewed in righteousness for a few seconds.

"Doris," I said, "did you know Fin was chasing Sophie?"

"That's what Buck told me. He said that the night after you guys found Fin in the barn. He said Rick killed Fin because he was trying to get in one of them movies."

"How'd he know about the movies?"

"Hell, how does everybody in Corden always know about everything?"

"How long had you been involved with Fin before he got you to Aquatown last year?"

"What's that got to do with anything?"

"You admit you were carrying on with him?" demanded Joey.

Doris looked at the ceiling and shook her head. "Look, I'm willing to tell what I can about Buck and tonight and okay, I was in the movie but I ain't gonna give you no history of my life so how about you just knock off all what I did with Fin and Buck and get down to what the hell you're after."

Joey stood up, walked a couple steps away and came back to lean down til his nose was only a foot from Doris' face.

"Now you listen to me—I'm gonna tell you one last time —you are in trouble. One—" he held up his forefinger, "tonight you were an accessory to attempted murder. That's a crime. Two—a year ago you were in an obscene movie. That's a crime and a shame. Three—you have had sexual intercourse with a man who wasn't your husband and that's a crime. And four—now we are trying to find out what the hell caused three people to get murdered and I figure you know enough to straighten it all out and by God you will tell me *all* you know without any damned coy stuff or every bit of what you been up to is gonna be known all over this state and you'll spend enough time in jail to forget what it's like to do something for fun. Have you got that?"

She folded a little with each number and was dribbling from both eyes by the time he stopped. Joey backed off and sat down, a little shocked at his toughness with a woman.

"Now," he said at last, "when'd you and Fin start messing around?"

"Couple years ago," she said and sniffed. Joey scowled at her and she went on. "Eddie got sick and Fin was running the shows alone. I went to a late show on Saturday night and he came down soon's it was over and caught up with me in the lobby and asked was I interested in seeing the projection room and I never had so I said sure and he showed me how he rewound the film and how they packed it in them funny shipping crates or whatever and one thing just sort of led to another—"

"Where'd you go?"

"We didn't go anywhere. We done it in the projection room."

"On the floor?" I asked.

"Naw—on the chair."

Joey was shocked again. "How can you—?"

She managed a half grin. "There's lotsa ways."

Joey was so shook he just goggled and I asked if she'd go on and tell how the movie thing got set up.

"Well, while we were still there in the projection room he asked me had I ever seen a blue movie and I of course said no and he said he bet I'd get a kick out of them and I said they sounded awful but I was curious about what in the world they did and so he explained about a couple and they didn't sound too bad. So later on we got together a few times and had a couple drinks and I asked about the movies and he finally showed me one. It wasn't so dirty—I mean—the people looked pretty good and like they had a lot of fun and they were funny. I figured they'd be disgusting but they weren't—well—except for some things—"

"So you agreed to be in one?"

"Not just like that. It just sort of came up that some fellows were going to be making a movie and Fin said maybe I'd like to watch and see how it went and at first I said no but he kept talking it up and it finally seemed such a lark I decided, what the hell. The fellas were real nice to me—the tall one said I was a dead ringer for Mae West—I think he liked it I wasn't skinny as the others girls they had. And then we had a lot of drinks and I asked Fin what the girls got paid and he said $100 and the tall fellow said if I was interested he'd pay me $150 but I had to promise not to tell the others I was getting more."

Joey whispered, "A hundred and fifty dollars!" and shook his head.

"I said he was kidding and he took out a wallet and counted it out in twenties. He said to make it easy he'd give me $160. I said did I have to do it with Buck and he said not if I didn't want to and I could do it with him and I thought he was so nice and he wanted it so bad that it just didn't seem proper to turn him down. He was older than any fellow I'd ever been with, and more of a gentleman."

"So you didn't actually mix with Buck?"

"No. Actually I wasn't going to do it even with the nice fellow but he kept talking so beautiful and Fin kept handing

me another drink and everything got pretty fuzzy. I figure
they put something in my drink to make me—you know—
more sort of loving. It was like I was hypnotized—"

I guessed the most hypnotizing thing was the folding
green stuff.

"I hear Fin had a little row with the hotel owner," I said.

"Oh yeah—old man White got all excited when Fin
asked his grand-niece to stick around. That was when we
were all just having a party in the afternoon. They didn't
have the cameras going yet. She was just a kid, kind of
funny looking—all teeth and big eyes—you know the kind.
Anyway, Fin was real taken with her, offered her a drink—
she couldn't been more than sixteen or so. White got her out
and then yelled at Fin."

"Did Buck threaten the old man?"

"Threaten? No—I don't think so. Well, he came over
when White first told the girl to go downstairs. Buck didn't
say anything but I guess he meant to scare him because he
kept scowling real mean the way he does. He can really
scare a person that way. But old man White, after the girl
had gone, he was shaking he was so mad and he said if Fin
so much as looked at the girl again he'd regret it. Fin just
laughed and told him to have a drink and relax, he sure
didn't plan to use virgins. Then Fat Fritz talked to White and
they went out together and the old man didn't come back."

We learned that Fat Fritz ran nearly everything but let Fin
give directions for the movie when it started. Fritz was from
Chicago, the tall "gentleman" came from Minneapolis and
the camera men were floaters—Doris thought one had
worked a while in Hollywood, "At least Fritz said he did."

The "gentleman" told her his name was Paul but she
heard him called something else by Fritz and guessed he lied
to her. He'd been a very active fellow for a man of advanced
years (Doris guessed he was about forty-five) and she was a
little disappointed that he performed with two of the other
girls after he'd been with her. I think she figured she should
have been more than enough for any one man in one night.

I asked about Buck's performance and she said he was a
washout—all noise and show. After his first big number he

couldn't get started again and they made such fun of him he drank himself sodden and went to sleep.

"They used him like a hunk of furniture," said Doris almost laughing. "He got mad when he saw the movie— thought he was gonna slug Fin."

"Where's that movie now?" I asked.

She shrugged. "I suppose Fat Fritz has it—he paid for it. Look, guys, I'm shot—I gotta sleep."

"You're just lucky you weren't shot, you'd get to sleep permanent," said Joey.

She didn't want to think about that and pretty soon she wouldn't talk any more and we'd heard more than enough anyway so we put her in my room at the hotel, locked her in and called it a night. I bunked out on the parlor sofa.

Sunday was the last day of July and while the sun had peaked six weeks before you'd never have guessed it from the way it was ladling out hot that afternoon as I hiked the hill up to Larson's house.

Joey had moved Doris from the hotel into the city hall jail and was taking Buck to Aquatown where they'd agreed to make him their guest so I had the assignment of telling Iris what had happened. A smarter and tougher guy would have figured there was nothing to do but lay it all out since town gossip would eventually tell her more than ever happened anyway. But I'm a simple type, about as tough as a melted marshmallow so I spent all the walk trying to dream up a way to make what I had to say a little easier on Iris.

When she met me at the screen door I still didn't know what I was going to say.

She'd applied a complete paint job—rouge, powder, lipstick—her cologne smelled light and cool and her graying hair was beauty parlor neat. Under it all she gave me a portrait smile.

"Doctor tells me it's all over," she said, "the mystery is solved and yours is the credit. It almost seems that you have a charmed life."

Somehow charms and my life seemed remote as the poles but I smiled and nodded and took the offered chair and agreed to a cup of coffee.

"I never could believe that Buck killed Fin," she said. "I

knew you thought so and I can understand why you thought it made sense, but he was *so* devoted—I knew he couldn't have been the one."

I built a cigaret and asked where Cora was.

Iris beamed at me. "She's upstairs packing. Now that everything's settled here, she's decided to go back to Minneapolis. I just hate to see her go—she's been such a dear—but there's really no reason for her to stay any longer."

I guessed not. I couldn't even admit to myself that I'd hoped she'd think I was worth sticking around for.

"When's she leaving?" I asked.

"Tomorrow morning. A little after 7:30. She'll be down soon—said not to let you get away without her seeing you."

That was something—I wasn't sure what.

"I suppose you'll be drifting off again soon," she said. "There isn't much left for you to do in Corden just now, is there?"

I leaned back and squinted at her through my cigaret smoke.

"It sounds like you're wrapping up this little business complete and shipping it off first class," I said.

She laughed lightly. "Well, it's all over, isn't it?"

"I don't know. Where's Angie?"

"Angie? Why—I'm not sure—probably with her friends —why do you ask?"

"I just wonder how much she knows about what's happened."

The laughter went out of Iris. "She doesn't know anything about what's happened—how could she?"

"She's got ears and friends. Last night's no secret in town—not much is. She must've been told."

"Well, she knows Buck confessed to killing that young couple and that they killed her father."

"They?"

"Well, the girl was involved, wasn't she?"

"I guess you could say so, in a way. If Buck's right, she probably was a witness to the killing at least."

Iris's head tilted a little forward as she narrowed her eyes.

"What do you mean 'If Buck's right?' Are you questioning what he says?"

"Uh-huh."

"Well, for goodness sake—why else would he kill that couple?"

"He was willing to kill me at least without any more reason than not liking me."

"Well, in a way I suppose he felt last night was in self-defense. When was the other time?"

"At the swimming hole the night Fin got it."

"Oh yes—he threw some stones at you—well, he thought he was serving Fin—he believed you had ravished Angie. Actually that just illustrates how obvious it is that he was devoted to Fin."

"Uh-huh. But it doesn't mean he was any more right about the Marksons than he was about the ravaging."

"Well, the circumstances were much different—that night was all impulsive, they were acting under the influence of liquor. The thing with the Marksons was—you know—more deliberate."

"Yeah, which all goes to show that quick or slow, Buck is murderous and stupid. It doesn't prove he knew what he was doing and it about convinces me he didn't."

"Well, in any case, the issue seems settled so there's no point in poking around any more."

I gave her a polite frown. "You mean you don't care if maybe Fin's killer is still loose and happy?"

"I don't think he is and I don't see any sense in pursuing the sordid matter any further. Would you go up and visit Cora? I'm sure she'd be pleased."

I suppose my eyebrows climbed an inch but I took up the offer.

"Which room?"

"First on the left at the head of the stairs."

Cora was sitting on the bed beside her suitcase, reading a letter when I stepped in her doorway. She looked up at once, startled, and blushed. I couldn't tell whether she was embarrassed at her start of surprise, or at being caught reading a letter. It struck me that I was totally unaware of any people she knew outside of Corden and that I didn't want her to know people who were strangers to me.

"Iris sent me up—she tells me you're leaving."

She stood, folded the letter and tucked it into a pocket on the side of the suitcase.

"Yes, in the morning."

"How come?"

"Well, there's really no reason for me to stay now. Iris is able to take care of herself."

"Maybe you've got something going on Minneapolis?"

She glanced toward the suitcase and smiled. "No, the letter was from a girl I know—it was nothing." She took a couple of steps toward me and spoke in a lower voice. "Aunt Iris is going to California. She's taking Angie with her—to get away from all that's happened."

"Is she paying your way back?"

She blushed. "Yes. Why do you ask?"

"I wanted to be sure you were okay. When's Iris leaving?"

"She didn't say—except that it'd be soon."

"I guess maybe she suggested you leave, huh?"

She laughed shortly. "You've fallen into the habit of detecting, haven't you? Yes—it was fairly subtle—but clear. Not 'Here's your hat, what's your hurry?' but more, 'here's a ticket, don't waste it.'"

I realized suddenly that she was very upset—close to tears.

"You might be interested to know," I said, "that she suggested maybe I was about to start traveling again. Didn't offer me ticket money but she reminded me there wasn't anything to do in Corden for a fellow of my talents and background. I'm beginning to think she wants the whole town vacated."

"More likely she'd like it to be obliterated—with all its history."

"Well, considering Fin's life that's not too surprising."

Since she was through packing everything she wouldn't be using before departure, I suggested we take a walk and she agreed. Downstairs Iris beamed at us while Cora explained that she wouldn't be gone long and then we were outside.

I told her we'd ought to have a little party that night but

she said she didn't think so—there wouldn't be anyone to invite.

"I haven't made any friends, somehow. I thought Iris and I had become close but the death changed that. To tell you the truth, I can't wait to get out of Corden."

We walked a little ways in silence before I asked, "Did Fin tell her he was bringing you to take care of the house before he actually did it?"

"I'm not really sure. She seemed so much the invalid when I arrived that I didn't get any impression of her being surprised or otherwise. And very soon I learned she didn't want to discuss anything about Fin. Angie didn't seem to expect me but she was so withdrawn all the time that it was impossible to know what she knew or didn't know."

"All right," I said, "just the two of us will have a party. I'll treat you to a sundae after dinner and then we'll go swimming—how's that?"

She looked at me suspiciously and I grinned at her.

She didn't grin back. "Look, what almost happened that night a while back—it's not going to happen. I'd like to think I found one friend here and I'd like to think you weren't just after something—that you *liked* me. Is that too much to ask?"

"No," I lied, "it's okay. We're pals."

"Don't get sarcastic, Carl, please."

"I'm not sarcastic—I just think being lovers is closer than being friends and I guess I'd risk the pal business for the other but I think enough of you to leave it the way you want. Okay?"

"I think so." She took my arm and walked along close to my side.

I wished it were dark and a lot of other things but it stayed light and we had nothing to talk about that was going to change things. I said she should let me know where she'd be staying and maybe I'd come around pretty soon and she said fine, she'd like that and would write to me when she got settled. For a while she'd be staying with the girl friend whose letter she'd been reading. She didn't offer her address.

When we separated a little before supper time I had a

feeling she was relieved that she had got over an awkward situation with a minimum of damage.

"Maybe you'd rather I didn't come around tonight," I said.

"It isn't that—" she looked pained.

"Of course not. Okay, take care of yourself."

I kissed her a little more firmly than you'd call polite but she wasn't so carried away she begged me to come back and I walked down to the street thinking that was the last God-damned kid I was going to try messing with but the resolve wasn't convincing, let alone encouraging.

I don't know whether it was the frustration caused by Cora or all the talk the past few days about dirty movies but after supper I found myself needing action in the worst way and decided, what the hell, I'd go visit Lil.

Normally she wasn't open for business on Sundays—not so much because she had puritan views one day a week but because business was usually lousy that day anyway and she figured she deserved a rest if it didn't cost anything. However, all the news I had to offer, plus the jug I brought along, softened what little resistance she had and before dark we were on her bed.

We'd been stretched out bare after the workout, not touching because it was hotter than a baker's brow in July and nothing came through the window but cricket fiddling and a mourning dove's call. I was wondering why you almost never hear but one dove at a time when Lil propped herself up on her elbow and frowned at me.

"You really believe Buck was right about the Marksons?"

"I'm not convinced," I admitted, "but I don't know how to prove otherwise."

"It wouldn't be too hard," she said, "except nobody'd take my word in court."

"What's that mean?"

"Well, the night Rick Markson was supposed to be sticking a fork in Fin, Rick was up here sticking something else in me."

I sat up and stared at her. "What time?"

"When he had it in? Hell, I don't have a time clock on it

but he got here around midnight and didn't leave til it was getting light out—I'd say 4:30 or so."

"How come he wasn't watch-dogging Sophie?"

"Because she was having her period and he didn't figure he had to worry."

"He told you that?"

"Sure. Everybody tells me everything."

"Jesus Christ." I got up, rolled a cigaret and sat on the edge of the bed, working it all over in my mind. "So it was Buck after all. But why'd he kill Sophie and Rick?"

"Who knows—maybe he had a headache."

I started pulling on clothes. "It was something about the dirty movies. Fin had propositioned Sophie and she knew about them. Fin was scared she'd blab. That's gotta be it."

"You're telling me Fin made dirty movies himself? How come he didn't ask me to be in on it?"

"He probably figured you'd charge professional rates."

It was near ten when I strolled past Clayt's home. All the lights were out and I figured he must be over trying to enjoy final good-byes with Angie, so I headed for the Larson's place. There were lights on upstairs in two bedrooms—Iris and Cora's—the rest of the house was dark. I walked by the front, stopped at the corner and came back.

I almost missed him—he was next to a box elder on the south edge of the lot and he'd been keeping the tree between us until I saw his elbow when he moved. I kept walking south, circled around and came down from the alley. He'd assumed I was gone and was standing beside the tree, staring up at the dark window of Angie's room. I stopped by the neighbor's garage and waited with him.

Iris's light went out just a few minutes later. Soon Cora's followed suit.

I figured the wait would be fairly short and shoved down my craving for a smoke. Ten minutes passed, then fifteen. I shoved away from the garage and walked toward him. He didn't even turn his head when I came within three feet.

"She's not coming," I said.

"I know."

I got out my makings, built a cigaret and offered it to him but he shook his head. I lit up and hunkered down.

"Who broke it up—Angie or her ma?"

"What difference does it make?"

"Oh, it could make all the difference. If it was Angie it means you two had a falling out over what happened to Fin. If it's Iris, it means she knows what happened and is being righteous, in a nice quiet way."

He took his eyes from Angie's window for a moment and turned his face toward me. It was too dark to see any expression—if he had any.

"So you got it figured out," he said.

"No—I'm afraid I got it handed to me, one way and another. So Fin followed Angie out to her meeting with you, didn't he? Caught you two in the barn and went wild—tried to kill you—?"

He moved away from the tree and I tensed up but he only began walking toward the alley. He walked slowly and I stayed with him.

"When you let me out of the car that night after the swimming hole thing I didn't go in the house. I walked back to the Larsons and waited under that same tree. And in a little while, Angie came out the back door. She was still mad at her old man—said he'd made a fool of her in front of everybody. She'd been mad at him lots of times before, but never like that time. She scared me. When I tried to say he was only worried about her she flared up at me. I got kind of tired of the talk about him by the time we got to the fairgrounds—I just wanted to talk about her and me—but mostly I wanted to kiss her. I must be crazy that way. I can never think of anything when I'm with her but kissing and stuff—not for more than a minute anyway."

We walked a little ways without saying anything until finally I said there wasn't anything unnatural about a young fellow thinking of loving all the time.

"Huh!" he said in a nasty tone, "I wouldn't expect you'd think so."

"I'm no different than most—just more honest."

He wanted to make a debate of that but I managed to steer him back to the night he'd started with and asked if he'd any notion that Fin was following them.

He shook his head. "I suppose it was dumb, but I was

listening to Angie and watching her and I never looked back. She slowed down some when we got to the grounds and I had to coax her a lot to get her into the barn. Before we always went to the grandstand and climbed way to the top corner. From up there you can see anybody coming from far away—you know? And Joey never flashed his lights up there—he never bothers anybody not in a car."

"So you went into the barn. Then what? Was it already open?"

"Oh sure. I'd opened it early in the spring. I'd been thinking it was a perfect place and one night before I thought I might get her to go with me, I snuck a crowbar out of our basement and just took the braces off. At night it was a little musty—but nice."

"Then what?"

"Well, we went inside but Angie wouldn't let me close the door. If she'd let me, Fin couldn't have surprised us so bad—he'd have had to make a lot of noise opening the door. But Angie said that'd make it too dark and she made me open it wide so there was moonlight coming in. It came in from the east, real bright. We stood a ways back inside, almost inside one of the cattle stalls. I wanted her to sit down but she wouldn't—she let me kiss her and then she looked all around. I was trying to kiss her again when she saw the shadow on the dirt floor and she screamed. God that scared me! My legs turned water. I let go of Angie and swung around and there he was—carrying a baseball bat. He yelled something at me and I just panicked—I *knew* he'd kill me. I ran back into the dark—there was a ladder to the loft—well you know that. Anyway I figured I could climb up and maybe get away, but then I heard Angie scream and I turned around and saw he was fighting with her so I ran back and I looked for something to hit him with and there was the pitchfork, just leaning against the stall divider—"

We'd been walking west, uphill, and then north a little beyond the last sidewalk at that end of town. He looked around vaguely, then started walking again. Soon we were beyond the last houses in Corden.

"It was an awfully old pitchfork—the handle was broken off short. I couldn't use it for a club so I held it with the tines pointed at him and I yelled, 'leave her alone!' I wasn't weak anymore. He'd dropped the bat when he was trying to get clear of Angie and I guess he saw me but I don't think he knew I had the fork. Anyway he threw Angie away—just threw her! And then he yelled and rushed at me. He'd probably have killed himself if I'd just held the fork steady but Carl, I'll tell you the truth—I was scared and mad and I jammed it into him with all I had—"

We had come to the deep sandpit and Clayt stopped a ways from the edge and stared down into the darkness.

"He fell after making an awful sound . . . I tried to hang on to the pitchfork but it wouldn't come out and I stumbled over his legs and fell on him as he went down. Right away I got up and tried to pull it out again. I don't know why it seemed so important—but it did. I'd jerk and his head would bob like he was nodding at me and finally I stepped on his face and gave an awful pull and the fork came loose so quick I had this notion he'd been hanging on and suddenly let go. I was still standing there with the fork in my hands when Angie grabbed my arm and asked was he dead and I said yes but I didn't really know—I thought he must be but I didn't dare touch him to make sure."

"What'd Angie say then?"

"She said, 'Good!' "

He kept staring into the darkness below. I waited, letting him remember it. He sighed and sat down. I hunkered down close by his side.

"She said 'Good!' and I thought oh God, I've done it now. I'll hang or go to the chair or whatever—but at the same time I was glad Fin wasn't coming after me with the bat. But what's worse, you know what I was thinking about as much as anything? I was thinking that now I wouldn't get to neck with Angie in the hay there. Does that seem possible?"

"Sure. So what happened next?"

"She started talking to me—she said we've got to bury him. I said I didn't have a shovel and she said wouldn't the pitchfork work and I said no and she said well, hide him under the straw and then she said we'll close up the barn and throw the fork where nobody's gonna find it and I'll go home and you go home and nobody'll ever guess it was us. Right from the start she said it like that. Us. We did it. So while I covered Fin with straw she took the pitchfork out and threw it away and then came back and got me to brace the doors and told me how I could get out by climbing to the vent window and that's all there was to it."

I asked was he willing to go down and tell Joey all about it and he said no. I said he could get off on self-defense and he said he didn't see why he should go through all that and drag Angie along and it made sense from his view and even in mine.

"What happened to Fin's bat?" I asked.

"Angie took it home with her."

# * Chapter *
# XXII

Cora's train was to leave at 7:20 a.m. so I got up early and went down to see her off. It was another bright, still morning, promising an oven day. Iris drove up in the big black Buick and fussed over Cora on the platform, pretended surprise at seeing me and after some more fluttering, kissed Cora's cheek and left us. Except for a peddler sitting on a chair beside the depot door and the ticket man inside, we had the place to ourselves. I took Cora's elbow and walked her slowly over the red bricks to the east end of the platform.

"Well," she said, "will you come to see me?"

"If you let me know where you are, yeah."

She rummaged in her purse, took out a little notebook and pen, had me hold her purse and wrote out the address in neat round letters. Then she carefully tore the page out and handed it to me.

"That's my girl friend's place. I probably won't be there long, but she'll know where I move when I do. It would probably be better if you didn't visit me there—we'd have no place to talk or anything. Her mother's very narrow—I mean just the most absolutely prim and proper person with a nasty suspicious mind."

I could imagine what a woman like that would think about a guy like me visiting.

"Do you ever write letters?" asked Cora. "Will you write to me?"

"I might. Would you answer?"

"Oh yes, I love writing letters and I adore getting them. You know—I'm going to miss you, Carl. You've been a special experience for me."

"I'd have been a hell of a lot bigger one if you'd allowed."

She laughed, completely unembarrassed. "In a way, I wish it had been like that, but I think it was better not. I'm really not that kind of girl and you're just not a one-woman man. You can think of me as the one that got away and then maybe I'll be remembered as something much more special than I am."

"I thought you wanted me to come and visit?"

"I hope you will, but it won't come to anything but friends meeting for a talk—you kow that, don't you? And that's why you won't really come."

The train whistled from the east and I hated the damned thing.

She glanced down the tracks, looked back toward the peddler near the depot door and stepped closer to me.

"Kiss me goodbye before it gets here. Just once—okay? Maybe it won't be like I think right now—maybe when it's been a while I'll see things differently. But I want to be honest and I don't believe I really mean anything to you and we're not really much alike and I just couldn't have an affair—you'd have to be all mine, you know—"

I shut her up by kissing her and we stayed at it until the engine rumbled and huffed up past us. She never opened her mouth but she pushed hard and hugged tight and that was enough to get me steamed up worse than the train's boiler.

When she was aboard and the train began moving out I headed toward the fairgrounds. At the corner of the depot Joey joined me. I was a little too preoccupied to pay any attention to how he looked or to wonder what the hell he was doing there and he had to tell me his message twice before I caught it.

"Buck's escaped," he said.

I shook Cora out of my mind and stopped still to stare at him.

"How?"

"He belted a guard and left. I guess his arm wasn't in as bad shape as he tried to make us think."

"When'd he do it?"

"I got the call last night and went over to keep an eye on his place—thought maybe he'd show up there but he didn't. Now I got to get some sleep so I was wondering if maybe you'd take over."

"What's wrong with your deputy, Jepson?"

"He's feelin' poorly. I think it come on when he heard Buck was loose. Anyway I already talked to the judge and he says it's okay if you take a day off as long as the village pays you and it will so how about it?"

I agreed and walked back to the hotel where I found Hank in the lobby and told him he was in charge of the fairgrounds project. He wanted to know if that meant he got a raise. I told him he'd get a raise from the toe of my boot if he didn't get a move on so he went and I walked back to Buck's.

Buck lived in an apartment over Barney Swanson's funeral parlor. It was a brown brick building in the middle of the block off Main with an empty lot on the south and an alley on the north. A closed-in stairway led to the second floor from the alley side.

Joey had kept watch from the empty rooms across the street over Clint's Variety Store. I decided I'd wait inside the apartment. Before I went over there, Joey had given me a pistol which didn't look much bigger than a French 75 and when I stuck it in my belt it damned near dragged my pants down.

"Hell," I told Joey, "I can barely lift this thing, how in the hell am I gonna point it?"

"You better practice," he said, "because Buck took a gun off the guard he muscled."

I could see why the deputy had suddenly turned sick.

Carrying the gun made me feel like a damned fool and I decided if I managed to get inside the apartment and could surprise him, there'd be no shooting.

I approached Buck's from the alley, worked close to the stairway door and copped a quick peek up before starting the climb. Halfway up I unlimbered my cannon, just in case Buck had crept in without old Jed Perkins seeing him (Jed had told Joey he'd keep a good watch but I knew if he got a customer he wouldn't notice a cattle stampede through his front door).

There was an empty glass on the sideboard but otherwise everything was put away neat as a barracks before Saturday inspection. I went through the open entry into the living room which was also the dining room and the bedroom. It ran about twenty by eighteen feet with the longer part running east and west. The only furniture was a sagging day bed against the north wall, a morris chair in the northwest corner and a small table with two straight-backed chairs. A curtained-off square in the northwest corner served as a closet where his clothes hung on an iron pipe or were stacked in a wooden bureau. I gave the bathroom a quick look and noticed that even a guy as neat as Buck couldn't keep the rust stains from spreading all around the drain and faucets. I took a leak to keep my ballast light and then went back and plunked down in the morris chair and prepared for a long wait.

The place seemed big because there was no little furniture and I realized that even though Buck had been working steady all his life and hadn't a chick or child, he was no better off than me, materially. What the hell did he do with his money and time? The meat market wasn't all too profitable, I guessed, and he probably spent everything on eating out and boozing with Fin. I also guessed he wasn't much of a winner at snooker and he played about every night so the losses could mount up. Chuck Nelson bragged once that Buck was his pension and it figured.

I stared out the front window at the dusty street and considered the view of Perkins' drug store, straight across, the dime store to its right with its red front and big windows and next to that Pete's Shoe Store. A tow-headed kid plodded along the sidewalk, carrying two quarts of milk from the creamery, cradled one in each arm, like twin babies, and carefully avoided stepping on cracks to preserve his mother.

It was warm when I arrived in the apartment at 8:00 a.m. By 11:00 a.m. it was a wall-papered oven. I opened the windows enough to let in some air but couldn't do it enough to really help without being obvious from the outside. I drank enough water to float the Titanic, peeled off my shirt, parked the cannon beside the morris and prowled around the apartment, first hoping to find some hootch and then just to be doing something. I went through all the clothes hung in the curtained closet and found one dirty picture in each pocket big enough to hold a three by four card. Each one showed a naked woman, always alone, usually with long, loose hair and a coy expression. Most of them were too heavy for my taste.

I thought about old Buck, working at the butcher shop, talking to Lutheran and Congregational ladies while he had one of those pictures in his pocket, and wondered if he went to the backroom and stared at the nudes between packaging pork chops and ground round—or if he just wanted them there because it seemed a little risky.

In the bottom drawer of his bureau I discovered a shoe box filled with more pictures—some with couples in action, several more coy singles but all of them pretty ugly.

I put them all back where Buck had left them and went for another gallon of water. At noon I decided the hell with it, put on my shirt, stuck the gun in my belt and went downstairs where I persuaded Barney Swanson to call City Hall if he heard action overhead.

Across the street I asked Jud to tip us off if he spotted the fugitive and he was more than willing.

At City Hall I found the deputy miraculously recovered from his recent bout of feeling poorly and he told me that Joey was still asleep at home but would show fairly soon. I said fine, left him my cannon and went back to the hotel.

After lunch Joey was sure enough back on duty but he was sleepy and sour. He made a few bitter remarks about some people's patience and I made nasties about some folks sleeping in comfort while others sweat their balls off for free. Eventually we agreed that Buck wouldn't show until after dark—if ever—and I went back out to the fairgrounds.

The judge had broken down when he saw the place beginning to look almost decent and decided to paint the stadium so he'd brought out paint and brushes and the guys were slopping things around like Tom Sawyer's gang at the fence. They'd already worked themselves out of shade and the sun was hot enough to make the devil sweat. I took a brush and pitched in.

I'd only been helping about half an hour when Chip suddenly hollered, "Hey—look!"

He was pointing southwest and at first I couldn't figure what he meant for us to see—I guess I half expected it'd be Buck coming across the field—and then I realized there was no horizon. It wasn't clouds or anything I remembered seeing before. Just a big mass, almost like an artist took a turpentine-soaked rag and wiped out the corner of a landscape on his canvas. It came slow at first, erasing sky and earth.

"Dust storm," I said, "let's get the hell out of here."

We grabbed our paint and brushes and raced to the barn, put the brushes in turpentine, slapped the lids on tight and high-tailed for town.

It didn't make a sound until it reached us and then we heard the wind howling and moaning and the dust came on, making dry lips crusty and nostrils hot. I wrapped my bandanna around my face, bandit-style—the boys held their hands over their noses and mouths.

Hank and I were into the hotel before the worst hit and within minutes it was so dark Elihu turned on the lights. We closed every window and Ma began moistening rags and lining the doors and window sills—starting with the parlor and working out. The building creaked in the wind and dust, so fine you couldn't see it until it piled up, came sifting through every crack in the place—and we had millions of them.

Elihu swore, Ma prayed and once I'd helped block all the obvious cracks I sat down, rolled a smoke and sat by the window, gawking out while sipping a glass of iced tea. Most of the time I could just see across the street.

It kept on through supper. All the food tasted of dust— even what we drank seemed dry. I called Joey around nine and the deputy said he'd gone over to wait at Buck's place. That struck me as devotion to duty beyond good sense but I was glad it was him and not me. It seemed plain that by now Buck would guess his place was staked out and not go near it. The trouble was, Joey couldn't think of anything else to do so it was natural for him to give it a try.

A little after nine-thirty I decided the hell with everything—I'd go up and see what it was like to get a full night's
sleep. The hall creaked underfoot loud enough to hear over
the howling wind as I ambled to my room thinking cheerful
thoughts of waking under ten feet of dust.

The fifteen watt bulb in the hall across from my room
threw just enough light inside when I opened my door to let
me see the overhead light string and as I reached up I all of a
sudden knew I wasn't alone.

"Turn it on," growled Buck, "and keep your hands up high."

I started to turn and he jabbed me with the gun barrel hard
enough to make me grunt. The light blinded me and I stood
there squinting while he checked me for artillery.

"Get down on the bed," he told me, "and keep your
hands behind your head."

I did it. He pulled the straight chair from beside the bureau and leaned toward me, holding the gun with both
hands. It had a short barrel and a very big muzzle. He held it
steady.

"You surprised me last time," he said, "but you won't
again. Nobody's faster than a slug, so you listen good and
answer quick—see?"

"Right," I said, quick.

"Where's the movie?"

"I don't know."

He leaned closer and the muzzle of the gun looked wide
as a train tunnel.

"It wasn't in the trunk. I looked the night after Fin got
killed and it was gone. The Marksons didn't get it—that just
leaves you."

"You killed the Marksons on account of the movie, huh?"

"That's none of your Goddamned business—just tell me
what you did with it, see?"

"Buck, I never knew a damned thing about any movie
until after Fin was dead. I didn't know about it 'til I went to
Aquatown and talked with people at the hotel. How the
hell'd I know before then?"

He thought about that for a moment while the wind
moaned outside and my drawn window shade stirred and
billowed.

"It was probably the guys from the city," I said. "More likely they killed Fin and took it."

He gave me a disgusted look as he drew back a little.

"You think they'd kill Fin with an old pitchfork? Don't be a damned fool. Anyway, Fritz called and asked for the film —said their copy'd been taken by cops in a raid."

"Who's Fritz?"

"The guy that paid for the girls—bankrolled the whole thing. He wants that movie and he's gonna get it."

"Haven't they got the negative?"

"Fin had it. That and the print—they were both in the trunk of his car. I know because he told me so the night we went out after you."

"That's a damned fool place to keep it—if he left the car in the sun the film'd be ruined."

"He was gonna take it to Minneapolis the next day."

"Why didn't Fritz have everything—he paid for it—"

"All he needed was the one print until the cops hit where he was showing it. He figured the rest was safe with Fin."

"What makes the movie so special—your whanger?"

"That's part," he said modestly, "but the other's the fact that Doris looks enough like Mae West to let 'em pretend it's her. Guys were breaking their ass to see Mae in action."

"So your schlong only got second billing, huh?"

"Guys aren't that hot on dongs. Listen, I got to find that film—and you're gonna help me."

"Why should I?"

"'Cause if you don't, I'm gonna blow your brains out."

"When do we start?"

"We'll go up to Fin's house—maybe Iris knows."

"How the hell would she know?"

"That woman knows all there is to know—don't you forget it. Come on."

The gun was persuasive as hell—more than hell—since I was looking directly into it. I got up. Buck went to the door, waved me back toward the window, looked out down the hall and then waved me forward.

"You're gonna get a lot of attention downstairs," I told him.

"We'll go down the back steps, then out through the kitchen. Bertha's in bed by now, ain't she?"

"By God, you really been studying the place."

"Damn right—I been watching you ever since Fin died."

"Why'd you kill the Marksons—really?"

"I figured he killed Fin and stole the film. He was a pig-headed son-of-a-bitch, you know? The only thing I'm sure of now, is that Sophie didn't know where the film was. I worked on her long enough to be sure—she'd have told me anything."

"So why kill Rick?"

"Because that pig-headed son-of-a-bitch was set on finding Sophie and pinning the murder on me. And anyway, when he came back to the car at the sandpit and I asked him, real polite, where the film was, he came at me like a maniac. I caught him with the pipe I was carrying just as neat—"

"Yeah, you told me and Joey that already—except you skipped the part about the movie. So you don't know that Rick didn't have it stashed away someplace."

"If he'd found it, he'd have told Sophie. She told me he thought she'd already made a movie with Fin—she admitted she was gonna if he paid her. That little bitch'd have done anything for money—she didn't get enough time, is all."

"So you saved her from a fate worse than death, huh?"

"Haw haw," he said without smiling, "get in front and move slow. Just remember I got nothing to lose and I'd purely enjoy drilling you."

"Don't worry—I wouldn't want to miss any of this."

"*You* worry," he said, and jabbed me over the left kidney. It made my eyes water but I didn't grunt and we hiked briskly down the hall to the servant's stairs where I pulled the little gate open and started down. He kept the gun so close it bumped my neck twice before we reached the private dining room and as we walked around the big table I felt the muzzle in my ribs. I kept thinking about whirling to catch it with my elbow but it was so chancy I kept putting it off and suddenly we were out the back door and walking behind city hall.

"Don't you want to stop and say hi to Doris?" I asked.

I got another good poke for that and shut up.

At the end of the block we turned right. I kept thinking we had to meet somebody and I'd get a chance to jump Buck but every soul in town seemed to be in the sack. Buck kept step with me and our feet ground into the graveled street or beat the pavement like one set. A dog barked in somebody's back yard and right away another picked it up.

In front of the Larsons he made me stop and sit down.

He squinted up toward the house. I'd seen a light in the front bedroom before Buck stopped me but the rest of the house was dark.

Buck hunkered down, holding the gun close to my nose.

"Go knock. Tell Iris you wanna talk to her. When she opens up, I'll come in behind you."

"Listen, Buck get smart—take off right now. Get the hell out while you can—don't kill anybody else for nothing."

"I ain't gonna kill nobody for nothing, except maybe you. I can get five grand for that movie—maybe more—I ain't ever had that kind of money all at once in my life and I Goddamned earned it and I'm gonna get it, now get off your ass and keep your mouth shut until Iris answers that door. You blow it, and I'll kill you both, don't forget that."

It seemed like a thing I could remember easy so I got up and knocked on the door.

Iris, who took her time answering, squinted hard at me through the screen when she finally arrived.

"It's me, Carl—I gotta talk to you."

"Don't be silly, it's late—come tomorrow."

"It won't keep, Iris—it's about Angie."

She hesitated, sighed, said all right and turned to go back in the house. Buck came out of the shadows and followed me inside to the living room. As Iris reached to turn on the lamp, Buck spoke.

"Leave it be—we'll talk in the dark."

Iris started—her back was to us but she recognized the voice. Slowly she turned and raised her hands to her robe collar.

"Iris," said Buck, "I want the film Fin made, I'm gonna get it no matter what I got to do, I got to have it. Now call Angie down here."

"What ever for—?"

"Just do like I tell you—*now*."

Iris tried to see me but it was too dark for her to get any satisfaction and she turned back to Buck.

"Angie doesn't know a thing and I'm not going to expose her to this."

Buck kicked the end table that held a milk glass lamp and set it sailing into the nearest wall where it shattered and crashed to the floor. Iris screamed, not because she was touched by the glass but because the violence scared her witless.

Buck kept the gun on me and for several seconds we three stood there like dummies in a clothing store window. A door opened upstairs and steps moved hesitantly along the upper hall.

"Mama?" called Angie.

"I'm all right, honey. Don't come down—"

"Shut up," Buck told her. "Angie—come down here!"

The hall light came on and Angie descended the steps slowly. A pink robe covered her night dress and she stood in the doorway, barefooted, tousle-haired and goggle-eyed.

"Mama?" she said, peering into the darkness.

"I'm all right—you shouldn't have come down."

"Come in here and sit down," said Buck. "Iris, you sit on the couch and Wilcox—you sit beside her."

He got Angie into the big chair at his side and stood near it, pointing the gun at Iris and me as we sat stiffly on the couch.

My back was to the front windows and I faced the dining room and kitchen. A movement in the kitchen suddenly reminded me of Clayt's vigil under the tree in the yard.

"Now," said Buck, "we can make this real easy, or it can be damned messy. I want them films. Fin had 'em in the Buick trunk. Wilcox don't know where they went, the Marksons didn't—but somebody has to and I figure it's you —or maybe Angie. Somebody got 'em and it hadda be somebody with keys. Now get this straight—I killed Sophie and Rick to get the movie. The town cop knows it, everybody knows it or will—so I got nothing to lose. If you don't tell me now, I'm gonna go to work on Angie."

"You're crazy," I said, "if she starts screaming the whole town'll show up."

"Her ma screamed and I don't see no crowd. Now let's cut the shit and spill it—Iris?"

"Why must you have this film?" she asked. Angie's presence seemed to calm her—her voice was low and steady.

"Because it's worth money, that's why."

"How much?"

Buck hesitated, then said in almost a normal voice. "Ten thousand."

"You told me five," I said.

"Shut up!" he yelled, "it was ten."

"I can give you money," said Iris. "You don't have to have the film."

"Yeah? What can you give me?"

"Well, I could write a check—"

"Jesus Christ—you think I'm a moron? What've you got in cash?"

A shadow moved in the kitchen and I pulled my feet in close to the couch. Apparently Iris had seen it too, she seemed to be stalling.

"I have jewelry upstairs, it's worth a good deal more than ten thousand. Angie, dear, go up and get my case, it's in the left hand drawer of the vanity—"

"Hold on," said Buck, waving the gun, "Angie's not going anywhere—you go get it."

Iris shrugged. "If you insist."

She rose slowly, stepped in front of Angie and stopped to stare past Buck toward the dining room.

"Hit him, Clayton," she said calmly.

Buck jerked right, starting to turn, realized she might be bluffing to give me an opening and swung back to shoot at me. The little move pulled the muzzle off my middle and while the blast was deafening I only sensed the passing of the slug as I hit the floor in a tight roll, arched from the shoulders and slammed both feet into his chest. He went over the chair into Clayt and they both sprawled into the dining room. The women screamed when the gun went off a second and third time. I rolled to my feet, grabbed the easy chair arms and slammed it into the rolling bodies as the bigger one started to rise. The gun went off again and I heard Clayt grunt from the impact. The chair only staggered Buck but by then he'd decided to leave and he wheeled toward the kitchen, stumbled against the right doorjamb and dropped the gun with a clatter.

He was up and halfway through the kitchen when I caught him in the small of the back with a flying tackle that knocked him to the floor and sent him skidding into a cabinet head first. I bounced up and tried to punt his thick skull through the upper cabinets but he managed to twist and raise his arm so I wound up on my ass which put me in a hell of a mood. I was honest to God happy when he came to his feet and I could start punching.

As he charged like a rhino I skipped to his left, speared him once with a sharp jab to the temple and tried to club him behind the ear with my right as he shot past but I only grazed his skull. He collided with the kitchen counter, bounced back, wheeled into a solid right cross, staggered, caromed off the doorjamb, caught two more licks and hit the floor hard enough to make the dishes rattle.

While he was trying to get up on his knees Iris turned on the wall switch, pointed the gun with both hands and shot him dead.

Later Joey asked why didn't I try to stop her. I said I didn't try to stop lightning, floods or tornadoes and at the time she was as unreachable as any of them. I sure as hell didn't worry about saving Buck at the risk of my neck.

When the gun was empty and she'd dropped it on the floor I said something like she needn't have shot him——he was all through. Slowly she raised her eyes from the body at her feet and gave me a long stare.

"He'd have hurt Angie. Now he won't hurt anybody."

"What'd you do with the movie?" I asked.

"I burned it."

"Why didn't you tell him?"

"He wouldn't have believed me. Not until he'd hurt

Angie. He'd never believe anything he didn't want to. He couldn't believe that Fin despised him."

Clayt died three days later. I figured it was what he wanted—having killed Angie's father he thought it was a price he had to pay and Iris had been more than willing for him to do it. If she hadn't sacrificed him there's no telling how it all would have ended but chances are things would have been worse.

I didn't have a damned thing to be proud about. I'd never been on top of it, never got the girl and didn't make a nickle. The morning after Clayt died I went around to the judge, told him the fairgrounds were as neat as I was going to get them and said I was quitting.

"The job ain't done 'til I say it is," he told me.

"Well, it's done for me. Hank and Chip can finish up."

"You got a funny way of proving your reliability."

"I never figured on proving anything like that—all I was working for was thirty cents an hour and all that proves is I needed money too bad."

I spent a couple hours jawing with Joey and after lunch sold my truck before stopping by Boswell's shack where we lifted a few to the recently departed. I ate supper with Ma and Pa, kidded Bertha some and in the early evening sat out in front of the hotel and watched Corden shrink to Main Street when darkness came and the streetlights turned on. It'd been hot all day and the sidewalk near fried the bugs that fell from the light and buzzed around.

Wilt Bowman came across the graveled street and sat down next to me without waiting for an invite.

"Well," he said, "a lot's happened since we talked last."

"Uh-huh—got a cigaret?"

He frowned, fished out his pack, shook one loose and handed it to me as if it were his last penny.

"Just think," he said as I lit up, "you hadn't been out of prison a week, Iris Larson was sick up on the hill, Fin, old Buck, Sophie Markson, Rick Marson and Clayt—all of 'em was alive and well. Now they're all gone but Iris and she's feeling fine and gonna move away with Angie. Corden's shrunk by seven people. That's a lot when you figure we only got about thirteen hundred all told."

I allowed as how he had a firm grasp on the whole scene.

"Iris won't be able to sell that house," said Wilt. "Not a soul in Corden'd pay what it's worth today."

I quit listening and watched my nephew, Hank, come out of the soda fountain across the street and stroll down the walk with Ellie. The judge had made him foreman of the two-man fairgrounds crew and he couldn't enjoy it because guilt pangs hit every time he thought about Clayt.

"Hey Carl," said Wilt, leaning too close, "about that dirty movie—was Doris really in it with Buck?"

I gave him my fish eye and considered butting out my borrowed cigaret in his left nostril. He drew back, looking nervous.

"That's what people are saying—I just wondered—"

"I never saw the movie—if there was one. And now I'd like to plan my future so why don't you drift and leave me to it?"

He was indignant, figuring the least I could give in return for the cigaret was the time it took to smoke it, but he got up and went.

So I plotted my future and that night, just before twelve, I hopped a freight heading for Minneapolis.

# MORE MYSTERIOUS PLEASURES

**HAROLD ADAMS**
MURDER
Carl Wilcox debuts in a story of triple murder which exposes the underbelly of corruption in the town of Corden, shattering the respectability of its most dignified citizens.               #501   $3.50

THE NAKED LIAR
When a sexy young widow is framed for the murder of her husband, Carl Wilcox comes through to help her fight off cops and big-city goons.
                                                        #420   $3.95

THE FOURTH WIDOW
Ex-con/private eye Carl Wilcox is back, investigating the death of a "popular" widow in the Depression-era town of Corden, S.D.
                                                        #502   $3.50

**EARL DERR BIGGERS**
THE HOUSE WITHOUT A KEY
Charlie Chan debuts in the Honolulu investigation of an expatriate Bostonian's murder.                                  #421   $3.95

THE CHINESE PARROT
Charlie Chan works to find the key to murders seemingly without victims—but which have left a multitude of clues.      #503   $3.95

BEHIND THAT CURTAIN
Two murders sixteen years apart, one in London, one in San Francisco, each share a major clue in a pair of velvet Chinese slippers. Chan seeks the connection.                                      #504   $3.95

THE BLACK CAMEL
When movie goddess Sheila Fane is murdered in her Hawaiian pavilion, Chan discovers an interrelated crime in a murky Hollywood mystery from the past.                                       #505   $3.95

CHARLIE CHAN CARRIES ON
An elusive transcontinental killer dogs the heels of the Lofton Round the World Cruise. When the touring party reaches Honolulu, the murderer finally meets his match.                             #506   $3.95

## JAMES M. CAIN
### THE ENCHANTED ISLE
A beautiful runaway is involved in a deadly bank robbery in this posthumously published novel.  #415  $3.95

### CLOUD NINE
Two brothers—one good, one evil—battle over a million-dollar land deal and a luscious 16-year-old in this posthumously published novel.  #507  $3.95

## ROBERT CAMPBELL
### IN LA-LA LAND WE TRUST
Child porn, snuff films, and drunken TV stars in fast cars—that's what makes the L.A. world go 'round. Whistler, a luckless P.I., finds that it's not good to know too much about the porn trade in the City of Angels.  #508  $3.95

## GEORGE C. CHESBRO
### VEIL
Clairvoyant artist Veil Kendry volunteers to be tested at the Institute for Human Studies and finds that his life is in deadly peril; is he threatened by the Institute, the Army, or the CIA?  #509  $3.95

## WILLIAM L. DeANDREA
### THE LUNATIC FRINGE
Police Commissioner Teddy Roosevelt and Officer Dennis Muldoon comb 1896 New York for a missing exotic dancer who holds the key to the murder of a prominent political cartoonist.  #306  $3.95

### SNARK
Espionage agent Bellman must locate the missing director of British Intelligence—and elude a master terrorist who has sworn to kill him.  #510  $3.50

### KILLED IN THE ACT
Brash, witty Matt Cobb, TV network troubleshooter, must contend with bizarre crimes connected with a TV spectacular—one of which is a murder committed before 40 million witnesses.  #511  $3.50

### KILLED WITH A PASSION
In seeking to clear an old college friend of murder, Matt Cobb must deal with the Mad Karate Killer and the Organic Hit Man, among other eccentric criminals.  #512  $3.50

### KILLED ON THE ICE
When a famous psychiatrist is stabbed in a Manhattan skating rink, Matt Cobb finds it necessary to protect a beautiful Olympic skater who appears to be the next victim.  #513  $3.50

## JAMES ELLROY
### SUICIDE HILL
Brilliant L.A. Police sergeant Lloyd Hopkins teams up with the FBI to solve a series of inside bank robberies—but is he working with or against them?                                                        #514   $3.95

## PAUL ENGLEMAN
### CATCH A FALLEN ANGEL
Private eye Mark Renzler becomes involved in publishing mayhem and murder when two slick mens' magazines battle for control of the lucrative market.                                                        #515   $3.50

## LOREN D. ESTLEMAN
### ROSES ARE DEAD
Someone's put a contract out on freelance hit man Peter Macklin. Is he as good as the killers on his trail?                                 #516   $3.95

### ANY MAN'S DEATH
Hit man Peter Macklin is engaged to keep a famous television evangelist *alive*—quite a switch from his normal line.             #517   $3.95

## DICK FRANCIS
### THE SPORT OF QUEENS
The autobiography of the celebrated race jockey/crime novelist.

#410   $3.95

## JOHN GARDNER
### THE GARDEN OF WEAPONS
Big Herbie Kruger returns to East Berlin to uncover a double agent. He confronts his own past and life's only certainty—death.

#103   $4.50

## BRIAN GARFIELD
### DEATH WISH
Paul Benjamin is a modern-day New York vigilante, stalking the rapist-killers who victimized his wife and daughter. The basis for the Charles Bronson movie.                                                      #301   $3.95

### DEATH SENTENCE
A riveting sequel to *Death Wish*. The action moves to Chicago as Paul Benjamin continues his heroic (or is it psychotic?) mission to make city streets safe.                                                      #302   $3.95

### TRIPWIRE
A crime novel set in the American West of the late 1800s. Boag, a black outlaw, seeks revenge on the white cohorts who left him for dead. "One of the most compelling characters in recent fiction."—Robert Ludlum.                                                          #303   $3.95

### FEAR IN A HANDFUL OF DUST
Four psychiatrists, three men and a woman, struggle across the blazing Arizona desert—pursued by a fanatic killer they themselves have judged insane. "Unique and disturbing."—Alfred Coppel.       #304   $3.95

## JOE GORES

### A TIME OF PREDATORS

When Paula Halstead kills herself after witnessing a horrid crime, her husband vows to avenge her death. Winner of the Edgar Allan Poe Award. #215 $3.95

### COME MORNING

Two million in diamonds are at stake, and the ex-con who knows their whereabouts may have trouble staying alive if he turns them up at the wrong moment. #518 $3.95

## NAT HENTOFF

### BLUES FOR CHARLIE DARWIN

Gritty, colorful Greenwich Village sets the scene for Noah Green and Sam McKibbon, two street-wise New York cops who are as at home in jazz clubs as they are at a homicide scene.
#208 $3.95

### THE MAN FROM INTERNAL AFFAIRS

Detective Noah Green wants to know who's stuffing corpses into East Village garbage cans . . . and who's lying about him to the Internal Affairs Division. #409 $3.95

## PATRICIA HIGHSMITH

### THE BLUNDERER

An unhappy husband attempts to kill his wife by applying the murderous methods of another man. When things go wrong, he pays a visit to the more successful killer—a dreadful error. #305 $3.95

## DOUG HORNIG

### THE DARK SIDE

Insurance detective Loren Swift is called to a rural commune to investigate a carbon-monoxide murder. Are the commune inhabitants as gentle as they seem? #519 $3.95

## P.D. JAMES/T.A. CRITCHLEY

### THE MAUL AND THE PEAR TREE

The noted mystery novelist teams up with a police historian to create a fascinating factual account of the 1811 Ratcliffe Highway murders.
#520 $3.95

## STUART KAMINSKY'S "TOBY PETERS" SERIES

### NEVER CROSS A VAMPIRE

When Bela Lugosi receives a dead bat in the mail, Toby tries to catch the prankster. But Toby's time is at a premium because he's also trying to clear William Faulkner of a murder charge! #107 $3.95

## HIGH MIDNIGHT
When Gary Cooper and Ernest Hemingway come to Toby for protection, he tries to save them from vicious blackmailers.　#106　$3.95

## HE DONE HER WRONG
Someone has stolen Mae West's autobiography, and when she asks Toby to come up and see her sometime, he doesn't know how deadly a visit it could be.　#105　$3.95

## BULLET FOR A STAR
Warner Brothers hires Toby Peters to clear the name of Errol Flynn, a blackmail victim with a penchant for young girls. The first novel in the acclaimed Hollywood-based private eye series.　#308　$3.95

## THE FALA FACTOR
Toby comes to the rescue of lady-in-distress Eleanor Roosevelt, and must match wits with a right-wing fanatic who is scheming to overthrow the U.S. Government.　#309　$3.95

## JOSEPH KOENIG
### FLOATER
Florida Everglades sheriff Buck White matches wits with a Miami murder-and-larceny team who just may have hidden his ex-wife's corpse in a remote bayou.　#521　$3.50

## ELMORE LEONARD
### THE HUNTED
Long out of print, this 1974 novel by the author of *Glitz* details the attempts of a man to escape killers from his past.　#401　$3.95

### MR. MAJESTYK
Sometimes bad guys can push a good man too far, and when that good guy is a Special Forces veteran, everyone had better duck.　#402　$3.95

### THE BIG BOUNCE
Suspense and black comedy are cleverly combined in this tale of a dangerous drifter's affair with a beautiful woman out for kicks.　#403　$3.95

## ELSA LEWIN
### I, ANNA
A recently divorced woman commits murder to avenge her degradation at the hands of a sleazy lothario.　#522　$3.50

## THOMAS MAXWELL
### KISS ME ONCE
An epic *roman noir* which explores the romantic but seamy underworld of New York during the WWII years. When the good guys are off fighting in Europe, the bad guys run amok in America.

#523　$3.95

**ED McBAIN**
**ANOTHER PART OF THE CITY**
The master of the police procedural moves from the fictional 87th precinct to the gritty reality of Manhattan. "McBain's best in several years."—*San Francisco Chronicle*.                    #524  $3.95

**SNOW WHITE AND ROSE RED**
A beautiful heiress confined to a sanitarium engages Matthew Hope to free her—and her $650,000.                    #414  $3.95

**CINDERELLA**
A dead detective and a hot young hooker lead Matthew Hope into a multi-layered plot among Miami cocaine dealers. "A gem of sting and countersting."—*Time*.                    #525  $3.95

**PETER O'DONNELL**
**MODESTY BLAISE**
Modesty and Willie Garvin must protect a shipment of diamonds from a gentleman about to murder his lover and an *un*civilized sheik.                    #216  $3.95

**SABRE TOOTH**
Modesty faces Willie's apparent betrayal and a modern-day Genghis Khan who wants her for his mercenary army.                    #217  $3.95

**A TASTE FOR DEATH**
Modesty and Willie are pitted against a giant enemy in the Sahara, where their only hope of escape is a blind girl whose time is running out.                    #218  $3.95

**I, LUCIFER**
Some people carry a nickname too far . . . like the maniac calling himself Lucifer. He's targeted 120 souls, and Modesty and Willie find they have a personal stake in stopping him.                    #219  $3.95

**THE IMPOSSIBLE VIRGIN**
Modesty fights for her soul when she and Willie attempt to rescue an albino girl from the evil Brunel, who lusts after the secret power of an idol called the Impossible Virgin.                    #220  $3.95

**DEAD MAN'S HANDLE**
Modesty Blaise must deal with a brainwashed—and deadly—Willie Garvin as well as with a host of outré religion-crazed villains.
                    #526  $3.95

**ELIZABETH PETERS**
**CROCODILE ON THE SANDBANK**
Amelia Peabody's trip to Egypt brings her face to face with an ancient mystery. With the help of Radcliffe Emerson, she uncovers a tomb and the solution to a deadly threat.                    #209  $3.95

## THE CURSE OF THE PHAROAHS
Amelia and Radcliffe Emerson head for Egypt to excavate a cursed tomb but must confront the burial ground's evil history before it claims them both. #210 $3.95

## THE SEVENTH SINNER
Murder in an ancient subterranean Roman temple sparks Jacqueline Kirby's first recorded case. #411 $3.95

## THE MURDERS OF RICHARD III
Death by archaic means haunts the costumed weekend get-together of a group of eccentric Ricardians. #412 $3.95

## ANTHONY PRICE
### THE LABYRINTH MAKERS
Dr. David Audley does his job too well in his first documented case, embarrassing British Intelligence, the CIA, and the KGB in one swoop. #404 $3.95

### THE ALAMUT AMBUSH
Alamut, in Northern Persia, is considered by many to be the original home of terrorism. Audley moves to the Mideast to put the cap on an explosive threat. #405 $3.95

### COLONEL BUTLER'S WOLF
The Soviets are recruiting spies from among Oxford's best and brightest; it's up to Dr. Audley to identify the Russian wolf in don's clothing. #527 $3.95

### OCTOBER MEN
Dr. Audley's "holiday" in Rome stirs up old Intelligence feuds and echoes of partisan warfare during World War II—and leads him into new danger. #529 $3.95

### OTHER PATHS TO GLORY
What can a World War I battlefield in France have in common with a deadly secret of the present? A modern assault on Bouillet Wood leads to the answers. #530 $3.95

### SION CROSSING
What does the chairman of a new NATO-like committee have to do with the American Civil War? Audley travels to Georgia in this espionage thriller. #406 $3.95

### HERE BE MONSTERS
The assassination of an American veteran forces Dr. David Audley into a confrontation with undercover KGB agents. #528 $3.95

## BILL PRONZINI AND JOHN LUTZ
### THE EYE
A lunatic watches over the residents of West 98th Street with a powerful telescope. When his "children" displease him, he is swift to mete out deadly punishment. #408 $3.95

## PATRICK RUELL
### RED CHRISTMAS
Murderers and political terrorists come down the chimney during an old-fashioned Dickensian Christmas at a British country inn.

#531  $3.50

### DEATH TAKES THE LOW ROAD
William Hazlitt, a universtiy administrator who moonlights as a Soviet mole, is on the run from both Russian and British agents who want him to assassinate an African general.

#532  $3.50

## DELL SHANNON
### CASE PENDING
In the first novel in the best-selling series, Lt. Luis Mendoza must solve a series of horrifying Los Angeles mutilation murders.  #211  $3.95

### THE ACE OF SPADES
When the police find an overdosed junkie, they're ready to write off the case—until the autopsy reveals that this junkie *wasn't* a junkie.  #212  $3.95

### EXTRA KILL
In "The Temple of Mystic Truth," Mendoza discovers idol worship, pornography, murder, and the clue to the death of a Los Angeles patrolman.  #213  $3.95

### KNAVE OF HEARTS
Mendoza must clear the name of the L.A.P.D. when it's discovered that an innocent man has been executed and the real killer is still on the loose.  #214  $3.95

### DEATH OF A BUSYBODY
When the West Coast's most industrious gossip and meddler turns up dead in a freight yard, Mendoza must work without clues to find the killer of a woman who had offended nearly everyone in Los Angeles.  #315  $3.95

### DOUBLE BLUFF
Mendoza goes against the evidence to dissect what looks like an air-tight case against suspected wife-killer Francis Ingram—a man the lieutenant insists is too nice to be a murderer.  #316  $3.95

### MARK OF MURDER
Mendoza investigates the near-fatal attack on an old friend as well as trying to track down an insane serial killer.  #417  $3.95

### ROOT OF ALL EVIL
The murder of a "nice" girl leads Mendoza to team up with the FBI in the search for her not-so-nice boyfriend—a Soviet agent.  #418  $3.95

**JULIE SMITH**
TRUE-LIFE ADVENTURE
Paul McDonald earned a meager living ghosting reports for a San Francisco private eye until the gumshoe turned up dead . . . now the killers are after him.                                    #407   $3.95

TOURIST TRAP
A lunatic is out to destroy San Francisco's tourism industry; can feisty lawyer/sleuth Rebecca Schwartz stop him while clearing an innocent man of a murder charge?                           #533   $3.95


**ROSS H. SPENCER**
THE MISSING BISHOP
Chicago P.I. Buzz Deckard has a missing person to find. Unfortunately his client has disappeared as well, and no one else seems to be who or what they claim.                                  #416   $3.50

MONASTERY NIGHTMARE
Chicago P.I. Luke Lassiter tries his hand at writing novels, and encounters murder in an abandoned monastery.           #534   $3.50


**REX STOUT**
UNDER THE ANDES
A long-lost 1914 fantasy novel from the creator of the immortal Nero Wolfe series. "The most exciting yarn we have read since *Tarzan of the Apes.*"—*All-Story Magazine*.                      #419   $3.50


**ROSS THOMAS**
CAST A YELLOW SHADOW
McCorkle's wife is kidnapped by agents of the South African government. The ransom—his cohort Padillo must assassinate their prime minister.                                          #535   $3.95

THE SINGAPORE WINK
Ex-Hollywood stunt man Ed Cauthorne is offered $25,000 to search for colleague Angelo Sacchetti—a man he thought he'd killed in Singapore two years earlier.                             #536   $3.95

THE FOOLS IN TOWN ARE ON OUR SIDE
Lucifer Dye, just resigned from a top secret U.S. Intelligence post, accepts a princely fee to undertake the corruption of an entire American city.                                           #537   $3.95


**JIM THOMPSON**
THE KILL-OFF
Luanne Devore was loathed by everyone in her small New England town. Her plots and designs threatened to destroy them—unless they destroyed her first.                              #538   $3.95

## DONALD E. WESTLAKE
### THE HOT ROCK
The unlucky master thief John Dortmunder debuts in this spectacular caper novel. How many times do you have to steal an emerald to make sure it *stays* stolen?                                    #539   $3.95

### BANK SHOT
Dortmunder and company return. A bank is temporarily housed in a trailer, so why not just hook it up and make off with the whole shebang? Too bad nothing is ever that simple.                         #540   $3.95

### THE BUSY BODY
Aloysius Engel is a gangster, the Big Man's right hand. So when he's ordered to dig a suit loaded with drugs out of a fresh grave, how come the corpse it's wrapped around won't lie still?              #541   $3.95

### THE SPY IN THE OINTMENT
Pacifist agitator J. Eugene Raxford is mistakenly listed as a terrorist by the FBI, which leads to his enforced recruitment to a group bent on world domination. Will very good Good triumph over absolutely villainous Evil?                                              #542   $3.95

### GOD SAVE THE MARK
Fred Fitch is the sucker's sucker—con men line up to bilk him. But when he inherits $300,000 from a murdered uncle, he finds it necessary to dodge killers as well as hustlers.                          #543   $3.95

## TERI WHITE
### TIGHTROPE
This second novel featuring L.A. cops Blue Maguire and Spaceman Kowalski takes them into the nooks and crannies of the city's Little Saigon.                                                  #544   $3.95

## COLLIN WILCOX
### VICTIMS
Lt. Frank Hastings investigates the murder of a police colleague in the home of a powerful—and nasty—San Francisco attorney.
                                                            #413   $3.95

### NIGHT GAMES
Lt. Frank Hastings of the San Francisco Police returns to investigate the at-home death of an unfaithful husband—whose affairs have led to his murder.                                              #545   $3.95

## DAVID WILLIAMS' "MARK TREASURE" SERIES
### UNHOLY WRIT
London financier Mark Treasure helps a friend reaquire some property. He stays to unravel the mystery when a Shakespeare manuscript is discovered and foul murder done. #112 $3.95

### TREASURE BY DEGREES
Mark Treasure discovers there's nothing funny about a board game called "Funny Farms." When he becomes involved in the takeover struggle for a small university, he also finds there's nothing funny about murder. #113 $3.95